WRECKER

SUMMER WOOD

BLOOMSBURY
LONDON · BERLIN · NEW YORK · SYDNEY

First published in Great Britain 2011

Copyright © 2011 by Summer Wood

The moral right of the author has been asserted

Bloomsbury Publishing, London, Berlin, New York and Sydney

36 Soho Square, London W1D 3QY

A CIP catalogue record for this book is available from the British Library

ISBN 978 1 4088 0931 0
10 9 8 7 6 5 4 3 2 1

Typeset by Westchester Book Group

Printed in Great Britain by Clays Limited, St Ives plc

www.bloomsbury.com/summerwood

for K, and for our sons
all of you
beloved

In this city, life happens in the street. A man walks out for a salami sandwich and comes back in love. A housewife turns into a taxi driver; a taxi driver trades his union card for some high heels and fishnet stockings—and nobody blinks an eye. Even the poor, beleaguered elms crack the sidewalks with their inspired reach for the sun. And since the year is 1965 and this city is San Francisco, home to saints and sinners and seekers of every stripe, it comes as no surprise for a young woman dressed in the madras skirt and flowing cotton blouse of a bohemian to lie back on a grassy stretch of Rolph Playground and give birth to a large, perfect, beautiful baby boy.

Presto! Change-O!

Become a mother.

Three years later, she lost him.

CHAPTER ONE

It was the middle of the afternoon, January 1969, and a half-hearted rain dampened San Francisco and cast a gloomy pall over the hallways of the Social Welfare building.

Len stood waiting for his life to change. He was a skinny man with a long face that showed its creases despite the stubble on his chin and cheeks, and he kept moving his hands from the brim of his cap to the pockets of his jeans as though he couldn't be held responsible for what they might do if left unsupervised. Finally a door creaked open and a young woman edged into the hall.

"Sir?"

Len lurched forward. He stopped abruptly when he saw the boy. This one? He was barely a child. They'd said he was three, but Len hadn't . . . were three-year-olds that tiny? Len had expected something along the lines of a good-sized calf, seventy pounds or so, take a little muscle to roll—but this kid would have a tough time toe-to-toe with the goose that patrolled the ragged edges of Len's yard. Did geese hurt children?

Len said, "Hey." He meant to sound friendly, but his voice caught in his throat and sputtered like a gas engine with a lazy spark.

The boy turned his face to him, and Len peered closely. He hadn't seen Lisa Fay since he'd married her sister fifteen years back, but there was something of the family resemblance in the snub nose, in the delicate oval curve of the chin. There was little else that seemed delicate on this boy. In spite of his small size he was robust and muscled. His pale hair was cropped short and badly, and his corduroy pants were bunched by a belt at his waist, the elastic gone slack. Kid had the right to look bedraggled, Len thought, yanked from his mother that young. He had the right to look forlorn. This boy didn't look forlorn, he looked ferocious. Len cleared his throat and glanced away.

The plain truth? He hadn't wanted a kid. Had no idea, with Meg the way she was, what to do with one. This boy was too small to bring to work with him and too young to leave on his own and would probably not take kindly to being penned up all day. Len looked sideways at the young woman who had maneuvered the boy into the hall. There was no other kin to take him, she'd said. Of course, if Len preferred he be raised by strangers—

"Do I sign something?"

Miss Hanson flashed him a weary smile. "Why don't you and Wrecker take some time to get acquainted?" She gestured toward the boy. "I'll meet you in ten minutes in the office and we can take care of the paperwork."

It was settled, then. Len took a hesitant step forward. His body was a compact knot from thirty years of working the woods, cramped worse from six hours in the truck on the drive south. "Okay." He grimaced upon squatting down. "All right." Should he call him sport? Son? Fifteen years to go, and already ten minutes seemed like an eternity. He reached out his hand. It looked giant and threatening, even to him, and he slid it back into his pocket. The kid stood his ground. Battle-worn, renegade—Len wasn't a praying man, but a few minutes alone in the company of this boy and it was starting to feel like something a good bit bigger than he'd bargained for. "I'm your uncle Len."

The boy made a low sound, mixed outrage and dismay.

That about summed it up, Len thought.

Len drove north out of San Francisco and watched the city fall away behind them. He followed the line of traffic across the Presidio and over the water, gray and choppy, that flowed beneath the Golden Gate. On the far side the truck rumbled past the entrance to San Quentin Prison. Len snuck a glance sideways. The boy's absent mother was shelved someplace like that. Lisa Fay had been sentenced for so long to the state slammer that they might as well have thrown away the key. Len frowned, and his fingers itched for a cigarette. He hadn't smoked in years, but it had been a very long day.

A muffled snore escaped from the boy, and Len risked a look in his direction. Wrecker. What kind of a name was that? Slumped against the door with his neck bent at an unnatural angle and his short legs jammed straight out on the seat. Len shifted his grip on the wheel and blinked his gaze forward. The highway buckled into green hills between each sleepy little town. Two hours down, now, and they still had four to go, a hundred miles north on narrow roads before they turned and threaded night-blind through the giant trees, up and down the winding mountain nearly to the sea. When the few buildings of Cloverdale loomed ahead, Len pulled in and parked in the lot of a diner. He was too weary to make a straight shot of it. "Boy?" Len said, and reached a big hand to jiggle the kid's shoulder. Wrecker. It would take some getting used to. "You want something to eat?"

Wrecker blinked a few times and reached a hand to wipe away the spit that dampened his cheek. Len hadn't noticed the boy's blue eyes before. Stormy. The color of sea-squall, not clear sky. "I have to pee."

"Pee? Oh." Len wrinkled his forehead. "That." He got out of

5

the truck and crossed to the other door and unbuckled Wrecker and lifted him down, and they stood there awkwardly for a moment, while Len wondered if he should carry the boy, or take his hand, or simply walk ahead and hope he would follow. He had settled on the last when the door to the diner flapped open and two men and a woman walked out.

Len sagged. Four hours from home, and his Mattole neighbors were marching straight at him. Charlie Burrell bleated a greeting, and his wife moved in to lay a sympathetic hand on Len's elbow. "Hullo, dear," she said. Greta was a decent woman with a face as broad and bland as a saucer. "How's Meg?"

Len's gaze swerved aground. Six months had passed since his wife had gone in for a root canal and come home with an infection that spread into her brain and rampaged like a wild beast. Penicillin saved her life, but it couldn't save her mind. "Meg?" Len answered gruffly, glancing back up. "Meg's fine." The same, he clarified. The doctors didn't think she'd change much from how she was now.

Charlie shuffled and grunted. "Hell of a thing," he mumbled. He glanced at his wife, and his voice veered toward belligerence. They'd had some news. "Junior got his draft notice," he announced. The son, thick and sullen, stood behind and pretended deafness. "I believe he'll go, but Greta here . . ."

Len watched the woman's lips tighten and her body inch away from her husband's. She kept her gaze trained on a spot just past Len's shoulder, and answered in clipped tones. Their neighbor had troubles of his own without them burdening him with theirs, Greta said. She flashed Len a quick glance, and her voice softened slightly. He should take care of himself, now. She would stop over to see Meg soon. Len nodded. He breathed out as they left. He settled his cap back on his head, paused a moment to reset his balance, and remembered the boy.

"Wrecker?"

Len circled the truck and scanned the parking lot.

"Kid?" He called twice, his voice tight and low. He swung his head toward the road to make sure the boy wasn't trapped in traffic, and then he hurried across the lot at awkward angles, checking between the cars. Len rushed inside and anxiously searched the faces. A boy, he stammered, taking hold of the waitress. Had she seen him? A little one. His eyes lit on a stool at the counter. "Maybe this tall."

"Whoa, there," she said, steadying him. "You lost your kid?" She studied Len's panicked face and then turned to the diners. "Any y'all seen this man's boy? 'Bout yay high." She gestured to her hip and then turned back to Len. "How old?" Her eyes widened. "Good God. Get looking," she shouted. "Three years old and on the loose. Spread out," and the people left their napkins by their plates and did as she ordered. "Norton," she yelled to the cook. He came out wiping his hands on the dingy apron that girdled his body. "Check down by the river. And fast."

Len felt his heart seize. If anything had happened to the boy—

"You set there," the waitress said. She placed a hand on his shoulder and forced him into the cracked padding of a booth. "You look like death. Can't have him see you like that," and Len felt himself collapse under her soft push.

The room emptied. Len counted slowly to five, forcing each breath into his lungs. And then he stood and followed the cook's broad back down a path to the river. He paused when Norton did, watched the cook straighten from his bearlike slump, tap a cigarette loose from a crumpled pack, hold it to his mouth. Norton leisurely cupped his hands to light the cigarette and drew a noisy, satisfied lungful of smoke.

Len strained to see past the brush that blocked his view. Wrecker stood on a boulder not ten paces away, throwing smaller rocks into the swiftly flowing stream. He had a powerful over-hand and imperfect aim.

Norton ignored the kid and smoked with gusto. Then he snubbed out the cigarette on the sole of his shoe, tossed the butt into the bushes, and roared, "All right, Champ. Come on with me."

Len watched Wrecker lift his chin and glance at the fat man in the apron. His gaze swept around to gather Len as well. He kept throwing his rocks into the water.

Norton tapped his foot. "You want a cheeseburger?" he bribed. "I can make you a cheeseburger." The boy didn't stir, and Norton yawned, his mouth opening wide as a walrus's. "Fine," he said, unperturbed. "Hide out down here and eat these weeds. It's all the same to me." He started back up the trail. "Hold your nose when you chew on them," Norton shouted helpfully. "Helps cover the fish shit."

Wrecker held on to the rest of his pebbles. "Fish don't shit."

Len lifted an eyebrow. He hadn't been raised to use language like that. Hadn't been raised to wander off, either.

Norton snorted. "Don't kid yourself." He spit out of the corner of his mouth. "Everybody shits. You get hungry, come on up," and lumbered past Len back up the trail to the diner.

Wrecker threw the rest of his rocks, one by one, into the flow. Then he turned and followed the heavyset cook back to the diner.

Len couldn't eat. He watched the boy tuck into his burger, kneeling on the booth seat to be tall enough to reach the table, and thought, Oh. What in the world have I done.

It was half past ten when Len made his careful way at last down to the Mattole. He felt happiness swell a lump into his throat. Every part of him ached and his mind was frozen with fatigue, but he'd made it home.

The Mattole Valley lay nestled in the rain-soaked western reaches of Humboldt County. It was a bump high on the California coast that jutted into the Pacific and sheltered bear and mountain lion in a kind of sleepy, soggy paradise of the ages. Sure, Len thought. Until the nineteenth century roared in. He'd read his history. That was a new age, a freight train fueled with the promise of fortune, and lumber barons and oil drillers and commercial fishermen and cattle ranchers caught wind of a fine opportunity and came to gather what they could of the rewards. By the time Len and Meg arrived in '55, the biggest trees had been felled and the oil played out and what was left was just enough range to run a few hundred head of cows. The river rose in '56, wiped whole towns off the map. Nobody was getting rich anymore.

That suited Len fine. He came looking for remote and he found it, a sweet little forty-acre spread at the end of a dirt road the county quit fixing after the first ranch and behind four gates he had to get out and open, move the truck through, then climb back out and shut to keep the cattle from wandering off their range. He didn't keep cows, himself. Couldn't abide them. He had a hunting rifle his father gave him when he left Tennessee twenty-odd years before, and he rarely had to go farther than his own wood lot to bring down a deer. One animal would keep them through the winter, and one more let him trade with the fishermen up in Eureka. Every summer Meg kept a garden, and Len had his cordwood business and the little lumber mill to bring in some cash. Of course, that was when Meg had been well. Len felt the worry squeeze the box of his ribs. This was the first time he'd been out past dark since her accident.

The third gate was Bow Farm, and Len eased down to push the rickety thing aside. He peered down the rutted track that led to the farmhouse. There'd been stories of trespassers chased off the land by women bearing shotguns. In the stories they were

9

always big women. Big shotguns. Len had lived next door long enough to have figured out that the girls weren't all that big, or half as threatening. They weren't nuns, or Amish, or cult members, or all sisters with widely ranging fathers, as the rumors had variously claimed—and since the tree hugger had joined them, one of them was a man. Len had to hand it to them. Nobody thought they'd stick, coming up here from the city, paying too much for that run-down spread. It was too hard a life. Too wet in the winter and hot in the summer, too many earthquakes and landslides and wild animals who shrieked and snarled in the night. But they were into their third wet season, Willow and the others, and they had saved him, in a way. He didn't know if he could have borne the heartbreak of Meg's decline without their help.

The fourth gate, left open when he pulled out that morning, was his own. A single light on in the house poured its yellow into the yard. Len opened the truck door and smelled the wet dripping off the trees. Everything was damped-down and quiet. The road quit here in his driveway. Past that were dark trees and steep hillsides and a five-mile hike to the sea.

Len hadn't told anyone quite where he'd gone, or why. He'd asked Willow to stay with Meg until he got back, and he could see her sitting at the kitchen table, her back to the door. He glanced sideways to make sure the kid was asleep but caught sight of the boy's round face, his open eyes. Len swore slightly under his breath. He couldn't count on this one to stay put. He crossed around the front of the truck to the passenger side, scooped the boy against his chest, and carried him like a loose sack of grain into the house.

Willow lifted her head to greet him. She cut an elegant figure, with her honey hair swept up like a movie star's, her pearl earrings, those flat shoes that made her feet look dainty—not the clodhopper boots Ruth and that Melody girl favored. She was the only one of the bunch to put on lipstick, and anyone could tell she wore a bra. Not that Len was looking. Not exactly. He met her gaze and brushed past Willow to lay the sleeping boy onto the couch by the wood stove. Then he crossed the floor, boards squeaking underfoot, to find his wife asleep in the single bedroom.

Meg's face in the muted light was peacefully asleep. Len felt a wave of love and revulsion. It was easy to confuse Meg's new blankness with peace, but blank was blank. Blank was blank was blank. If the old Meg was trapped in there, Len had no way to get her out. The old Meg was peaceful. She had never talked much but there had been a calm, an ease to her that Len felt comfortable to be around. She was competent and even-tempered and had a way of running a hand under his shirt and up his spine that tingled the base of his brain and made him yearn, without reason, for the chill and tart flavor of raspberry sherbet. She had always been a modest woman, and now, quite simply, she was not. Len did his best to satisfy her but for him the pleasure had gone out of that part of his life. He felt for the wedding band on his left hand. Fifteen years grown into the flesh of his finger, they would have to cut his hand to get it off. Though why would they. There was no need. Len and Meg. Meg and Len. Even their names were similar, brief and to the point, the consonants crowding the short *e*. Len. Bed. Meg. Fed. Pen. Leg. Red.

Dead, he thought, and turned back to the other room.

Willow had her coat on, black wool with the high collar. She had draped the couch throw over the boy and tucked in its edges and was watching him intently, her slender hand stroking the soft blond of his hair. She looked up when Len entered, and he winced at the look on her face. That delicate, quizzical smile.

Len was helpless to answer. The letter had come from the state some weeks ago, and it sat on the kitchen table for days, yielding less and less to each reading until he couldn't even tell what they wanted, much less what he should do about it. But Len had gassed up the truck and drove the six hours to find out. He held Willow's gaze and then broke from it to turn a bewildered eye toward the boy. That was what he'd brought back. That one, there, inert and lying quiet on the couch. It was all the answer he could give. "It's late, Willow. I could drive you home."

She smiled and shook her head. Her yurt behind Bow Farm was an easy walk away. "I'll see you, Len."

"All right, then."

The open door let in a gust of night air. Len went to the closet and drew out an extra blanket and opened it over the boy, and then he went in to the bedroom and lay down beside his wife and fought for sleep.

A man alone can operate a sawmill if he's smart. Len lay on the narrow strip of bed Meg didn't take up the next morning, and let his mind wander slowly toward waking. Len had done it himself; but he'd had to be smart, Len thought, and he'd had to be careful. With winches and pulleys and roller tables a man could maneuver the logs into place, he could lift the chainsaw carriage and position it onto the timber, adjust the settings to skim the bark slabs first, then quartersaw the log so the wood smell—sharp, sweet, intoxicating—leapt into the air and gave him strength. There was Engelmann spruce in these woods, here and there cedar, lodge-pole pine, the strong and stringy Douglas fir. There was red-wood, too, but Len left that alone. It took more than one man to handle a redwood, and something about the tree spooked him, the big crowns casting the forest floor in a kind of twilight gloom and the wind in the dead branches above sounding like a dry hinge on a barn door.

A good part of the year it was too wet to get in to the forest. Len worked on the vehicles, then. Patched the roof of his house.

Sharpened the sawteeth. The forest here was wet and deep, and ferns grew tall as a man in places. In winter the creek jumped its banks and flooded the road and only the tallest vehicles could downshift and get across. Then everybody dreamed of the desert. Dreamed of being someplace they could dry out. They plodded along and listened for the suck and rumble of mudslides. They stoked their fires with Len's cordwood and watched the flames for prophetic gestures. Mud caked on their boots six inches thick. They met at the Grange Hall for pancake breakfasts and played top this. These past years, though, too many families had a son in that other wet place, the one they watched on the evening news. Or a son had gone to Canada to sidestep the war. Len had signed up himself in '44; they sent him to basic training and then called the war off and he was dispatched with his buddies to MP in the Philippines. He didn't know what he would tell a son of his to do. A son of his? Len remembered the kid on the couch and swung his legs over the side of the bed, dressed, and went in to restart the fire.

The scatter of blankets had shifted. They were bundled up now in a tangle on the armchair, and through their soft bulk Len could pick out an elbow, the dome of the boy's head, and sticking out of the bottom a bare foot. He stared at that. It was as long as the palm of Len's hand. It would need socks. It would need shoes. It would need flippers for swimming lessons at the Y and basketball sneakers and lace-up oxfords for catechism and how on earth did you size a thing like that, anyway? The kid came with a trash bag half full of who knows what. Len would have to go through that. But not now. He stepped out of the door and the sun poured magnificently over the stoop and he heard a warbler singing hard enough to burst and he was happy.

By ten o'clock Len was gasping for air. Pistol-whipped by noon. Knocked-down defeated by three in the afternoon.

Not that the kid was bad. Not exactly. But there was no way a person over three feet tall could keep up with a thing like that. He had speed on his side and a complete unconcern for his own safety and a kind of smoldering disrespect for the command of his elder—Len—which erupted into outright disobedience and ensued in a ridiculous chase that left Len winded and feeling foolish. The boy looked down at the ground and spoke with such a low voice when he did speak that Len was forced to crank the dial on his hearing aid (the gift of too many years around loud machinery) to top volume and even then found it hard to gather the meaning of the boy's garbled utterances. Len could not understand why he did the things he did. Who in his right mind would climb to the top of a stack of logs three times his own height—the logs themselves well stacked but always subject to tipping under pressure, a log that size a steamroller once it gets started—and let loose with a holler and jump? And then, earnestly *chastised* for his action, the danger *explained* in no uncertain terms, and with the elder in command *watching*—climb to the top and jump again? He was taken with the log truck, with the winch, with the machines. And every time Len turned his back the boy disappeared. Into the woods, into the lumber shed, drawing with a stick in the dirt between the vehicles. And once, it seemed, into thin air.

Len was searching the bushes by the outhouse for the second time, calling for the boy, when he heard a sound from the direction of the house. He stood up to listen. Yes, from the house, and it had to be the kid: not a high whimper like a puppy would make, but closer to a moan. It raised the hair on the back of his neck. He had penned Meg's goose to keep her from harming the boy, but God help him—he'd never thought of his wife that way. He took off at a run, leapt the front steps, and threw open the door.

Meg was no small woman. Broad-hipped and broad-shouldered, she had cornered the little boy and was advancing on him, her arms outstretched to bar his exit. Wrecker huddled in the corner of the room, moaning, his head tucked like a turtle as close as he could get it to his chest and his eyes wide with terror.

"Meg!" Len shouted, and wrapped his arms around his wife.

Wrecker saw his opportunity and shot like a bullet past the two of them, out the door and gone.

Meg slumped her whole weight against Len. He stepped back to support her and shifted his grip and saw where his hands had raised red welts on her forearms. He had never hurt her before, and a wave of guilt and horror crashed over him. He would never do that again. Never. Never.

"Oh, girl—," he started, but Meg opened her mouth wider than he thought possible and drained all the air in the room into her lungs and then let it out in a tremendous bellow so loud Len had to release her and frantically clap his hands over his ears and struggle to adjust the volume on his aid and roll his eyes up into his head to escape the pain of the sound.

And when that breath ended she drew another and bellowed again. And again. For breath after breath, despite Len's every effort to calm her, she kept up her wail. She clung to him as she bellowed, she held him tightly, and when she finally calmed—or tired—enough to stop, she took his face in both hands and said the first two intelligible words she'd uttered since the dental surgery had gone so wrong.

Her eyes wide, bovine, her mouth struggling to meet the unreasonable demands of language, Meg said, "My boy."

Len led Meg into the bedroom and settled her onto the bed. The early evening sun streamed through the window and left a bright patch on the spread. He lay next to her and stroked her hair and spoke softly. It didn't seem to matter what he said. He told her how he was going to have to borrow the grader to improve the track to the back lot, and how the welding generator would need an overhaul, and that he hadn't quite gotten used to seeing the new red roof on the lumber shed. He said she made the best buttermilk biscuits around and that the latch on the garden gate was working fine now and that he had more business to take care of in the city but that he'd be back as soon as he could. The sound of his voice calmed her, and she closed her eyes.

Len eased himself up from the bed. He'd kept his voice soft, but every nerve in his body jangled, knowing the kid was on the loose. He stepped down into the yard and quickly surveyed the perimeter. The sun was just a few degrees off the horizon and dropping fast. Len checked the log pile and the machinery and then circled the house in systematically widening bands. The shadows lengthened, a hundred pools of darkness that could swallow a boy that small. "Wrecker?" Len called, the name rolling like marbles from his dry mouth. His voice cracked and he called again, and then again as the sweat dried clammy on his neck. He stopped at last with the boy's name ringing in the air. His jaw trembled. What if he'd lost him for good?

And then it was dark, and Len realized he didn't know what to do. It was cold, this time of year, and too dangerous for a boy that small—he was a baby, for chrissakes—to spend the night in the woods. What a mistake he had made, taking this child. A son? A person didn't just collect a *son* from a government office. Len pushed the thought from his mind. When he found him he would load him in the truck and take him back to the city. Surely Miss Hanson would understand. There must be some nice home for a boy like that. A boy like—

Wrecker was asleep on the seat of the truck. Somehow he had gotten himself in. How? When he couldn't even reach the door handle? And shut the door and buckled himself into the seat belt. His wispy blond hair was plastered to his forehead. Asleep he looked like an angel, not the wild animal, the unbroken young mustang, Len had fought all day. He had Meg's family's chin. He had long eyelashes, and the shoelaces Len had tied for him throughout the day had come undone. He needed a bath and a bedtime story and an end to this nonsense. For god's sake, what was he thinking?

The boy needed a mother.

"Wrecker," Len said, his voice gruff but not harsh. The boy mumbled and turned in his sleep. "Wrecker." Len reached in and gently shook the boy. "Come on, son. Wake up."

Wrecker's eyes fluttered open and he pulled away from Len's touch. He looked around the truck and then back at the man.

"I have to take you back," Len said.

"Home?"

Len made himself meet the boy's eyes for as long as he could before he turned away. "I can't promise you that." His face looked stern, but he was only tired. "Look." He turned back to the boy. "If I go inside and get food and blankets for the trip, will you be here when I get back?"

Wrecker nodded.

Len squinted. "You sure?" he said. "I want you to be sure. Because if you go running off again I don't think I'd have the energy to find you."

Wrecker just looked at him. Len met his gaze and let it hold him up, like a fighter slumped in the arms of his opponent, too weary to punch.

Len returned to the truck with two peanut butter sandwiches and a block of cheese, and Wrecker tore into the food like he hadn't had a meal in days. He was wearing an old sweatshirt of

17

Len's—there didn't seem to be anything suitable for winter in the bag of clothes—and Len had had to roll the sleeves well past halfway to let Wrecker's hands free. Still, he needed help peeling the orange. He wanted cookies. He was thirsty.

"Let's go see Willow," Len said, and turned over the truck engine. "She'll give you something to drink." Len backed out of the drive and rumbled slowly toward Bow Farm. He pulled in to the small cleared area and parked the truck beside a battered VW bus. He turned to the boy and considered. It would save a lot of time if Len could go alone. "Listen," he said. "I'll come back for you." He furrowed his brow. "But you've got to stay put."

Len paced down the short trail to the log building that served as common space for the inhabitants of Bow Farm. "Hello?" he shouted. "Anybody home?" He stood under the yard light to let them get a good view of him, and waited.

"Who's there?"

Len turned toward the deep bark. "Just me, Ruthie. Len. From next door."

And then from the darkness, Willow's elegant drawl. "Come to borrow a cup of sugar, Len?"

"Something like it, Willow."

The porch lamp switched on overhead, and they stood together in the fringe of light. Len felt like a galoot in his faded work coveralls. Slight, sophisticated, Willow leaned against a porch post as though it were a city lamppost and gazed at him in a way that made him swallow hard. Ruth was neither slight nor sophisticated. Older than either one and broader than both combined, she stood bundled above dungarees in what looked to Len like layers of plaid flannel topped with a lumberjack's vest. Len only had business with Willow, but he knew there wasn't much chance of dodging Ruth. Hearty, helpful, the woman resembled a country monk but was nosy as a fishwife in a gossip den.

18

"I hate to ask again, Willow," Len said, his hat in his hands and the side of his boot scraping the ground.

Willow's eyebrows arched. "Leaving so soon?"

Len flicked his eyes at her and then at Ruthie, whose arms remained crossed on her chest. He hesitated. "I didn't expect to," he said. The women waited and Len could tell they wouldn't make this easy for him. "It's the kid," he said, blushing. He pointed with his cap to the truck. "I can't keep him."

"What kid?" Ruthie looked confused.

Willow cut her a glance. "Not that it's any of our business, Len," she said, and Len groaned inwardly, knowing he'd have to tell the whole sordid story if he wanted help with Meg, "but whose kid is he, anyway?"

"A kid?" Ruthie repeated.

In the distance the truck door squeaked open and the soft pad of footsteps ruffled the quiet night. They listened intently until the boy resolved out of the darkness and stopped on the trail, a few paces from the porch. Len cleared his throat. "This is Wrecker," he said quietly.

He glanced at the women. Something skittered briefly across Willow's face, something private and complex and beyond his understanding, and Len looked guiltily away. But Ruth's square face lit like the front beam of a locomotive and she followed its trajectory straight for the boy. "Johnny Appleseed! Melody!" she shouted over her shoulder, and a short, lithe man and a gangly woman emerged from the farmhouse at her call. "We've got a visitor." She squatted at his side and bobbed to balance. "Awfully glad to see you," she said. "I'm Ruth." Then she opened her arms, and Len watched, agape, as the boy walked into them. She hugged him close and carried him past Len and Willow and up the rickety porch steps. The screen door slammed behind her.

Willow flashed Len a wry smile. "Don't worry," she said. "The

19

answer is yes." She laid a cool hand on his forearm. "Come inside, Len. You've got some explaining to do."

From the outside, the farmhouse looked old and dilapidated, with paint flakes peeling off the logs and some of the windowpanes cracked, the putty crumbling out. Len stepped over the threshold and lifted his head in surprise at how welcoming they had made it within. Woven throws and hand-hooked rugs brightened the dark wood. Willow repaired precious carpets for her living, Len knew, but she had a loom, and a love for crazy patterns and color. A giant, calcified whale vertebra propped up a stack of books, and overstuffed armchairs circled a large pillow in the center of the floor. The boy lay fast asleep in the middle, his head cushioned on one arm and small snores escaping his open mouth. Len finished his story. "At least," he said quietly, "that's all they told me. There might be more."

He glanced around at them. Willow's face was serious and composed, and she nodded slowly, running an index finger absently along her lower lip. Ruthie's gaze was focused on the boy. A tear slid over her wrinkled cheek, and she brushed it away with the sleeve of her shirt. She looked up at Len. "Did they say why she's in jail? Or how long?"

Len hesitated. Miss Hanson hadn't told him the whole story, he said. Something about drugs, something about a gun, something about a cop—she'd be in a long time, he said. He didn't tell them she'd done the shooting. He couldn't square it with the picture he held of her, a little girl with an eager smile and anxious eyes. And the bullet had only grazed the policeman.

By the time Wrecker's mother had a chance at parole, Len told them, the boy would be grown.

"Why you?" Melody was the youngest of the bunch, a blunt-mannered blonde girl from somewhere down south. Len pictured

20

a beach town full of people like her, tall and handsome and trying hard to disguise themselves with odd clothes and messy hair and a way of sloping around like their bones were made of rubber. She had a braying laugh and perpetual bad luck when it came to keeping her car on the road. Three, four times already Len had winched her VW bus from the ditch. Careless, Len had ventured, but Willow would not have it. Haphazard and impulsive, she said. Slapdash. But generous, and as loyal as a person could be.

"What?" Len said, and blinked rapidly.

Willow looked from one to the other. "Meg's sister is Wrecker's mother," she clarified. "So Len is the boy's uncle."

"I know why they asked him," Melody said, dismissively. She sat up and shook her hand as though she were tumbling dice to gamble with. She did this reflexively, the way other people pop their joints or drum their fingers. Len wanted to grab her hands and still them. He wanted to chase after her and pick up all the little piles she left in her wake. He itched to step in and stop her from making so many mistakes—Steer into the slide, he advised her, each time he came to pull her out of the mud—but she turned a deaf ear. This girl listened to nobody. She dropped from the chair to lounge cross-legged on the floor. "Come on, Len. Why would you say yes? I mean—" She stared at him frankly. "Let's face it. You're loaded up with Meg."

Len's brow furrowed. Why? This was a kid, a child with no other relatives to look after him. Wouldn't Meg have said yes? You couldn't leave a child alone in the world. But now Len was saying no. Was this right? How could this be? He looked aside, morose. Accused, somehow. And plainly guilty.

Willow came to his rescue. "You do what you have to do," she said, "and you figure it out later." She looked around at them, challenging anyone to argue. Then she laid a hand on the sleeve of his work shirt and gave a gentle squeeze. "We'll help you however

21

we can, Len. Why don't you get a good night's sleep, call the agency in the morning, and go in the daylight. We'll take care of Wrecker until you're ready to leave."

"Would you—"

"Of course." Willow nodded. "It's no trouble at all. Meg will be fine until you come back."

Melody yawned. "I'm going to bed. See you all tomorrow." She stood and looked down at the sleeping boy. "You too, buckaroo." She glanced at Ruth. "I'll come take over in the morning. You staying with him tonight?"

The broad woman fluffed the pillow behind her. "Wouldn't miss it for the world." She turned to Willow. "You go on, now, too. He's just a wee thing. I can handle him fine."

"He's giving you the wrong idea," Len muttered. "Wait'll he wakes up. I'm telling you."

Ruthie leaned forward and balanced her hands on her knees. "How bad could he be? Three years old."

"Oh, pretty bad, all right," Willow said, standing anyway. She looked tired, her crow's-feet and laugh lines deeper than usual. "I don't doubt you, Len. At three they're too small to spank, even if you could catch them. But we're not talking a lifetime commitment, here. We're talking about you getting a good night's sleep and a little daylight before you drive six more hours through the trees. After the day you just had."

Len rubbed his balding head. "I could use the rest," he admitted. "I'd keep him at home, only—"

Willow waved him off. The picture he'd painted of Meg's murderous advance was still clear in her mind. "Take your time in the morning," she advised. "Don't worry about him until you're ready to leave." She paused and looked away. "It's been a while since I had a little fellow to look after." Len caught a startled glance from

Ruthie. "Who knows?" Willow added. The corner of her lip turned up, and again Len watched the fleeting expression lightly touch and vanish from her face. "I might even like it."

Len nodded. There were so many things he didn't understand. But Melody had gone, the one they called Johnny Appleseed had evaporated already, unobserved, and Willow was making her way toward the door. He needed to get home to Meg. "I can't thank you enough," he said, and meant it. The boy snuffled in his sleep and rolled onto his side. Len gazed at him. Then he turned on his heel and left.

The cab of his truck seemed oddly empty on the short ride home.

Ruthie slept in the chair that first night, waking often to make sure that the boy was still breathing, adjusting the blankets when he flung them off, once moving him back onto the cushion when his thrashing left him curled like a snail on the bare floor. She was too excited to sink deeply into sleep. His presence felt like an unearned reward, some random jackpot she didn't deserve and couldn't keep but which, however temporary, she was determined to treasure.

By morning her resistance was down. The light filtered in to play on the mottled pink wrinkles of her face, and her snores abraded the silence like the honks and squeaks of raucous waterbirds.

A catch in her own labored breathing startled her and she floundered toward consciousness, rubbing her eyes with both fists and creaking to standing. The boy was still there. Ruthie peered closer. Still there and awake, now. He had the blanket over his head and was observing her through the crocheted eyeholes. She stretched and yawned and looked out the window. "Well, I'll be chicken-fried," she said, loud enough for Wrecker to hear. "Snow?"

She blinked hard to make sure she wasn't dreaming. "I can hardly believe it." She turned to face the couch and said, "Kid. Get up. This'll melt by noon and you don't want to miss it."

A layer of white blanketed the world outside, ice riming the tree branches, the evergreen boughs dusted with snow. Inside, Wrecker froze in place beneath his blanket. Ruthie moved near him. She squatted down and put her face close to Wrecker's, so her eyes filled the eyeholes from the other side. She did something funny with her eyebrows. Then she crossed her eyes, tightened her lips, and wiggled her ears.

"Good morning, Wrecker," she said in a normal voice. "I'm Ruth. I'll be your pilot for this morning, so fasten your seat belt, secure your tray table, and prepare for takeoff."

"I'm hungry," Wrecker said, his voice muffled by the throw.

"Right this way." And Ruth didn't seem to mind that Wrecker followed her into the kitchen with the crocheted throw draped over his head.

Len held on to the pay phone handset so tightly his knuckles were white. He'd never had a line put in at the house. Who had the money for that? When he had a call to make, he'd drive down the mountain and use the booth outside the Mercantile. "Miss *Hanson*," he repeated for the eleventh time. "I'm holding for *Miss Hanson*."

"Please deposit forty cents for the next three minutes," the operator whined. Len searched his pockets. He had thirty-five cents. He dropped it into the coin slots.

"Please deposit—"

"This is Miss Hanson."

"—five cents more for the next three minutes."

"Miss Hanson!" But Len had no more change, and the operator terminated his call.

24

Len slumped against the grimy glass of the booth. He needed to reach the social worker to let her know he was bringing the boy back, could *not* keep the child. He flapped open his wallet to reveal three worn ten-dollar bills. He would walk over to the Mercantile and get change for one of them. He would return to the phone booth and feed quarters until, come hell or high water, the woman took his call.

"I'm sorry," the receptionist said when Len finally reached her again. "Miss Hanson has left for lunch."

"What time do you expect her back," Len asked, weary. He'd been at this all morning. He winced to think what kind of trouble the kid was stirring up at Bow Farm.

"She's scheduled to be out until Tuesday. Shall I take a message?"

"Tell her—," Len said, and then stopped. Tuesday? Len stood there in despair. He could think of nothing to say.

"Sir? Are you there, sir?" A long pause and a sigh.

And then the phone went dead in his hand.

It was not a matter of keeping up with Wrecker. Melody learned early on how impossible a task that would be. She marshaled the efforts of Johnny Appleseed, short and furry and rapid as a squirrel, and woke Ruth from her recuperative slumber and stationed her at the far end of the field, and the three of them kept the boy corralled, herded him toward the others when his curiosity stretched past the boundaries of safety. He didn't speak—they had begun to worry about this—but made noises to keep himself company: the rat-tat-tat of machine gun fire, the growls and snarls of wild animals, a tuneless humming that resembled singing but was not. They wondered if he was deaf, so inattentive was he to their directives.

He was not deaf. When Melody shouted across the field, "Johnny Appleseed! Got anything good to eat?" the boy swiveled his head first toward Melody, taller than the others and lanky and so casual in her movements as to appear almost clumsy—watched her with eyebrows raised, extreme interest—and then turned to the compact man they called Johnny Appleseed and watched him dig in the pockets of his pants.

"Some nuts," he called back. "Half a dozen dried figs. What's left of this chocolate bar and a couple of cubes of cheese."

Wrecker made a beeline for him and the others gathered, too. Johnny Appleseed had the sun behind his head. Wrecker squinted up. "Chocolate," he said.

Johnny Appleseed raised his eyebrows in comic surprise. "So you *do* talk?"

"I want chocolate."

Ruth laughed with something like triumph and relief. "Give him that chocolate, man!"

Johnny Appleseed knelt so his face was even with Wrecker's and looked into his eyes. The boy stood stout, his chest high and his face unmoving. Blond hair lay in a tousled mat over his scalp and his bad haircut showed signs of resistance. Pug nose, red lips, blue eyes steady as steel and behind them a whisper of gray Johnny Appleseed locked in on. He knew the language of trees and of wild things and he watched that gray like a deer watches the leaves of the trees for what moves behind them.

Melody flinched for him. Ruth watched, silent, helpless, and her eyes shone with tears. But Wrecker stood stock-still, eyes open.

Johnny Appleseed reached for the hem of the sweatshirt Wrecker wore. He lifted it gently to make a pocket that he had the boy hold. Then he reached into the pockets of his own pants and emptied each into the fold. Cheese, chocolate, figs and nuts, and a piece of polished sea-glass, blue, and a stone in the shape of a heart, and two pieces of gum still in their wrappers and a folded photo of a dog, the creases gone white, and some lint.

"What's mine is yours, kid," he said, and stood.

It was for the night; and then it was until Tuesday, until Thursday, until the next social worker hired to replace the absent Miss Hanson could review the case and there was quite a stack of folders before Wrecker's and would Mr.—Mr.—would *Len*, all right, please be patient with the department, there were children in far more dire need than his son (*not* my son, he shouted over the phone, driven to distraction)—Very well! Very well then, Mr. Len, but he'd have to be patient, they'd get to it as soon as they could.

Which he gradually understood to mean never.

At Bow Farm they took turns sleeping in the chair beside Wrecker and during the day they traded off spending time with him. What took three of them that first day later required only two, and when they became more adept—more wily, faster, developed more stamina (which is to say when Wrecker grew comfortable enough on the farm to agree to stay, when he began to prefer their company to that of his own, solitary)—one alone could spend the day with Wrecker in relative peace and safety. It's true that his feats acquired the status of legends. The day Wrecker jumped from the barn roof (two stories!) to bounce from the hay bales below. The day Wrecker was lost and they scoured the pond bottom for his body. The day Wrecker climbed into the pickup and released the brake, took it out of gear, and rode it all the way downslope into the field, where a big rock slowed it down by lodging itself in the oil pan. He seemed to need to feel his body collide with the physical world to know he existed. He threw his food, sometimes; he ignored them, he drowned out the sound of their voices by plugging his ears with his fingers and singing nonsense

27

songs; he sometimes refused to put away the toys they gathered for him; he demanded bedtime stories at breakfast and pancakes at dinner. They couldn't control him and so they gave up trying. But neither could he control them, and he, too, came to understand this, and the shimmering tentative thing that stretched between them those first days thickened into something workable, something like love in overalls, love with a spade in its hand.

The pile of firewood by the barn grew mountainous as Len struggled to repay them for keeping the boy. It had been five weeks, and something had to be done or they would be buried under the split rounds. Willow broached the issue one evening when Wrecker was asleep on the farmhouse floor and the others lounged around, warm-bellied from dinner and eager for spring. "Len's shrinking," she announced. The others nodded gravely.

"That man's between a rock and a hard place," Ruth agreed.

Melody furrowed her brow. "Not exactly *our* rock or hard place," she growled, and the others looked at her, not accusing, just mildly surprised. They blinked and looked back at the boy. Melody persisted. "Look. One more night sleeping in this chair and I'll turn into a lunatic. Where would we even keep him?"

Ruth faced her. "Well, he's too big for a shoebox," she said dryly. "And we'd be arrested if we stuffed him in the oven."

Melody reddened.

Johnny Appleseed, who stayed so silent most times they almost forgot he was there, said softly, "He's too small to sleep by himself."

Willow raised her eyebrows. "Any volunteers to sleep with him?"

Johnny Appleseed shrugged. "Sitka won't mind. She has the pups. I'll make a mattress for him on my floor with the dogs."

Ruth nodded. "Won't hurt him, spend some time in a pack like that." She tipped her head toward Melody. "What do you say? Harbor the fugitive a while longer?"

Melody cast guarded glances at them all. No one else seemed to think it odd, the arrival of this small interloper. None of the others seemed plagued by such rapid-fire emotion at his presence. He set something aflutter in her that was hard to name and harder to ignore. Melody frowned. She rose from her chair and then knelt on the floor beside the sleeping boy. He was curled like a question mark under one of Willow's blankets, his fist clinging tightly to a rusty metal pipe he had salvaged from the yard. Asleep, he threw off heat like a stoked furnace. He was no bigger than her duffel bag packed halfway, no heavier than a crate of oranges, aromatic in the sun. His lips moved and his mouth opened and he gave a long, soughing sigh. Dreaming. Melody understood. She dreamed like that, too. She tilted back onto her heels and faked nonchalance. "If it helps Len." Her voice betrayed her and she shrugged and cleared her throat. "I won't be the one to say no."

And so it was decided. Sooner or later the state would assign him a permanent family, but until that time he could call Bow Farm home. They thought of him as a puppy and they took him in.

CHAPTER TWO

Melody wrestled her bus along the muddy ruts of the farm road, gunned it uphill, and came to a valve-pinging, clutch-stinking stop on top of the small rise. Beyond this the drive gave way to weeds and water. They'd made a feeble effort to fix it the year before, digging channels and hacking away at the greenery for an hour until their hands blistered and Melody quit, dropping her shovel and slumping against a mossy rock. The forest wants the road that bad? She'd waved her hand royally, dispensing with the territory. Let it have it. We'll carry our shit from here.

Carrying their shit didn't seem like such a good plan at this point. Not when her shit included an eight-foot, hundred-pound post she'd just salvaged from a fish shack slated for tear down in Eureka. Melody got out and circled the Volkswagen. The bus was decorated with spots, painted one day in a pique of fancy (and with the assistance of mildly hallucinogenic mushrooms) to resemble a ladybug. It looked like a bread loaf with a bad rash, which is how Melody felt the day after, and she left it that way as a reminder to go easy on her body chemistry. She leaned back now and squinted up at her rescued treasure, strapped with loops of clothesline to the roof. There was no way she was going to get it off the bus, down the hill, past the farmhouse, and over the next hundred yards or so to the barn. Not by herself, anyway.

But Bow Farm was good that way. In a pinch there was always

someone to count on for help. Or to bitch to, or to gripe about, or to bum money off of, or to suffer alongside—yes, and thank you, Jesus, there was room enough to get the hell away from one another when they needed that, too. That was its raison d'être, really. To be French about it. Which Melody was not. But it gave it a kind of weight, made what they were choosing to do seem considered, intentional, instead of the crazy shot in the dark they were really taking. The bottom line was simple: do what you want and no one will stop you. The alpha and omega. Freedom.

Melody hitched up her jeans, glanced over her shoulder once more at the post, and headed down the rutted path. Buying the place had been her bright idea, and now, with three wet winters under her belt, she could start to take some credit for the accomplishment. It was touch-and-go for a while there, admittedly. She'd gone to college for drinking, sex, a little art history and some basic accounting courses, and dropped out before becoming truly proficient at any of them. Twenty-five years old, loose-jointed, lazy, and green as this afternoon's salad, she'd jumped off the path her parents had ordained and was beating her way around a miserable thicket. She'd been flailing for some years and had nothing to show for it but a number of psychic bruises and the growing sense that she would have to take action if anything were going to change. What she needed was a permanent address. A place to park her weary bones. It sounded like land to the more levelheaded of her friends, and land sounded like money. Ask your father, they suggested.

Melody said bluntly, No.

She winced, remembering. Ask her father? Hell, no. She would do it herself. Somehow. When she was eighty, maybe. When she was a hundred and twenty. But then she agreed to fill in for a friend at that beachfront gallery opening, and Willow turned up among the hundreds, and to avoid the crowd they ducked outside and walked and talked. Willow had just settled a divorce, changed her name, and begun to bend her considerable attention to forgetting the past twenty years. She had a good livelihood and similar aims, and in time Melody mustered her courage and launched her idea. Crazy, she knew. Harebrained, probably. But what if they were to go in on a piece of land, far enough north and neglected enough to afford, and cut loose from the rest of the world and its cranky opinions on how they should live?

Go in? Willow asked, her natural courtesy masking her natural skepticism. Did Melody mean split the cost? And did that mean—

Ask your father, Melody's friends insisted.

She wavered. But why not? He'd bought her everything she didn't want. Braces and prep school and two miserable years of college where she slept with every boy who asked her until she discovered, yawning, that that was just another brand of commerce. He'd paid her bail when she was busted sharing a blunt behind the local cemetery, hired his lawyer to clean up her record, bribed the newspaper to keep the family name off the roll of recent miscreants. Then he shelled out a healthy deposit for one of Miss Porter's extended trips to Europe, where she would be properly chaperoned and might be encouraged to develop appropriate remorse for the mess she had gotten her family involved in. She declined to participate. And forgot to visit them for two years.

Just ask, her friends said. All he can say is—

Melody broke down, scripted an appeal, and went to her father. Look, she said, desperate to keep the waver out of her voice. I know how to read and write and do math adequate for my own use. I can speak French, which is utterly useless to me now, and I can spot a con man a mile away. I am not vulnerable to those who would use my ambition against me, as I have none and am furthermore indifferent to the standard brands of happiness that are most frequently purveyed. Give me twenty thousand dollars and you may omit me from your will without incurring any bitterness on my part.

Her father was a man who knew a good deal when he saw one. He looked up over his reading glasses at this young woman standing in front of his desk. He adopted a look of deep concentration. Melody was not fooled. If she had said one hundred thousand dollars he would have had exactly the same look on his face. And then he would have written the check.

He wrote the check. He handed it to her and when she reached to take it he continued to hold on. Their skin didn't touch, but they were connected through the medium of that piece of paper.

Melody did not dare let go. It had taken all of her courage and more humility than she thought she owned to come this far. If she released the check she would not have had the strength to lift her arm and reach for it again.

She held on. He let go.

Thanks a million, Pops, she said. She wanted him to know what a bargain he had struck.

It's nothing, he said perversely. Don't spend it all in one place.

But she did.

Hadn't she been vindicated, though? Bow Farm was paradise. Melody paused at a level patch halfway down the hill. Ahead of her squatted the farmhouse, and beyond that the barn, gone to gray and tilting off its foundations like a drunken matron, her dear old home sweet home. And now she was going to have to lug that post all that distance to it. Shit. She had embarked on a restoration project that rivaled any other and couldn't seem to curb her impulse to collect materials to sustain it. Nothing was paid for but nothing was stolen, either—although a few broken slabs of marble had been liberated from the back side of an old bank without explicit permission. Real work hadn't actually commenced on the project; apart from some basic tasks like replacing broken panes of glass so the rain would stay out and making a monumental effort (okay, Ruth's monumental effort) to clean the hayloft so she could set up a bedroom, she was still in the collecting phase. So? They owned the place. She, Willow, and that finance company Willow had finagled a loan from. She could work on it for the next half century if she lasted that long. Sure, there was the balloon payment to deal with—but that was fifteen long years in the future.

The trees that flanked the path to the farmhouse were scruffy little scrub oaks that gave way to stately buckeyes in the dooryard. Melody shuffled on, glancing east when a break in the brush let the view yawn before her. Loggers had hauled out the best timber decades before, but there were still patches of old firs tucked among the scrub and hardwoods. There was something comforting about them. Generations of disasters befell them, and look, Ma—still standing! She glimpsed a movement below and heard the screen door of the farmhouse slam. Ruth. No mistaking that distinctive waddle. The boy buzzed around her, an errant electron tethered by affinity to the massive nucleus Ruthie presented. Melody skirted the log farmhouse and followed them around to the backyard.

Ruthie's mouth was puckered with clothespins and she reached to clip a sacklike flowered nightdress alongside some voluminous undergarments. She toed the wicker basket of wet clothes Melody's way. "Make yourself useful," she mumbled.

"Kid can't reach?" Melody dipped into the basket and shook out a miniature pair of corduroy pants before pinning them to the line. At least he was out of diapers.

Ruth used the last of her clothespins to pair socks. "Reach, nothing. He's got a vertical leap Tarzan would envy. I had to retie

34

the line after he was swinging on it." She nodded toward the kitchen. "I sent him in to play. I've washed this load twice already and I wouldn't mind seeing it dry without dragging in the mud first."

Melody glanced at the sky. "You must think spring is coming."

"Oh, ye of little faith."

"Don't say I didn't warn you." In Mattole they measured rainfall by the foot. Winter came and the creeks flooded, the land slid, and what looked like paradise in the golden rays of autumn turned into a muddy mess. How else would they have managed to buy the land so cheap? That, and distance. If San Francisco was the center of the universe, the Mattole Valley hovered in its nether reaches, a day's drive north and so rugged and remote that even the coast highway surrendered its ocean view and headed inland for more stable footing. But Melody's hopes had soared when they stumbled across Bow Farm. Remote, dilapidated, the neglected farmstead covered eighty acres of cleared meadow and mixed conifers and a year-round spring, the water sweet tasting and cold enough to set their teeth. The huge barn was weathered to a slant but still standing, the farmhouse itself frayed but sound. It was perfect. And thirty thousand dollars more than they were prepared to spend. Melody stood behind the real estate agent and scribbled furiously on the back of an envelope. OLD TREES! she wrote. ROSE BUSHES! She tapped her pen against her front teeth and tried not to scuttle the deal with her breathlessness. Willow cast an amused glance her way. In thirty seconds she had the agent charmed; in ten minutes he was looking for creative ways to finance; in three weeks Bow Farm was theirs, with a mortgage they could handle and a lump sum due at the end of it.

Ruth took back the basket. "I'll finish this. Go in. He was asking for you."

"Everything okay?"

"Bad night, Johnny said."

Melody ducked under the line and jumped the steps. The back door to the kitchen had a half-window in it and she peered in to see the boy hunched, splay-legged, on the linoleum. He held something in his hand. Melody pushed open the door.

Wrecker tilted his dirt-smudged face toward her. "Oh. Deedee." His voice was munchkinlike, piping but throaty—a flute that aspired to run away from the orchestra. This nickname business, it was a new thing. The last time she'd been called anything but her own name had been in college, and the tag had to do with her prowess at knocking back shots.

"Hey, little man. Show me what you've got." Melody ran a hand over the velvet of his head. Ruth had just taken the clippers to his mop, and his ears lunged from the sides of his head like vulnerable creatures suddenly stripped of shelter. She examined the wad of paper he handed her. It was folded into a dense, bulky triangle. "What is it?"

"Watch." He reached up to retrieve his toy and with his left hand he carefully stood it on one point. The sinews on the back of his neck guarded a tender hollow no bigger than the nail of Melody's thumb. She'd never been around kids, much. Not up close. She couldn't get over it, how small he was, and how much noise and energy and willfulness and—and *person* there was. She squatted down to observe his preparations. He made a circle with the index finger of his right hand and then he let loose and flicked the wadded football hard. It bounced off the lower cabinets and ricocheted back to collide with Ruth's shin as she entered the kitchen.

"Finesse, buddy." Ruth set down the basket. "And keep it out of my stew."

"Stew? That's what smells so good." Melody followed Ruth to the woodstove and peered over her shoulder as she clattered about, lifting lids and rattling utensils. Ruthie was queen of the kitchen. When she arrived there was still a layer of grease on the windowpanes left over from the previous owners, and the refrigerator coils were lost in a thick matting of dog hair and dust. No dirt, they soon learned, stood a chance against Ruth's eagle eye and elbow grease. She cleaned with a fury and she cooked that way, too, staking a claim to the four-burner woodstove and turning out real meals with whatever she could find. Eggs from Johnny Appleseed's wild chickens fried in butter; scalloped potatoes with a thick coating of salt and cheese—she had a penchant for grease and sweets, and was killing them with it. Ruth dipped a spoonful of stew for Melody to taste. "Got barley in it." With a defensive edge to her voice, she added, "It's good for you."

"Stew?"

"Hold on, little sweetheart. It's still cooking." Ruth dragged a chair out from the table, its legs screeching against the linoleum, and pushed it up against the sink. "See what you can do to lose some of that dirt."

Melody watched Wrecker climb onto the chair and twist the faucet, wet his hands, and wipe them dry on the front of his shirt. They were a pair, those two. The boy had been at Bow Farm for two months, now, but it hadn't taken any time at all for him to peg Ruth for a kindred soul. Wrecker gravitated to commotion, and even when Ruth dozed her breathing made a distinct wheezing whistle. She was sliding down the backside of middle age, losing the war against gravity, and wore her considerable weight in a soft wide landing pad around her middle. The better to hug him with, Melody figured; the better to do the Bump as they boogied around the kitchen. Ruth had fallen for the boy hard and thought nothing of spending the whole day in foolery to coax an unexpected smile from the foursquare of his face. Melody had watched Ruth sneak glances at Wrecker throughout each day; together they'd seen his sober face go quickly livid with anger or frustration, watched it brighten with delight until he noticed and swallowed it, embarrassed. The change was quicker and more intimate than the weather. He was scarred and volatile and more luminous than any celestial body. There had to be a way to defuse some of his explosive anger, Ruth worried, before the boy blew himself up by accident.

"I made you something," Ruth said, her eyebrows lifting and wiggling like nascent caterpillars. Wrecker chortled, a cascade of raspy giggles that Melody matched without meaning to. He had wrinkled his face, trying to duplicate the burlesque routine Ruth performed with her bushy brows. Ruth turned away and reached under the sink, rustled about with some clinking sounds. She creaked herself back up. In her hands shimmered a sheet of crushed soda cans wired together. "Get over here," she commanded. When Wrecker advanced toward her, she fed his arms through holes in the sides and let the tunic-shaped contraption dangle about him. She stood back and beamed. "You're invincible, buddy. Nobody can mess with you now."

"Dinty Spaceman?" Melody ventured.

"In the flesh. Newly outfitted with his ray-deflecting armor." Ruth gave him a gentle shove and the tin cans jingled. "Now get out to your spaceship and make the galaxy safe for mankind."

Melody stepped narrowly out of his path as Wrecker bulldozed his way for the back door. The woman was obsessed when it came to the boy's happiness. Ruth lived in a makeshift room under the rafters of the farmhouse and came down most mornings to find him waiting impatiently for her in the kitchen, and each day Ruth outdid herself, inventing games no one had played before and tableaux Wrecker could reenact for hours. She folded paper airplanes that fell from the sky, grew expert at farting noises made under her armpit. The two of them invented knock-knock jokes with incoherent punch lines. Twice a week she would fill the metal tub and scrub Wrecker raw, banish dirt from behind his ears and between his toes, and discuss twenty-car pileups. But none of that held a candle to Dinty Spaceman-a-Go-Go, with his metal colander for a helmet and rocket ship docked in the yard. In the absence of rocket fuel, Dinty Spaceman had to dance on the hood to activate the thrust engines and prepare for takeoff. Indeed, any time he noticed a decrease in power he had only to climb through the window and stomp a few steps—the wilder the better, as Go-Go was never mild—on the wide hood to revitalize the engine. He could fly to the moon, then. He could zoom through the Milky Way.

Sure, and he could slip off the rain-slicked car hood and crack his head so his brains poured out, Melody thought, but so far there had been no serious injuries.

Melody watched the boy through the kitchen window and glanced toward the front door when the hinges squeaked. Sitka the dog entered first, with Johnny Appleseed the human close behind. Johnny Appleseed the *mostly* human, Melody corrected herself. Her friend was as far on the spectrum as a person could get and still belong to the same species. Tiny, leathern, silent as the night, he pictured himself some hybrid form of plant and animal in a base of dirt and water. The women moved over to make room for him at the window. Melody lifted her chin and gestured toward the boy. "He gave you some trouble last night?"

Johnny shrugged. "He's no trouble to me. Just to himself." He tipped his head toward the boy in a gesture of respect. The day before, as they were driving the Mattole Road toward South Fork, the motor of Johnny's beloved Ford Falcon had burst into flames. "That was the end of it," he told them, his dark eyes drooping sorrowfully. With Wrecker's help he had shoved the rusty vehicle from the bridge into the river below. Aghast and euphoric, they'd watched it dip and bob in the current, and then they'd trudged the nine miles back to the farm. The boy rode the last four, exhausted, clinging to Johnny's back, and hadn't complained once. "It was a long day. More than he could handle, maybe." Johnny held Melody's gaze for a long beat before turning to Ruth. "Most nights he's fine."

Melody, shoulder to shoulder with Ruth, felt the older woman falter. If a train were barreling down on the boy, Ruth would heave herself in front of it to save him. But this train was stealthier, colliding with him in his sleep and leaving him squalling or, worse, nearly silent, his eyes wide and his pajamas soaked in sweat—and there was nothing any of them could do to stop it. Melody glanced at Johnny. They all knew it was more than just exhaustion that had clobbered the boy. Whatever he'd been through before had left its mark on him. "What do you think happened to him?" She kept her voice low. "Before he got here, I mean."

They watched as Wrecker quit bouncing on the roof and slid back into the car through the open window. His face was half shaded, half in sun. He had just powered up the rockets and was intent on navigating.

"He's here, isn't he?" Johnny Appleseed dispensed his words like drops of water from a bedouin's goatskin canteen. "He can't go back. So help him go forward."

"What's done is done," Ruth said crisply, as if she believed it.

Melody wasn't so sure. Everyone at Bow Farm seemed to have some private, unresolved reason for being there. The land had a way of calling to its own. That first August they'd dragged Ruth half dead out of the sea, bullied her back to life only to discover that she'd been making an honest effort to leave it. Whoever she'd been before—her old name, her old home—had drowned in the attempt. The March after that Johnny Appleseed

40

had wandered mysteriously from the woods that fringed the bowl of cleared meadow. Now the boy had arrived, with his blue eyes and his short fuse and that trash bag for a suitcase, and made himself at home.

"Maybe," Melody said. Still, she couldn't shake the feeling that something important had changed.

Ruth and Johnny helped Melody haul the post down from the roof of the bus. They'd lugged it as far as the farmhouse when the drizzle began, and they dropped the post and ran for the laundry.

"Go ahead in with Wrecker," Willow told Ruth, arriving in time to cross the yard and offer Melody some shelter with her umbrella.

Melody was sick and tired of the rain by this time of year. She pushed inside with the laundry basket under one arm while Willow sat on the porch bench and removed her muddy boots. That was Willow: the picture of preparedness. She kept a spare pair of shoes next to the door so she wouldn't track dirt into the farmhouse. Melody had trouble keeping track of her rain hat. Her keys. Half the time, her mind. But Willow was Willow, which meant Bow Farm had cloth napkins and matching cutlery nesting together in a drawer in the kitchen. They had olives, the occasional bottle of good wine, cured salami, Gorgonzola cheese, a decent assortment of fruits and vegetables. Ruth was averse to commerce and cooked with whatever the others brought home. Johnny Appleseed—who would have been content with moss and small grubs—raised hens for their eggs, traded for meat, and produced cases of canned goods he acquired through mysterious channels. Melody offered beans and grains from the Mercantile that had to be soaked overnight and cooked for hours to become palatable. She was committed to eating natural foods but hid a valuable stash of Snickers bars and Cracker Jack boxes in the barn for bad cramps and midnight cravings. It was her secret. Wrecker knew, but she'd paid for his silence with chocolate.

Ruth lifted the lid from the soup pot and ladled it into bowls.

"Told you it would rain." Melody reached for her bowl and parked herself at the round kitchen table between Wrecker and Johnny Appleseed.

The boy had finished half his stew by the time Ruth eased herself down. "Mind your manners," Ruth told him. "Nobody eats until everybody sits." Melody looked up guiltily and laid her spoon beside her bowl. Ruth glanced at her. "Rain?" she scoffed. "That was a sprinkle. Spring's here."

"Not by a long shot." Melody lifted her spoon again and went to work on the stew. "Pretty good stuff, Ruth."

Johnny Appleseed nodded reverently. "You're the best, Ruthie." He turned to Melody. "She's right, you know. Winter's over." He glanced around the table. "Day after tomorrow, I start planting."

There was a moment of shocked silence.

"What?" Melody shook her head and laughed at him. "Are you crazy?" She gestured toward the boy. He sat at her elbow, shoveling the stew in as fast as he could. "You can't go yet. Where would he sleep?"

Johnny's face clouded. "The ground's ready," he said softly.

Melody put her spoon down and stared at him. She cupped her hands over Wrecker's ears. "No fucking way, Johnny." She enunciated slowly and forcefully so that there would be no confusion. Johnny had his dates wrong. Once he left for his planting contracts they wouldn't see him for weeks. He lived in the forest with his crew of wild boys and worked dawn to dusk, planting seedlings over acres of lumber company clear-cuts. On the side he tended his own crop, hidden in obscure patches on federal land.

"Will you excuse us?" Willow rose from the table, cleared her bowl, and gathered Wrecker from his seat stacked with pillows. She gave Melody a meaningful glance. "You three work it out. Whatever you need from me, I'll try to do," she said, and carried the boy into the living room.

Melody felt the red creep into her cheeks as she watched Willow settle the boy down against the base of her armchair. She hadn't signed on for this. Things were fine so long as Johnny took care of him, nights, but if Johnny left—she swung her head toward Ruth and spoke in a low mutter. "I thought we were in this together. Tell him, Ruthie. If he goes now, there's no one to cover for him."

Johnny Appleseed sighed. "I'm right here," he said. "I'm listening." Melody glared at him as Willow's voice floated in from the other room. Some nights she read to Wrecker from Sinbad or Aladdin, the language a great wafting cloud of image and incomprehension; other times she made up stories, launching her characters—almost always two big boys and their smaller sister—into the unknown on the back of a flying carpet. This night's story began with a lion, his mane thick and luxuriant, the muscles on his back a cushion for the small boy who rode up there. "Hold on, Wrecker," she called softly, swaying him back and forth between her calves and introducing sound effects—the soft swish of the wind, the bark of hyenas in the night—that filled the stony silence in the kitchen.

"I can't wait, Melody," Johnny said. His eyes were dark and dewy, softly beseeching. "When it's time, it's time."

"Ruthie?"

Melody already knew the answer. Ruth would spend all day with Wrecker, would feed him and pick up after him and wash his clothes for him and mend his scrapes. She would do anything Melody asked her to do. She just couldn't let Wrecker sleep up in her room with her. It was killing her to say no. "If he bugs you

43

too much," Ruth promised, "he can go back to the living room. I'll sleep in the chair. It wasn't so bad."

Melody scowled. Together they turned to look at Willow and Wrecker. Genies, camels, sand dunes, and an elephant of the king, to whose palace Wrecker was invited for royal tea—but not a single word about who would look after him in real life. "Why bother," Melody muttered to herself, morose. Willow was fond of the boy, but she had set her boundaries. She did everything on her own terms.

Willow continued. "The king had a beautiful daughter. He had horsemen and minions and a magnificent library with shelves that stretched four stories high. He lived in a palace surrounded by water that was greener than emeralds and warmed by springs that went deep to the center of the earth."

"A moat?" Wrecker clung to wakefulness, shipwrecked in an ocean of sleep.

"A moat," Willow said, hardly louder than a whisper. Melody had to strain to hear her. "Yes. And when the elephant reached the moat he knelt down. First one giant leg"—she extended her left leg—"and then the other giant leg"—now the right—"and with his lo-o-o-o-ng trunk, he reached over his head for the little boy."

"For me," Wrecker mumbled, his lids sinking.

"For you." Willow's voice was softer still, more melodious than ever, and she smoothed the hair around his ears. "And a boat was waiting." Sleep billowed over the boy and he relaxed his neck and let the weight of his head fall into her hands. "And the boat slowly carried the boy across the emerald water." She wrapped her arms around his shoulders and held him snug. "And into the land of sleep." Willow glanced toward the kitchen and held Melody's gaze. She lifted him onto the pillow and covered him with a throw.

There was a tentative knock at the door.

Willow stepped forward and opened it. Len hadn't washed up from the afternoon's work. He wore a stripe of pine sap across one cheekbone and clutched a full paper sack in both arms. "I forgot to give these to you." He extended it toward her. "Your library books."

Willow opened the door wider and motioned him forward.

He hesitated. "Is something wrong?"

Willow leaned toward him to take the books and said something softly.

Len swallowed. He looked stricken.

Willow led him into the kitchen. "Hey, Len," Johnny Appleseed said, and Ruth and Melody nodded.

Len's voice was gravelly. "I'll take him tomorrow."

Ruth gave a small cry, and her hand flew to cover her mouth.

The color drained from Melody's face. "What?"

Len's gaze darted from her face to Willow's and back again. "I thought—"

"Is there a family for him?" Ruth asked.

"No, but—"

Melody shot Willow a look and turned her back to them. She shook her hands, thinking. Her shoulders rose and fell with each breath. When she turned again, her mouth was set in a resolute line. Len's jaw dropped. Melody watched him glance quickly at Willow and the others. Was it that obvious? Panic, but she was fending that off. "Fine," Melody said. "He'll start sleeping in the barn." Her voice quavered slightly. "What the hell, right? While Johnny's gone, Wrecker can stay up there with me." She glanced at Ruth. "You'll help me get it ready?"

"Of course," Ruth murmured.

"I'll spend tomorrow with him," Johnny said. "Give you some time to prepare."

Melody nodded. Her right hand started flicking, but she stilled it by gripping a chair, pulling it out from the table. "Sit," she told Len. "Eat."

Len was in no position to argue.

"Give it up, already," Melody said. Ruth was starting to irritate her, apologizing, trying to make amends. They were rigging a makeshift wall in the barn loft to prevent the kid from pitching over the side. They had already commandeered a mattress for him and rearranged the space to make room for it. "It's fine for him to be here. I said so. Let's just go over the instructions once more."

If he choked. If he fell down the steps. If he broke a limb. If he needed to pee in the night. If he wanted a glass of water. If he spit where he shouldn't. If he couldn't get to sleep. If he woke up in the night and she couldn't calm him. There were a thousand things that could go wrong, and Melody wanted to be prepared. At least he was small enough for her to throw him over her shoulder and run for help.

Everything would be okay, Ruth assured her. He was a good boy.

And if he got under her skin?

The truth was, things were getting out of hand. No one knew how long it was going to take for Len to work out some permanent arrangement for the kid, and the longer he was there—well, it didn't take a rocket scientist to figure out that the longer he stayed, the more at home he'd make himself. And the more he'd weasel his way into their affections.

Weasel? Wrong animal. This boy was a dog straight up and down, though it pained Melody to admit it, bothered her that a person—especially a kid, way too young to have figured out what kind of persona to move in through the world—a person could be so completely what they were. He had a doglike way of attaching himself to any person who fed him or made him feel good, and a way of muscling through the world that was as much like a dog as any other animal Melody could think of. He ran directly at things, stopped to smell them, tested their resistance to his enthusiastic battering, and ran directly on. He was interested in everything, fearless and physically skilled enough to engage in nearly any activity he could think up—enough so that Melody and Johnny Appleseed and certainly Ruth, who hadn't the advantage of youth, wore themselves out worrying over his safety. He was different with Willow; quieter, better behaved. Melody understood this. She loved Willow's arch wit and prodigious intelligence and her singular sense of style, but there was something in Willow that inspired an odd formality. Around Willow, you wanted to do your best. They all felt it. No one wanted to disappoint her.

With Wrecker, there was this other thing, too. The boy didn't seem to need petting, but when he was tired he didn't resist it. Even Melody had carried him around, felt his body grow heavy with sleep and slump against her. On trips to town he would keel over on the seat and sleep with his head in her lap. Melody was awkward with her body, strong but gangly and not much given to hugging, but the boy might come up beside her on a walk and without any self-consciousness slip his small hand into hers and walk that way until something caught his attention and he went sprinting off. It stung her. She could never initiate that affection—couldn't sweep him up in a bear hug as Ruthie would do, or pat her lap for him to climb into after supper—but it surprised her, the flood of emotion that arose when, unbidden, he leaned his weight against her or wrapped his arms around her neck for a free ride to anywhere.

They were going to have to find him a home, soon. Because

she was starting to wonder—just to herself, she would admit this to no one—how she could manage to let him go.

Ruth fixed a special dinner for Johnny's last day before planting. She roasted beets, pan-fried some venison Len had brought over, opened a can of string beans, baked a blackberry cobbler with fruit she'd put up the season before. Wrecker finished most of his plate before he fell asleep at the table. Ruthie was impressed. "Where'd you take him? He didn't even make it to dessert."

"He's a tough little kid." Johnny allowed a small smile. "We went all over."

Yeah, Melody thought, she bet they did. She'd tagged along on a couple of Johnny's marathon routes. It was hard to keep up with him as he leapt over grassy hummocks, wove through stands of madrone, skidded down steep slopes, vaulted the trunks of fallen trees—her legs were longer, but he knew the territory like it was his own skin. She could picture Wrecker motoring along beside him, pumping through brush and undergrowth, his clothes dampened with sweat and the rainwater that glistened on sheltered leaves. He adored Johnny and the dogs, and would sooner tear his heart out than let himself be left behind.

The kid was amazing, physically. But for all his kinetic energy, there was a part of Wrecker that was stunned and paralyzed. No one felt this more than Johnny. He knew what it meant to yearn for something hopelessly distant. Distant and essential. Distant and so wished for, so furiously sought, it warped your dreams. Time after time he had stolen glances at the boy's face, watched the want rise palpably into his features. The kid had been yanked without warning from his people, set adrift in paradise, when all he wanted was to be back on home ground. Whatever it was his mother had done, Johnny told them, it wasn't bad enough to turn her son. Even at this distance his heart tracked her like a plant hungry for light.

It was six years already since Johnny Appleseed—John Chapman in those days, youngest of seven, idly loved and adequately fed and largely overlooked—had walked away from his family, his job, the tule fog of the Sacramento River delta, and the honest and earnest affection of a young woman who craved the very things that John yearned to be free of. Carpets. Bedspreads. Movie dates and backyard swings and someday kids to swing in them. John aged up from apprentice to journeyman printer at the *Sacramento Bee* and couldn't shake the feeling that trees were better fit in a forest than cut for the pulp he printed on. He craved chaos, the wild disorder of duff to sleep on and acorns and morels to eat. When Johnny first heard about Humboldt it struck a bell so deep in him the vibration had not yet stopped sounding. Land so wild no human had set foot there, in some places; trees unclimbed before, unmeasured, maybe even unseen. He bought his girl a ring. The freedom ring, he called it on the note he sent along with it, and he walked out the door and headed north, didn't stop until the trees towered so high he couldn't see the tops of them. He took a job planting seedlings. He honed his senses. He watched the shadows, he listened to the breeze. Deeper and deeper into the woods Johnny Appleseed went in search of the wildest thickets and the world's tallest trees.

"Best dinner ever," Johnny said softly, and walked his dishes to the sink.

Johnny hefted the sleeping boy in his arms and carried him the long route to the barn. Melody hovered behind as he climbed the ladder to the loft. "Nice," he said, glancing at the changes. He delivered the boy into the bed she'd made for him and straightened the blankets to cover him. Below, Sitka and her pups circled and huffed, settling into the wood chips Johnny had spread for them. "You don't mind taking care of the dogs while I'm gone?"

"Come back soon, buddy."

Johnny Appleseed smiled. Melody watched his face soften and grow sober as he gazed at the boy. He put a hand to Wrecker's cheek and the boy snuffled and turned. Johnny smiled again, but his eyes were sad. Melody waited. "The dogs will be fine," she said.

"Of course they will." He gazed at her. "Remember that maple?"

"Up the hill? Where you can see the water?"

"I took him there."

He'd shown her the tree the year before. The tree stretched horizontally, a broadleaf maple so old, so *venerable*, Johnny said, it seemed as much a part of the hillside as the rocks and soil. Venerable? She didn't know, but it was as broad as the back of an ox, and it looked like it had poured itself down the hillside, spurning the sky above in favor of the adjacent air. Its corrugated bark was softened with moss. She'd sat up there and slowly inched her way forward for the view. The ribbon of Mattole glinted past the manzanita, and past that, so far it was no more than a hint of different blue beside the blue sky, was the sea. Melody squinted at him. "Did he get scared?"

Johnny glanced again at the sleeping boy. Not exactly, Johnny said. Melody watched him stumble for the words to describe it. He'd held on to Wrecker as the boy slid his way forward, gripping the ridges of the bark, easing his legs around limbs that branched off, feeling the fresh new leaves brush his face. Soon the ground dropped away. Johnny had hold of Wrecker by the waist, and he could feel him tremble. Why wouldn't he? He was a little boy in the middle of the sky. It was a different world aloft, humid and softly sussurant, the air buzzing as though the tree breathed with them. A horned owl gave a low hoot, coasting from tree to tree below them in the dusk. The boy's small back was pressed snug against Johnny Appleseed's chest, the top of his head tucked under Johnny's chin.

Melody shut her eyes and pictured Bow Farm the way Johnny drew it, a few roofs scattered across the patchy acreage and Ruth a small figure in the yard of the farmhouse, working the hand pump to fill a bucket. Down the path stood the barn where Melody had set up camp. Past that—they all knew how far, by foot—was Willow's yurt, a cupcake house planted on the edge of the meadow. Farther on Len's place with its roofs the color of rusty nails; farther still the rollicking Mattole, the river black and broad and giddy with runoff. And then the forest closed in dense and green. In every direction were miles and miles and miles of trees. And glinting fiercely with the low-slung sun, the sea.

Beyond the sea—

"'Is it there?' I asked him," Johnny said. His voice was low and his face half in shadow as he glanced at Melody and then back at the boy. "'What you're looking for?'"

Melody opened her eyes and blinked at him quizzically. "Is *what* there?"

Johnny laughed softly. "The same sea. How far can a kid swim if he wants that badly to go home?" He turned his head to gaze at Wrecker. The boy sighed in his sleep. "Remember your mother, I told him. Remember everything. It's bound to be a long while." He cleared his throat and focused on Melody. "Before he gets back, I mean."

Melody gave her head a little shake. Wrecker had escaped all that, she said.

Johnny Appleseed dipped his head and flashed an enigmatic smile. "You think it was bad, what he left behind."

"Wasn't it?"

He looked at her for a long time. And then Johnny bent forward to rest his cheek on Wrecker's forehead. He straightened himself, breathed deep, and stood to leave. He had thousands of seedlings to set where a grove had been clear-cut, and he gathered his crew of wild boys about him and took to the woods.

Wrecker had cried, soundless and trembling, for an hour, Johnny said.

Was it bad? Johnny had looked at her with something close to pity in his eyes before he answered.

It was everything.

Weeks passed, and still Wrecker did not fall down the stairs, nor break a bone, nor throw a tantrum from which he couldn't by chocolate and reasonable patience be retrieved. The nightmares came less often. Melody rummaged through the free box at the Mercantile for hand-me-downs that would fit the kid. He'd stretched out of everything he had come with and had busted through two pairs of shoes since his arrival. Five months? Six, almost. Long enough for all the relationships at Bow Farm to subtly shift to accommodate him. And according to the papers Len had on him, Wrecker was about due to turn four.

All signs pointed to a party. It was the height of summer, and everything alive was bursting its seams with the pure urgency of growth. The days were long, and the night sky, when dusk finally surrendered to dark, was filled with stars and meteor showers and the unspeakably rich odors of deep grass and damp riverbank and tree sap and the family of skunks who had taken up residence under the tumbledown shed that housed Ruth's farm implements. Johnny Appleseed had a few days to lay low at the farm before heading back to the forest. Ruth's garden had produced a champion watermelon. It was time to celebrate.

Johnny sent word over the green wire, and in pairs and threes his wild and unkempt treeboys trickled in from the woods. Melody's coworkers from the Mercantile piled into pickup trucks to get there; they brought children and dogs and guitars and draft-dodging cousins who'd caught wind of how easy it was to get lost in this untamed stretch of overgrown coast. Len ironed his clothes before coming. He brought six pairs of new socks and a savings bond for the boy. And Willow summoned her friend Daria, who raised white doves; she brought them to offer Wrecker the spectacle of their flight, and he laughed and clapped his hands with the others when she set them free and they circled the farm twice, a pageant of wingbeat and white fluff, before heading for home.

It was late in the afternoon on the third day, a day fat and full and green and with enough of a breeze to keep them from broiling, that the last of the guests shook off the celebratory stupor occasioned by Ruth's extraordinary blue sheet cake and made their way home. Melody lay sprawled in the hammock, one foot trailing out to gently press the ground and keep it rocking. "Know what I think?" She proceeded, undaunted by silence. "I think we should go to the beach."

Willow peered over her book, raised her eyebrows, and went back to reading. She turned the page. "Ruth won't go."

"Ruth never goes," Melody said. Ruth had swallowed enough seawater the day they found her to sweat ocean brine for the rest of her life. "What about you?"

Johnny Appleseed came around the corner of the farmhouse. He held an elk ivory drilled for a wire loop and strung on a piece of rawhide. "Wrecker around?" When the boy crawled out from under the porch, twigs and dry leaves stuck to his scruffy hair, Johnny stepped forward and looped it around his neck. "Happy birthday, kid. May it keep you strong and free."

Wrecker fingered the creamy tooth. He had on a pair of shorts and no shirt and the tooth was bright against his tanned chest. He grinned. Johnny Appleseed dazzled him. Wrecker said, "Want to go to the beach?"

"With you? Anywhere."

Melody reached out a foot and nudged the leg of Willow's lawn chair. "Come on."

Willow shook her head.

Wrecker padded closer to her. He stayed a few feet away, as though he needed permission to enter her force field. When he caught her attention he lifted the ivory to show her. His face was earnest and he stood his ground. Melody watched Willow reach out and gently take hold of the tooth. "Nice," she said. She looked down at her book and sighed, then folded it shut. "All right," she said. "For a little while."

They picked the easiest beach to get to. Forty minutes of twisting mountain roads to suffer through, but once there they could park the van and walk directly onto the sand. It was state-run and more developed than the out-of-the-way black sand beaches Melody favored, but it was wide enough for Wrecker and Johnny Appleseed to race along and send airborne the newsprint kite they'd hastily assembled. Melody found herself a drift log to flop against and watched the cheery flyer pit itself against the swells. In a pile next to her Wrecker had deposited his collection of shells and slimy kelp and a fluorescent orange Frisbee with teeth marks all around the rim, and the briny, old-rot smell made her oddly happy.

She pulled her knees to her chest and listened to the waves. Ahead, Willow made her way to the edge of the water. The older woman faced out to sea and twisted her elegant body into yoga poses. No surprise, Melody thought. They all knew Willow could do anything. Speak Russian, for one. Operate a small aircraft. Make a pair of historically accurate breeches for a town production of

Gilbert and Sullivan's *Mikado* two hours before the performance and take her seat unflustered, every hair in place and no trace of sweat or frustration. There were only a handful of people in the world as skilled as she at restoring precious carpets, and her work for international collectors was amply rewarded. But when she turned her hand to the thing she loved best—turning spun wool into weavings that dazzled the eye and caught the heart—something much more vital than competence came into play. It was magic, Melody had to admit. A simple array of colors and textures could remind you of someone you'd loved and lost. It could call out the person you'd once hoped to be. It could make you think (why not? the weavings said; who else?) there was still hope.

But Willow didn't drive. Melody took some comfort in this. Not that Willow couldn't, Melody was sure, if she'd wanted to; but to know that there was one thing—for one moment, anyway—Melody could do that Willow did not gave her a cheap thrill of satisfaction. Honestly, it was hard to be around such competence all the time. If she'd been haughty or condescending they could at least ridicule her privately. But she wasn't. She loved them all, in her way. She loved Len and Melody best. She just stopped short, Melody realized with sadness, of loving the boy.

Melody scanned the beach and found Wrecker a ways off, dragging a piece of driftwood toward a pile Johnny Appleseed guarded. She let her eyes return to Willow. She was sharp-focus, while Melody was all broad-spectrum. Did that just mean lazy? The thought tired her. She had plenty of qualities, but it would take some effort to remember what they were. Better just to curl herself against the log and drift to sleep.

She was deep in a dream when something startled her awake. She blinked hard. Her head felt gelatinous. Willow's face came in close and unsmiling and she gripped Melody's elbow. "Get up," she said, and stood back while Melody pushed herself to standing. "We can't find the boy."

Melody rubbed her nose and tried to make sense of the words. "What do you mean," she said, her heart beating faster as the thought settled in, "you can't *find* him?"

"We were gathering driftwood." Johnny Appleseed came into focus. "I thought he came back here. I thought you had him."

They all turned to stare at the waves. Collectively, with horror, they searched for a bob of blond hair, for a flash of red sweatshirt. The water looked calm and satisfied, and Willow turned away first. "I can't imagine he'd go in for a swim," she said, her voice calm, nearly nonchalant. "It's too cold for that."

Melody felt a chill ripple through her body. She wanted to tear Willow's head off. And then she wanted to reach up and tear off her own. Her legs weakened under her, and she sat hard in the sand. "Oh God," she said. He could not be gone. The thought filled her mind with a blackness that came on so fast and so thoroughly there was nothing she could do to resist it. She could not stop it from roaring out of her chest.

It involved hours of waiting. It involved Willow's Zen-like calm and Johnny Appleseed's steady rubbing of the stone bear talisman he carried in his pocket and Melody's thoroughly humiliating hysteria. It involved numerous prostrations to the earth mother and the god of the sea and just for good measure several tight-lipped appeals to Saint Anthony, patron of lost things, and some unmentionable promises of exceptionally generous behavior before Wrecker was returned to them. Melody held him tight.

"I ought to wring your neck," she said, her voice rough as a crow's caw.

Willow said, "What were you thinking?"

Johnny Appleseed said nothing. He gazed at the boy with the appraising eye of a fellow traveler.

He had walked down the salt river and past the lagoon and beyond the parking area and along the road. He was headed for the highway. An old couple vacationing with their towed trailer had pulled over, alarmed at the sight of a small boy walking alone on the pavement. He was the same size as their youngest grandson. They offered him cookies and wiped the dirt off his face with a travel wipe. They asked him his name and he told them. They asked him where his mother was.

San Francisco, he said, stumbling over the syllables.

And did he mean to walk there?

Yes.

It crashed over Melody like a wave, a sense of what he had lost. The bitter, open ache of it.

They were angry, now, this pair. Righteously indignant. They wanted to know how any mother could be so inattentive as to let her son wander off like that. And at the beach, no less! Wasn't she watching? Didn't she know a mother has got to have eyes in the back of her head? They hadn't raised four children for nothing. They could tell her a thing or two.

Melody felt her anger rise in her like an upward flow of lava, steaming and corrosive. Who were these people? What could they possibly know? But she looked down and caught Wrecker's blue eyes watching her carefully. Maybe it was the sky that had clouded over, but those eyes had half again as much gray in them as they'd had that morning. Steady on her.

How close she had come to losing him.

She laid her hand softly on the back of his neck. She squatted until they were eye to eye.

Something shifted in her, then. A rock rolled away from a chamber of her heart she had not even known was there. She could not guess what her future would bring but suddenly it did not matter, so long as it held him.

"I'm so sorry," she whispered.

CHAPTER THREE

Lisa Fay lay in a hospital bed—the smell of antiseptic gave it away, and the faded cotton gown she wore—but could not recall how she'd gotten there. She remembered the green grass of Rolph Playground. Some stabbing pain. A sunset that bled orange behind the lump of Potrero Hill. She remembered crying, and not being able to help it. And she remembered him. Not clearly; just a fuzz of shape and sound and emotion, but enough to make the space between her hips ache hard with its emptiness. In a bed arranged not far from hers, a very pregnant woman moaned and winced through labor. A glass of water stood on the bedside table, and Lisa Fay drained it in one long pull. Her throat felt scraped raw. "Where'd they take him?" she croaked. "Where's my baby?"

The woman in the opposite bed turned her head toward Lisa Fay. "Call. The nurse," she huffed, sweat beading on her broad forehead. "Whoo. Get her to bring him." When the pain eased she lifted a tired hand. "I'm Yolanda," she said, patting her chest. "Nice of you to finally wake up. It was getting lonesome in here."

Lisa Fay found a call button wedged against the side of the bed and pressed it. When nothing happened, she pushed it again, hard. "Nurse!" Her voice was a dry rasp that barely carried, and she fumbled for the button to buzz it again.

"Let me do mine," Yolanda offered. A nurse poked her head in from the hall at the signal. "What would it take for you to get this woman her baby?" The nurse nodded curtly and disappeared. "Don't hold your breath. It'll be a little while," Yolanda said. "This one's my third. You figure out what to expect." She cocked her head to one side. Her skin was the same polished brown as the butt stock of the hunting rifle Lisa Fay's father kept locked in a cabinet back home. "Not that you bothered coming in to have your baby. Went ahead and delivered him yourself right there in a—oh, Lord." Yolanda was a full-bodied woman who wore her hospital gown like a negligee, and her belly jiggled with laughter that sent ripples along the sheet. "In a *public park*, girl!" She tried to contain herself. "I heard the nurses talking," she explained. "Bunch of magpies."

"What else did they say?"

"Ambulance brought you both in. Baby's fine, they said. Big. You lost some blood. Don't you want to call nobody?"

Lisa Fay frowned and looked away. The people she knew didn't have a telephone.

"The baby's father? Nobody?" Yolanda narrowed her eyes at Lisa Fay.

The door opened wider and a nurse pushed in a bassinet on wheels. "I've got someone here who wants to meet you," she said, and lifted a flannel bundle out of the cart. She cooed down at the blue lump. "Say hello to your mama."

Lisa Fay hesitated, her heart pounding, but the nurse went right ahead and placed the warm little package in her arms. She looked down and gasped. Then she loosened the blanket and gaped at the baby in awe. One, two, three, four—ten fingers. Ten toes. Two eyes, two ears, a nose and a mouth in a head the size and shape of a pumped-up Florida grapefruit. "No wonder I passed out. You're a bruiser." She couldn't take her eyes from his wrinkled face. "Hello, boy." She felt suddenly shy. She had waited for this moment for so long, and now that it was here—now that *he* was here—she had no idea what to do.

The nurse bustled about with equipment. "Got a name picked out?"

Lisa Fay gazed at the baby's face in dismay. None of the names she had thought of would fit. He wasn't a Buzz, or a Jonas; not a Raymond; certainly no Kincaid, a name she'd seen plastered on the side of a bus. And he wasn't an Arlyn, like his father. Her heart curled in on itself with the pain of that absence, and for a moment Lisa Fay lifted her eyes to the open doorway and willed Arlyn to walk through it. He had vanished, plain disappeared, before she'd had the chance to tell him what they'd made. She squeezed her eyes shut, then forced them wide. She would not cry. She shot a bewildered glance at her roommate. "What's he look like to you?"

"Baby that big? Ought to call him Zeus."

Gently, tentatively, Lisa Fay lifted the boy. His head lolled on the stump of his neck. "Zeus," she said. "Hello. Zeus?" The baby opened his rosebud mouth and started to cry. She quickly brought him down. "I don't think he likes it."

"Try Angelo. Or Tyrone." Yolanda gazed into the distance, cogitating. "James."

"It'll come to you," the nurse said. "Right now, he'll need to eat." Lisa Fay looked over, alarmed. "This your first? Don't worry. He does all the work." She reached in to free Lisa Fay's breast from the gown and settled the baby to suckle there. "See?" She tucked the blankets around them. "I'll be back in to check on both of you in a little while."

Lisa Fay gazed down in wonder as the baby nursed. His little cheeks flexed and his hand crept up to rest on her breast. It was a miracle, really. Yolanda breathed her noisy way through another contraction and Lisa Fay watched her son suck furiously until his tiny eyelids fluttered closed. It wasn't the way she'd planned it, losing the basement squat, having her baby outside. She hadn't planned any of this. She hadn't planned *him*—but now that he was here, she would do whatever it took to keep him safe.

To keep him at all. How long would it take for the hospital to find out she had no money and no place to live? They could be checking on her right now. They could snatch him back as quick as that. "Yolanda," she whispered. She was tired, but there was no time to wait. "I need to borrow your clothes."

The huffs and moans had settled to quiet whimpers and Yolanda held her in a long gaze, considering. Then she sighed, and tilted her head toward the suitcase at the end of the bed. "Give me that baby while you dress yourself. You got someplace to go?"

"Anywhere but here." Lisa Fay chose a plaid skirt and a pressed white blouse with a Peter Pan collar and slipped into the bathroom. Steal her baby? They'd have to beat her to it. A minute later she poked her head out the door. "Is it safe?"

Yolanda took one look and guffawed. "You won't be winning no beauty contests like that, girl. Fit two of you in there." She gestured to the end of the bed. "Hand me my purse." When Lisa Fay came around the side Yolanda had scribbled a name—Belle— and an address on the torn back of a card. She handed the scrap and the flannel bundle to Lisa Fay and rustled in her handbag, drew out two five-dollar bills. "All I've got right now," she said, passing them over. "Go by Mama Belle's and she'll take you in. You and little . . ."

Lisa Fay nodded her thanks. Tucked the address and the banknotes in her sock and settled the baby in her arms. "I'll pay you back."

"You better. And I want that skirt back, girl. Clean. Don't go sitting in no grass like y'all do."

Lisa Fay grinned and saluted. Turned and slid secretively into the hall.

Yolanda's voice floated after her: "André. Jubilee. Harrison."

She called him HeyBoy or BigBoy or Beauty; she called him Honey and Sweetie and Champ. For a whole year she called him Luxe, for Deluxe, meaning the best and luckiest thing that had ever happened to her. When she was angry with him she called him Son, and he held his neck stiff and waited to hear what he had done wrong. One day, gazing around at the trail of broken things strewn in his wake, she said, "Kid! Can't you leave off wrecking things, for once?" And he turned his round face, his plum lips, to her and said, "I a wrecker." It made her laugh. "A Wrecker?" And he nodded his head, serious, sure, and on that day it was settled.

There was a man on the moon. All across America children sat cross-legged on shag rugs and watched *F Troop* and *Gilligan's Island*, *Gigantor*, *Bewitched*. Lisa Fay didn't own a TV. She worked the swing shift at the Hills Brothers coffee factory on Second Street at a job Yolanda scared up for her, lived in a room with a hot plate and a cast iron bathtub above a Greek grocery, took the bus every weekday afternoon to leave Wrecker with Yolanda's mother, Belle, in the Fillmore and the late-night bus back to pick him up after work. Weekends belonged to them. Lisa Fay was put together in a marginal way, and anybody could believe that the stress of caring for a baby—a big, rowdy baby like Wrecker—might wear her past the tolerances machined in. Instead, it worked the other way. Lisa Fay took to raising Wrecker like a boat takes to water; he gave her the ballast she needed to ride steady; he was rudder and anchor and sail. Sunday mornings she'd load him in the secondhand stroller and push the boy all the way to the Presidio. Wrecker never missed a parade. He learned to walk and quickly to run and terrorized the ducks in Golden Gate Park. Tow-headed, blue-eyed, brawny as the Christ child in a Renaissance oil, Wrecker feasted on delicacies from the Greek grocery below and wore the love of the bums on Townsend—the ones who clustered each afternoon for a hot meal at the Salvation Army—like a coat of armor to shield him from the cruelties of life.

Which cruelties? Lisa Fay didn't abandon Wrecker as a baby in a trash bin. She didn't force him to spend long hours alone in a dark closet, nor hold his small feet in boiling water, nor use the sharp end of a safety pin to inscribe his skin, nor forbid him food when he was hungry, nor force him to eat sand or clay or feces. She did not touch his small body in damaging ways or allow others to do that. She loved her son more than she loved her own life.

But she didn't always know what to do when he cried. Wrecker was a healthy baby, and still sometimes he cried so hard it made him throw up. Some mornings—once in a while—he woke dull-eyed and coughing and his nose ran green and his forehead and the skin of his arms and his chest were much too hot. Lisa Fay thought she should take him to a doctor but she didn't know where to find the right kind or how she would pay for it. She fed him the little orange dots of aspirin. Time and the candy-flavored pills seemed to cure him.

Mostly she looked at her son and was delighted to see how strong he was, how happy, how soft and perfect and resourceful. Sometimes she looked at him and was horrified. He grew more or less on his own—his body seemed to know how to form itself, it followed some basic instructions that seemed built in—but what if she made a mistake? No. What if the mistakes she made (of course she made mistakes, how was she to know how to raise a child like this, any child) mounted up and somehow tipped the scale toward bad? What if she made—a monster? It would be her fault. Everyone would know she had been a BAD MOTHER.

Sometimes she thought it was absurd that she was a mother at all. Sometimes—not very often, hardly at all—she left him to sleep in the bed and she quietly shut the door to the rented room, locked it with the knob and the deadbolt, and quietly fled down the steps into the city night. Jazz at the pier and someone to buy her a drink. Remind her. What? Remind her she was a woman. A woman of San Francisco.

Jerry Skink slunk around corners; he moved like a polecat with a hard-on, stunk of sweat and perfume, chased skirts and money-making opportunities as long as they didn't look like much work. He combed his wispy light brown mustache and let his hair flop over his forehead to hide the scars from teenage acne. No one knew how old he was. Forty? Fifty? Thirty-four? He was a wolf in sheep's clothing; a sheep in pimp's clothing; a pimp in a waxy body that gave nobody pleasure, not even him. He took it out on every-one around him. He smiled at them and gave them the creeps.

Except Lisa Fay. He gave her gonorrhea and a habit Hills Broth-ers couldn't even begin to pay for.

It was 1968, and the year ripened from an innocent spring into the summer of love. Wrecker turned three and independent in June, no longer content to hold her hand, running everywhere, finding tall places to jump from. He was his mother's nightmare and his mother's joy. He was the only toddler who could pump the swings at the playground, pump them high and leap off to fall and tumble in the sand. He outran eight-year-olds, climbed ev-ery tree he could get a grip on or con a leg up, splashed without worry in the fountains, in the ponds. He made the city his own with the slap of his feet, the slam of his small body bouncing off its rough edges. He near-strangled the ducks he caught and smothered in affection. He stood in awe of the cranes that worked the waterfront, the cement trucks that rolled and disgorged the wet mix, the backhoes and loaders and forklifts and graders that wrestled earth and stone with yellow glee. He wanted to drive them. He was a boy in love with heavy machinery.

Lisa Fay was a woman quite taken with the idea of a little relief. She met Jerry Skink at the Fourth of July Hills Brothers cookout at the marina; he was somebody's brother-in-law, or cousin, or business acquaintance; he was a skunk who disguised his stripe with Grecian Formula 16 and a touch of Brylcreem. She found him amusing. She rebuffed his advances until dark and the explosion of the fireworks finale—a grand display of positive attitude that everyone thought reminded them a little too much of the war going on in Asia—and Wrecker, asleep in his mother's lap (spilling out of his mother's lap, for he'd grown too big to fully fit) was still for once and then Lisa Fay let Jerry place his soft hand over hers and, very gently, kiss her on the cheek.

"Just so you know—" Lisa Fay mitigated, but Jerry stood and helped her up and took the baby in his arms.

"I've got a friend with a pad on Haight," Jerry said, hopeful.

Lisa Fay walked with him as far as the bus stop and offered him her cheek and her address. "I haven't got a phone," she said. "Come for lunch some day." She climbed aboard the bus with Wrecker, paying her fare. "Come for food."

"Food," Jerry repeated stupidly, and as the bus doors closed on his surprised face Lisa Fay felt certain that was the last she'd see of him.

It was all right with Belle to leave Wrecker overnight—he was sleeping already, why wake him?—although the first night Lisa Fay slept away from her son she woke up gasping, her palms wet with sweat, thinking she'd lost him. Jerry Skink went on snoring next to her on the mattress and through the open door she could see dark spots on the floor of the next room, the bodies of people (Her friends? Were these her friends?) who lay where they had fallen. They had all smoked a little much, they had done too many mushrooms, dropped a bit much acid—*these were not her friends*. Lisa Fay threw off the sheets and stood. She found her clothes and a clock: 3:15. On the streets at 3:15 in the morning. But it had to be better than here.

Jerry Skink showed up on the outside steps to her room the next day in time for lunch. Lisa Fay looked gray and soggy. She had downed half the bottle of Wrecker's orange pills and felt no better for it. She was toasting white bread on the hot-plate burner, mechanically smearing on margarine and sprinkling sugar and cinnamon. She couldn't keep up with the kid's appetite but she was trying. Focus was hard. When she answered the knock on the door and stood looking at Jerry Skink, fresh-scrubbed and dandy in a new woven poncho, her efforts at focus slid off the plate of her mind. The son of a bitch. She stood waiting for his apology. She wasn't sure what he should apologize for but felt fairly certain he should.

Jerry lifted his little upturned nose, nonchalant, and sniffed. He meant to say, "What's for lunch?" but it came out, "Your kitchen is on fire."

Lisa Fay turned and watched the last piece of sliced bread go up in a flame of glory. Wrecker cried. He didn't like burned toast. He was still hungry.

Jerry stepped the three paces to the hot plate and switched it off. Then he smothered the flame with a cloth diaper that doubled as a dishtowel. He shot Wrecker a look that shut him up. Then he turned to Lisa Fay and said, all sugar, "I know a place on Gough makes great hamburgers. What do you say we go?"

67

Lisa Fay's mouth watered for meat. She meant to say, "I have potatoes in the drawer. I have to get Wrecker to the sitter by two and be at work at three," but it came out, "Medium rare. With fries and a vanilla shake and Wrecker likes pickles."

Jerry smiled. "I have a car," he said. "Let me take you out."

Every silver lining has its cloud. Jerry Skink had time on his hands and access to a borrowed car and enough cash to every now and then treat mother and son to a day on the beach, to a meal out. They grew into a familiar routine. Saturday mornings Jerry Skink would come by with the car and ask Lisa Fay to cruise with him, down the peninsula some days, up to Muir Woods, and Lisa Fay would agree on the condition that Wrecker come along, and Jerry would suggest, tenderly but as the weeks went by more forcefully, that Wrecker be left with a friend, that he would have more fun with children his own age, that it was improper for a child to be kept in a car so long, that in fact much of the way Lisa Fay treated her son was not correct, that in fact the experts said—not that Jerry was an expert, what did he know about children, a single man, but he did *read*—the experts said, actually, to be fair about it, that Lisa Fay's style of mothering was all wrong.

Wrecker was napping. Lisa Fay was sitting opposite Jerry at the table, snacking on the cheese sandwich crusts Wrecker had left in his wake. She was lifting the bread with her right hand and slowly, unconsciously, her left elbow slid on to the table and moved forward to shield the plate from Jerry and her left hand lifted and positioned itself on her forehead to shield her face from his view. She put back the scrap of bread and left her right hand in her lap.

"Hey. Whoa." Jerry reached over to squeeze Lisa Fay's upper arm. "Didn't mean to hurt your feelings."

It was just—well. He was getting attached. He only wanted what was best for the little guy. Didn't she?

Of course she did. And so Wrecker's day-to-day life changed considerably as Lisa Fay submitted to Jerry Skink's tutelage. It was not best for Wrecker to spend his evenings in the care of Yolanda's mother in the Fillmore, and so Lisa Fay moved in with Jerry and his friends in the flat above Haight Street. There were plenty of extra people there to look after the boy while Lisa Fay worked. And it was not best that Wrecker sleep in the same room as his mother; surely Lisa Fay could see that. Jerry generously moved his crib mattress into the hall. Furthermore, it was not best that Wrecker be allowed to bulldoze freely through his environment. He needed discipline, to learn respect for other people's time and space and property—but Jerry could take care of that, too.

It did cross Lisa Fay's mind that it might not be best for Wrecker to have a mother so frequently strung out on the drugs Jerry dealt for a living, but some changes would have to wait.

Jerry's income increased, and so, correspondingly, did his work schedule. It was no longer advantageous for Lisa Fay to continue to work at Hills Brothers when she could ease his load—and contribute more fully to the family's needs—by assisting him. Life was still looser than before, it was Haight Street, it was the October of Love, but the day trips and evening excursions they took incorporated more and more business. For this, Wrecker was always welcome. And Lisa Fay, who felt like she rarely saw her son, who missed his pint-sized muscular body in bed next to hers, was glad for any chance to spend time with him. Even if it meant holding on to the stash. Even those few times when Jerry handed her the pistol and said, Put this in your belt, girl. I want you to be safe.

69

Wrecker didn't mind. He liked going to the parks. He liked playing on the swings. Jerry was almost always in a good mood at the end of those days and took them for ice cream at Mitchell's, where Wrecker could have any flavor he wanted, three scoops that came in a miniature batting helmet from the San Francisco Giants.

It was a new park in a different part of town. It was big. Not as big as Golden Gate—which was a city in itself—but bigger than Yerba Buena, where they usually went, or the little block parks they used to go to when they lived over the grocery. It had more space between the playground and the basketball courts, it had a place to play tennis, it had a very nice slide, long and fast and curved at the bottom, that dropped the children into the sandbox. Wrecker stood and brushed the sand grains from his lap. There was some sand caught in the elastic waist of his pants and the air was starting to cool. Wrecker was hungry. He gazed away from the sun to the grassy slope, past the slope to the street and beyond that to the tall stone fronts of the school building.

There was a backhoe parked by a barricaded hole on the street. Wrecker's eyes widened. A yellow backhoe with an open cab— just a canopy—and big wheels in the back and its stabilizers extended to keep it steady while the operator dug. But there was no driver Wrecker could see. It called to him. Oh! He glanced around to try to locate his mother, but quickly his gaze returned to the machine. He left his toy sword in the sandbox. He moved quickly. Lisa Fay had said Stay there, don't move from the playground, but he couldn't help himself.

A backhoe. A yellow backhoe.

His mother had said Don't go in the street, Wrecker. Never go in the street.

But he had to get under the barricades to be able to climb

70

up the big tire, gripping the treads, and scramble his way into the cab.

There was some noise. People arguing in a corner of the park. There was a big bang like an explosion, and then a lot of police cars with sirens and flashing lights. Someone was running and someone was chasing. There were dials and levers and pedals in the cab. There was a torn black seat Wrecker stood on and tried to reach the switch for the light but he was too short. He looked over to see a policeman tackle the running person. Wrecker wished he could turn the machine on. He wanted to move the arm; scoop dirt with the bucket. The policeman handcuffed the running person. He looked back again at the controls; pumped the pedals and pretended he had the key. He made a growl in his throat like the diesel engine warming up. When he looked up again, that corner of the park was deserted and the sky was dark.

Slowly a thought elbowed its way to the front of his brain. He rubbed his nose and tasted salt and dirt and snot.

That familiar shape? The one they had taken away?

That was his mother.

CHAPTER FOUR

They all sat around the kitchen table with the letter planted in the middle like a ticking bomb.

"Well," Willow began. "It could be worse."

"How?" Melody's eyes were rimmed with red. She struggled to get a grip in spite of the tears that kept streaming down her face.

Ruth shot a worried glance at Johnny Appleseed. He'd been home for a week and was still wild-eyed with the look of the woods. It would take time for him to remember how to function like a human. Time they didn't have.

Len could barely stand to look the others in the face. It was his fault the news arrived so late. The letter had come the week before, preceded by a slip in the mailbox that informed him he had certified mail and must appear at the Mattole Post Office between the hours of 8:00 and 4:30 to sign for it. Len quit work early and washed up before he drove to town. The postmistress showed him where to sign and he deposited the envelope in the chest pocket of his twill shirt. He stopped at the Mercantile and went around back to the feed store and dropped his laundry at the Wash'n'Fold on his way out of town. Back home, he cooked pork chops and scalloped potatoes while he rambled to Meg about his day, and then he washed the dishes, ran the water in the tub, undressed Meg and settled her in the bath, and began to undress and climb in with her—until he saw the green certified tag attached to the envelope in the pocket of his shirt. He hesitated. The return address was Children's Protective Services. Meg was splashing happily, humming with gusto. He stepped out of his shorts and socks and slid in behind her. It was the only way she would allow him to wash her hair, and now it was the rare night they didn't bathe together. He wet the washcloth and squeezed the water down her back. She squealed with delight. He dampened her hair, poured some shampoo into his palm, and began to rub it into her scalp. She melted against him. He would deal with the letter tomorrow. He gently scrubbed behind her ears and used the suds to soap under her arms and his own.

The next day he forgot the letter. It wasn't until the following week—until today—when he brought the next load of dirty clothes to the Wash'n'Fold that the envelope slid out from between his work clothes and Meg's rumpled blouses. He slid his thick nail under the flap to open it. He hunched slightly to read the small print and then he straightened up and ran the heel of his hand across his brow. He ignored the laundry he had just lifted onto the counter and he got in his truck and drove directly to Bow Farm.

"Len."

He looked up at the sound of Willow's voice.

"Come on. This was the idea, wasn't it?" She shifted her gaze from his face to consider each of the others in turn. "We'd look after him for a few days, or weeks, or a month? Until Len got something settled with the state?" Willow lifted the letter and read it through again. "It's not like he's going to an orphanage or anything. They sound like nice people."

"What makes you think that?" Ruth wasn't buying any of it. She eased out of her chair and started bustling about the kitchen, giving the clean counters another vigorous wipe. "A husband and wife who live up in Eureka. They could be ax murderers." The idea spawned a flare of fear and a sudden headache. She straightened up, pinched the bridge of her nose. "For all we know, they could have forty other children they've adopted this way. We don't know a thing about them."

Willow arched an eyebrow. She didn't suppose the agency would give out children without doing a background check, she said.

"They didn't check Len." Johnny Appleseed squatted in the corner with his elbows on his knees and his hands clasped pensively under his chin. Len looked over, startled. "Sorry, man," Johnny told him. "No offense. But they didn't exactly make sure everything was copacetic before they shipped Wrecker up to you."

Len was confused. He wasn't sure if he was being accused of something specific or if the tree planter was just making a point.

He felt terrible about all this. He couldn't take care of the boy. The first day had proved that, and nothing had changed on that front. But the girls could, and they'd proved that, too. He'd just forgotten about the state. He'd thought—if he thought about it at all—that they'd forgotten about him, too. He was fraying at the edges. He wondered what else he might have forgotten. What if he forgot something Meg needed? What if, one day, he forgot Meg? He flicked his gaze toward Willow but quickly dropped his eyes.

"What did you tell them, Len?" Melody's eyes searched his face. "Did you tell them Wrecker wasn't doing well? Did you say he needed something better?"

"Leave him alone," Willow warned. Her voice sharpened with irritation. "He took the boy because he was the only kin Wrecker had, and he believed it was his duty. You all know that." She looked around at them; waited for someone to challenge her. "Look," she said, and breathed out. She laid her hands flat on the table before her. "Len's been trying to work out the best thing for Wrecker. The boy needs a solid, reliable home."

Melody's eyes flared. "This isn't home?"

"This is summer camp." Willow's tone matched hers. "And all of us"—she moved her hand wearily to indicate them all—"we're all just camp counselors."

"Speak for yourself," Melody said, her voice low and angry.

"Melody." Willow shook her head when the young woman wouldn't meet her eye. "I know you've grown fond of him," she said. "We all have. It's hard to let him go." She softened her voice. "But you're not his mother."

Melody stood up abruptly. "And she is?" She jabbed a finger at the letter. "She is? She doesn't know a thing about him. She probably picked his picture out of a catalog. And you, Willow. You don't know him, either." Ruth lifted her chin in warning, but Melody blundered forward. "No wonder you're willing to let him go so easily."

Len wanted to cry. It was his fault alone that Wrecker was leaving. He opened his mouth to defend Willow but the look on her face made him clamp his jaw shut.

Willow paused several beats before answering. "It's possible that I know a bit more about children than anyone here," she said, her voice clipped, her face a shade darker with emotion. "But that's not the point. The point is Len is required to bring Wrecker to the CPS office in Eureka tomorrow. If he doesn't appear he'll be held in contempt of a court order. If he doesn't respond at all they'll send someone down to take Wrecker and they'll likely arrest Len." She took in each of them with her measured gaze. Those were fairly high stakes for a man with the responsibilities Len had, she said. Perhaps they could tell her who else stood to lose as much?

Melody swiveled toward Len. "Listen," she said, her voice

breaking slightly. "Tell them you'll keep him. That you made a mistake." She stilled her hands from their reflexive action and, gawky but deliberate, brought them together in appeal. "I promise you we'll take care of him." She looked at Willow and then back at Len. "Not just for a day or a week or a month. We'll stick with him. I swear."

Len felt her appeal slice at his heart. Yes; if only. But his throat was too swollen to let the words pass.

There was a long pause. When Willow broke it, her voice was softer than before. "Melody? Don't make this hard for him."

"I'm making this very easy." Melody leaned forward and addressed Len. "I'll take total responsibility. If you adopt him, I promise you we'll raise him. Ruth? Johnny Appleseed? Tell him. Please, Len."

"I don't mean for Len," Willow said quietly. She tilted her head toward the doorframe. "I mean for Wrecker."

The boy stood there and looked from face to face. They gaped at him as though they were rabbits startled in their warren by a sudden light. "What?"

Ruth asked, "Are you hungry, pal?"

Melody tipped the chair over in her rush out the door.

Len watched her go. All he wanted was to lay his head on the table and leave it there, but he had to get home to Meg.

It fell to Ruth to get the boy ready the next morning. She sent him out to play after breakfast and then called him in when she'd filled the metal tub in the kitchen for his bath. He squeaked and squalled as she ran the washcloth inside his ears, yipped and shivered when she lifted him out of the water and toweled him dry, dodged about naked as she chased after him with clothes. Wrecker was old enough to dress himself but she helped him pull on his best outfit, a pair of dungarees and a striped cotton shirt they had salvaged from the free box. The pants had fit him perfectly six weeks before but already showed an inch of sock. Ruthie hated to send him off this way. She turned aside so he wouldn't see her face. She hated to send him off at all.

Wrecker caught the frown and squinted at her, unsure, and Ruth made herself beam back hard. "Look at you, buddy," she growled, drinking in the sight of him. His damp hair stood askew in random cowlicks. "Handsome as a bug!" She squatted down to tie his shoes, and Wrecker reached for the doorknob. "Stay in for now," she ordered. If he went outside his sneakers, his pants, his shirt, his face, would attract dirt in thirty seconds. In a minute and a half he'd be filthy, and it meant something to her that at least he go clean. She gathered his army figures from a shelf and set them on the floor. He looked at the toys and back at her, sur- prised. "You're going to town." It was as much as she would say. Either Willow or Melody would have to break the news.

Neither woman had appeared. Out in the garden, Johnny Appleseed kept his own counsel. Ruth watched him through the kitchen window as he sifted the dark soil through his fin- gers, gathering the last of the harvest. He brushed the dirt from the golden bodies of the squash, stripped the yellow outside leaves from the kale, and neatly placed it all—one melon, the late peas and tomatoes, a last bouquet of marigolds—into a brown paper sack. He carried it into the kitchen and glanced at Ruth and the boy.

"Good morning," he said formally.

The boy hummed and Ruthie grunted. She stood at the sink and scrubbed the morning's dishes.

Johnny set the bag on the table and sat beside it and began to draft a note.

Ruth spied over his shoulder. *Dear . . .* he began. His pen hovered over the scrap of paper. She waited for him to continue, but he crumpled the page and began again. *Enjoy the vegetables*, he wrote. *Wrecker helped grow them*. He lifted his head. Wrecker was busy on the floor with his plastic GI Joes. Johnny hunched to write again. *If you'll let Wrecker have a dog, tell Len. He will bring him one he knows and loves*. He glanced over his shoulder at Ruth. She shrugged. He frowned and started to crumple that sheet as well but Ruth laid a hand gently over his. "It's fine." She lowered herself into a chair next to his. "Len will be here in a bit." She lifted an eyebrow and tipped her head toward the boy.

A vein pulsed in Johnny Appleseed's neck. His lips tightened and he nodded. "Wrecker?"

The boy twisted his head to glance at him.

Johnny Appleseed squatted on the floor beside him. "Listen, kid." There was no decent way to say this. "Len is coming to pick you up soon. He's going to take you to an office, and you're going to meet some people. They're going to be your new par—" Johnny stuttered and winced. Ruthie felt green, as though she'd eaten something that was going to have to come back out, one way or the other. "They'll be your new parents." It sounded stupid, the way it came out of his mouth, stupid and emphatic and wrong, but Johnny was in the middle now and couldn't very well stop. "You're going to live with them, Wrecker." He forced himself to slow down. "They'll be your family. Everything will be good. You'll see."

Wrecker's expression didn't change. He kept his eyes on Johnny's face for a lengthy period and then slowly his gaze drifted back to his toys. He reached a hand out to rearrange them. He devoted a sizable amount of attention to aligning the figures in battle position, and when he was done he had positioned himself so that his back shielded both the toys and himself from Johnny's view.

Johnny rocked back onto his heels. He stood up. He caught Ruth's eye to make sure she understood to send the note and the bag along, and he stepped outside.

Ruthie chewed her lip. Once they lost Wrecker, she knew, it wouldn't be long before Johnny moved on.

The windup clock in the kitchen ticked loudly, marking the minutes until Len arrived. Ruth had emptied the few items from her blue cloth suitcase and neatly packed it with Wrecker's clothes and toys. She tucked the rawhide cord with the elk tooth into an elastic pocket on the side. The army figures would be the last to go. Ruth was hoping he would be content to play with them until Len came to get him. The door to the kitchen opened and Willow stepped in. "Oh!" she said. "You're here!" Where, Ruthie wondered, did she think they would be? Willow's face adopted a more serious look. "Wrecker?" she said. "Put your toys away. There's something we need to talk about."

"He knows," Ruth said. Her voice was dry. "Johnny Appleseed told him." She bit her tongue before adding, *Somebody had to.*

Willow caught the undertone in Ruth's voice and looked up quickly. She opened her mouth to speak but the sound of Len's truck rumbling up the drive made them all start. Willow turned to Ruth. "I'll be outside," she said, and dropped her gaze.

Ruth felt a pang of regret. It wasn't fair to be hard on Willow. It wasn't her fault. It wasn't Len's and it wasn't Melody's and it wasn't her own and it sure as hell wasn't Johnny Appleseed's. It was something that happened; it was life—and she hated it. She hated this about life, the leaving. Huffing and creaking, Ruth folded down onto the linoleum beside Wrecker.

He glanced at her. A flicker of recognition chased across his face but he retreated again behind a stony gaze.

It wasn't anybody's fault, Ruth thought, but wouldn't he be the one to pay for it?

She'd done her own leaving, once. Walked into the ocean with Liz's ashes in a small box in her hands and laid herself beside them on the waves. But the sea had coughed her back out, her tattered heart preserved in her chest like a cheese sandwich in the dented chassis of a lunch box—and now she felt her heart squeeze tight again.

"Wrecker," she said gruffly, and waited for him to meet her gaze. "Pay attention, now. I want you to remember this." She raised her eyebrows and flared her nostrils and watched as his chin lifted and he looked at her sideways. "This is the *secret weapon*." She glanced about furtively and then lowered her voice to a whisper. "Never use this unless your life is in danger."

Ruth paused a moment to take it in: the slopes and curves of his small face, curiosity flaring brighter than anger across it, as he tilted his gaze toward her. She let her eyes linger there. And then she cupped her hands to her mouth and trumpeted the most graceful, elongated, musical Bronx cheer in the history of mankind.

"The story of my life, boy," she said soberly, and watched the smile spread across his face.

The door squeaked open. Len thrust his ruined face inside. "Son," he said. "It's time."

Ruth gathered his soldiers in a plastic bread bag. She tucked them into the suitcase, grasped it by the handle, and headed outside. Len and Willow stood talking to the boy. Wrecker's left leg was muddy up to the knee. They put him in the cab of the truck and he suffered their kisses and Len drove away.

Melody had parked the van several blocks away from the CPS office in Eureka. She had walked the neighborhood in successive loops, located a café, sat down for a plate of bacon and eggs, been unable to eat, paid her bill, left a tip, and continued to walk. There was a little park within view of the office and she stationed herself there to wait. A few young mothers watched their children play on the slides and swings of the playground. They provided camouflage, Melody hoped, for her stealth operation. She didn't want anything to interfere with what she planned to do.

Melody had dressed as conservatively as possible for her mission. She wore a simple navy dress and a cardigan and flats. She had styled her hair to fall in a French braid down her back. The day had turned out to be beastly hot. She couldn't remove the cardigan or it would be evident to everyone that she was not wearing a bra. She had meant to; she owned several, but none of them had surfaced that morning as she struggled to get ready. The sweat streamed from her armpits. She kept her arms clamped to her sides. It was hardly the effect she had aimed for but it was the best she could do given the circumstances.

She had arrived in plenty of time to intercept Len and the boy, and she came armed with a strategy. It was not sophisticated and she was not remotely convinced that it would work. She had plan B in case it didn't. Plan B was even less developed. But she was desperate, and willing to entertain desperate measures.

"Excuse me?"

Melody had been resting her eyes while she waited. She opened them to find a young woman blocking the horizon. Melody craned her neck to see around her.

The woman didn't move. "Could you help me out?" Her skin was wan in spite of too much makeup. "I've got this splitting head-ache? I need to run across the street to the pharmacy for some aspirin, but my kids"—she shot a sidelong look at a boy and a girl hanging upside down on the monkey bars—"they won't leave? Do me a favor and watch them while I run over there?"

Out of the corner of her eye Melody caught sight of Len's truck turning onto the block. "Oh!" she said. She shifted to keep it in her field of vision, but the young mother kept moving in ways that blocked the street. She heard two car doors slam and tried to edge toward the sound. "What?" Melody said, growing frantic.

The young woman spoke slower and louder. "I need you to—"

There was Len, crossing the street, clutching Ruth's blue suit-case in one hand and balancing a brown paper bag on the opposite hip. There was Wrecker. Her heart leapt. He came up to Len's elbow, now. He'd grown so much. How had she failed to notice? "I'll go for you," Melody said quickly. She had to reach Len before he got inside. "What kind?"

The woman reached into her purse and pulled out a dollar. "Any kind," she said brusquely, jabbing the bill toward Melody.

Melody hurtled down the hill toward the office but the door snapped shut behind Len and the boy before she arrived. She pulled up short. She couldn't very well burst in there looking for them. For her plan to work, she needed to make a strong impression of competence. It was important that she appear normal. Competent, normal—Christ. The heel of her dress shoe had come loose.

Melody limped across the street to the pharmacy, keeping her eye on the office door. Even inside she could keep track through the plate glass. She located the aspirin and chose the least expensive brand. Then she walked the aisles until she came across deodorant. She chose the spray can with pastel flowers. It advertised fresh scent. She needed industrial strength, but this was probably as close as she could come.

The woman in line ahead of her nodded sympathetically toward the aspirin. She was older than Melody—thirty, maybe, or a little past—and had a pleasant, open face. "Headache?"

"It's for somebody else," Melody said. But come to think of it, she *did* have the start of a dull tightness that wrapped itself around her skull. Maybe she should pick some up for herself. She glanced down at the box in the woman's arms.

"Humidifier," the woman volunteered. "My husband gets asthma occasionally. The doctors thought this might help."

"I used to get asthma when I was a kid. It went away when I got older," Melody said, scanning the street. "And moved out of my parents' house."

The woman looked up quickly and they shared a brief grin. "Sometimes that solves more than you think." She handed the box to the clerk and turned back to Melody. "Our kids will probably say the same thing about us."

"If we're lucky," Melody said, and blinked hard.

The sun hit Melody square in the face when she stepped back onto the sidewalk and crossed the street to the park. The children eyed her suspiciously. Melody handed their mother the aspirin and a bottle of orange Fanta she had thought, at the last minute, to buy. The woman tossed back two tablets, took a swig of the soda, and grudgingly thanked her. The children clamored for the rest of the drink. Melody wanted to smack them. She should have bought them a bottle, too. She should have bought herself aspirin. She should have stayed home. Why did anyone ever have children, she wondered, when they could turn out like this?

The door to Children's Protective Services swung open and Len appeared on the sidewalk. He looked dazed. Melody looked closer. No, he had always looked like that. Life had clubbed him between the eyes, and he was reeling from its continuous aftershocks.

The door swung shut behind him, and Melody waited two beats before she realized the boy wasn't with him. The force of that simple fact squeezed the air from her lungs. The plan? Was there a plan? She sat down hard in the grass. There was a noise in her head, a growing roar competing with the isolated fragments of ideas and observations that passed for thought. The small family watched her. Melody looked up at them and at the leaves of the trees and at the clouds behind the trees and at the sky behind the clouds. Everything seemed to hold itself at a distance. Far, far away, Len put his hat back on his head and crossed the street to his truck. The plan called for Melody to run to him, to force him to return to the office and beg for Wrecker back, but she couldn't suck in enough air even to sit up.

It wouldn't do any good to beg. Len didn't want the boy. Willow didn't want him. Johnny Appleseed was too extreme and Ruth too tentative in their own lives to be able to raise a kid. And Melody?

She could hear her father's laughter pulsing in the tight spot in her throat.

Len pulled open the driver's door and climbed in. The sun glared, blinding, off the windshield. He started the engine and pulled into traffic.

Melody turned her head away from the small family. Her gaze settled on the boy's striped ball pinned under the framework of the park bench. She felt the roar in her head diminish and she desperately wished for it back. The roar masked the silence that filled the place where her heart had been.

She lay back on the grass, caught sight of the clouds swirling high in the blue sky, and reached under the bench to grasp the ball and pull it out.

"Here," she said, her voice flat and small, and rolled it toward the boy.

It was quiet at the farm. Ruth didn't bother to cook for days and Johnny Appleseed made himself busy in the garden, tilling under the old plants and digging sheep manure into the damp soil; Willow stayed in her cupcake house and read, or rethreaded the delicate carpets, or cataloged her library; Melody went to the barn and stayed there. On the days she wasn't scheduled to work she slept, letting her slumber sop up the hours so she wouldn't have to decide how to use them. An awkward stiffness arose between the four of them when they bumped into each other, crossing to the outhouse or rustling for simple meals in the kitchen. But they exchanged a few words. They laughed a little. And gradually they came together again. Ruth made occasional dinners, they stayed longer after eating, they told stories. Still it seemed quiet. No one mentioned why. No one talked about him at all.

Melody thought about him every day. Not just about the things he had done but the things he would do. The kind of man he would become. She thought about the way his face opened and closed like a shutter when sorrow or anger or happiness ran across it. About the way his body twisted and stretched to reach the far apples on the tree before the branch broke. She thought about the way his hair smelled. She thought about the sudden strength and flare of fury when she'd crossed him; how she'd stepped back, startled by the fever. He could be ugly and she loved him then, too. He could be beautiful. He could be a manipulative little sonofabitch and he could remind her that the world was composed of absurd and humorous coincidences. It seemed obscene, somehow, to send him off. It seemed obscene to wish him well. She made herself wish him well. She made herself pray for this new family to love him. She made herself pray for him to love them back. She hoped, she wished, that he would not forget her. She would not pray for that. She knew it was foolish.

The meadow was golden with October's honey light when Melody followed the path to Willow's house. She'd been out walking the perimeter of the farm, reminding herself she was home, fighting the nasty nagging thoughts she'd felt arise again lately to flee, to change the scenery and start fresh somewhere new. Sure, there was no new. There was just the same old thing repackaged in a different wrapping, blah blah—but the thing was?

Sometimes that shiny paper, those loopy bows, were just the things to distract you from the burden of tightness that had taken up permanent lodging in your throat.

Melody gazed across the meadow at the yurt. Willow was the only one of them all to build fresh. She had planted her new home on the far edge of the property, its back up against the dark wood and its face opening onto the meadow. Her house had the sloped walls and the round, domed roof of an oversized cupcake. It was a fairy house; an elegant mushroom that seemed to sprout organically from its setting. In fact it had been shipped in pieces from a yurt manufacturer in Dayton, Ohio. A crew of skilled yurt-raisers accompanied the numbered crates and in two days assembled the finished structure on the wooden deck Willow had commissioned from an itinerant carpenter who had, in a gesture toward world peace, carved thoughtful prayers in Sanskrit into the perimeter floorboards. It was a work of art strung together with steel cables and advanced engineering. It was a wisp, a dream, guaranteed to remain standing under thirty pounds of snow load and in winds up to eighty miles an hour.

"Hello?" Melody shouted, and waited until Willow opened the door, stepped onto the deck, pushed her reading glasses onto her forehead and waved in response before she crossed the strip of meadow and climbed the deck to sit in the sun beside her.

"Nice day," Willow ventured. She lifted her face to take in the sky.

"Nice enough, I guess."

"You guess?"

Melody shrugged. "It's autumn. Autumn always makes me want to be someplace else." She crossed her legs and harassed an ant that had climbed onto her shoelaces. "Mozambique. Michigan. I don't care. Siberia." She flashed Willow a glance. "I'm thinking of traveling."

"Copenhagen's nice in the fall," Willow said. And on her way back, could she pick up a roll of stamps and the pair of pinking shears Willow had special-ordered through the Mercantile?

"Maybe I won't come back," Melody said.

Willow gave herself time to read the unfamiliar note in Melody's voice. Maybe it was a challenge piggybacking on a silent insult. But maybe it was grief, plain and simple, squeezed out through the one hole poked in the held breath.

"You miss him," Willow said.

Melody made a sound. "I just wonder what he's doing now."

So it was grief. Willow laid her hand on Melody's ankle, but Melody looked up sharply. "You think it was right to let him go."

Ah. There was the challenge. There was the insult.

"Right?" Willow gave a little laugh. "Do you think I know what is right?"

"You're supposed to."

There was a long silence. Finally Willow stood up. "Well," she said. "You wouldn't be the first to question my judgment regarding children."

Melody looked out at the shadows that were growing in the meadow. "Kathmandu," she said, the tightness closing in on her voice. "Sri Lanka. Detroit, Michigan, home of the Lions."

"The pinking shears," Willow said, and Melody nodded and got up and walked back to the barn.

Len's work suffered under the new conditions of his life. He had to be home before dark to feed and bathe and care for Meg, but the weather was turning and more people than ever had left orders for cordwood at the Mercantile where he picked up his messages. He split and delivered whatever he could of the rounds he had stockpiled, drying. He took people's money and tucked it in the glove box of the truck and forgot about it. He let the millwork go to hell. Unless he got into the woods and cut more green logs he would suffer next year. And he made the three-hour round trip to Eureka each week to check on the boy.

If he had a telephone, the social worker advised him, he could save himself the trouble. He nodded and grinned. He could have called from the pay phone outside the Merc. He didn't trust them to tell him the truth on the phone.

The truth was, the boy was adjusting. (Week One.) He was doing just fine. (Week Two.) He was fitting in with the other children. (Week Three.) He was enrolling in preschool. (Week Four.) He was being placed in the orphanage in Red Bluff. (Week Five.)

"Whoa," Len said. "Hold on just a minute. I thought he was adjusting. Fitting in? Doing fine?"

The social worker gave him a look of pained forbearance. "Children adjust in different ways," she said. "This boy adjusted by walking out of his preschool and causing a forty-hour intensive police and rescue unit search that found him twenty-two miles away, sleeping under a bridge and eating trash. He adjusted by biting the ear of his adoptive mother. He refused to have his hair combed. He would not sleep in a bed."

"Oh," Len said. "That."

She looked at him oddly. "That," she said, "was the least of it. This child would be better served in a group home with professionals who have been trained to treat the kind of behavior he presents."

"He's not a bad boy," Len protested. His voice was so soft the social worker had to lean closer to hear him.

"I'm sure he's not," she said. And added, her voice lowered to his pitch, "But he's not a good boy, either."

Len said he'd take him.

The social worker blinked. She removed her glasses and slowly wiped each lens before replacing them. She said, "I don't need to remind you that you already gave him back."

Len said, "Let me have him."

That decision, the social worker said, was not up to her. It was up to the judge. Len went to see the judge. The judge rustled the papers and cleared his throat. You are asking to foster this troubled boy? he wanted to know.

"I want to adopt him," Len said. He felt the sweat bead on the leathered skin of his neck. He felt it behind his ears.

"This child is related to you?"

"He's my nephew. My wife's sister's son."

The judge was a handsome young man with a baby face he attempted to dignify with a very bushy mustache. He twirled the ends. "Sir," he said, and paused. "You must understand. If you adopt this child it will be a binding decision. There will be no trial period. He lived with you and your wife for"—he rustled through the mountain of papers—"for—"

They had Wrecker for eight months, Len confirmed; and yes, he understood the decision was binding.

"That means," the judge said, making his voice as low as he could, "you may not give him back."

Len swallowed hard. He opened his mouth and he said, "I understand."

The man and boy rode together in the truck and the shadows lengthened. Len didn't know what to say. He stole looks at the boy. Wrecker seemed smaller and paler than when he had left. He looked out the window or at his lap or straight ahead, and he fell asleep for a short time but jolted awake when Len threw the blinker lever. They were silent all the way back.

Len pulled onto the dirt road toward Bow Farm. He got out to open the first gate. He glanced at Wrecker. The boy sat impassive in the seat. Len got in and drove on. At the second gate he joked, "Before long I'm going to make you get down and open these, son. Too much trouble for an old man like me."

Wrecker faced him. He said, "I'm not your son."

Well, Len thought, tell *that* to the judge. He drove past the parking area and stopped the truck at the farmhouse. "Want to get down?"

Wrecker shrugged. Len walked around and opened the door and unbuckled the boy. Wrecker slid down and walked ahead. It was the only time Len neither honked nor shouted first to announce his presence. They simply walked in.

The four of them were seated around the table, eating dinner. Len heard the sharp intake of breath when they saw the boy. He stood behind Wrecker and saw the boy pause; saw his shoulders give the slightest shudder.

Len said, "Wrecker's home." And he lifted his hand in a vague gesture to let them know to go easy.

Ruth stood up and crossed the room. She took his small hand and cupped it in hers. "Well, it's about time. Hungry, pal?" And she led him to a spot at the table, pulled up a chair, and laid him a heaping plate.

Len watched Melody. It rested on her.

He turned for home when he saw her face. Meg would be waiting. It was late, already. "See you tomorrow, Wrecker," he said, but the boy was oblivious to him.

They ate the meal slowly and talked softly about small matters, about things of no consequence, and then they moved together into the next room. Wrecker lay on the big chair with his head in Melody's lap and his eyes closed, though she knew he wasn't sleeping. The others clustered near enough to each other that any of them could lay a hand close to him. On the edge of the chair, or on its high back. On the soft down of his cheek. He had come with his shoulders high and his chin jutting forward, his every muscle on alert, but the plank of his body gradually softened as Melody smoothed the hair behind his ears. They let the flow of their voices surround him. No one said a word about the next day. Or the day after that. Or the long days to come, the string of days that swam like fish waiting to be caught.

When his breaths lengthened and he let go at last of the weight of himself, Melody lifted Wrecker onto her hip and carried his slumped body over the moonlit path to the barn. She woke him just long enough to let him pee outside and to climb the ladder to the loft, and then she helped him shed his shoes and socks and jeans, tug his shirt over his head, wrestle his inert body into a soft clean shirt of her own to sleep in. She pulled the covers up to his chin and she sat on the bed beside him with her knees up to her chin and, for a long time, she watched him breathe.

She would call in sick to work the next day. She would drive to Eureka and get him his own bed. A permanent one. For tonight he could have this half and she would sleep with one eye open to make sure he did not disappear again. A pulse in his temple beat like a butterfly trapped beneath his skin. There were dark circles under his eyes. Melody felt her own fear mount with each breath she took. If there were no one else to raise him up, if it were Melody alone rising to stand beside him, then God help him. She had never been enough at anything. If she failed at this—

"Melody?" Willow's voice filtered up from the darkness below.

Melody rubbed her nose and pressed her hands against her eyes. She took a deep breath. Then she rearranged the blankets so Wrecker would stay covered, and she quietly descended the ladder.

They stood outside and talked softly. Their voices made clouds of mist in the moonlit air. The light pooled in the hollows of Willow's cheeks and splashed in her eyes and Melody thought, Just because you're beautiful and charming does not mean you are always right. Sometimes you are plain wrong. "I didn't plan this, Willow. This is as much a surprise to me as it is to you."

"A surprise? Yes. Definitely a surprise."

"I won't let go of him again."

The briefest smile lifted the corner of Willow's mouth. "Don't you think that's a decision we should make together? Not just the two of us, but Ruth and Johnny, too?"

"Ruth and Johnny want him."

"Ruth and Johnny *love* him," Willow said quickly. "But they're not foolish enough to think they know anything about raising a child." Melody scowled but Willow reached to take hold of her arm. "I *do*, Melody. I *do* know. And you know what? It's no walk in the park."

"I don't expect it to be easy."

"*Easy*?" Willow gave a little laugh. "Easy's not even on the spectrum. Try all-consuming. Try heartbreaking. You might start by giving up everything you ever wanted just to do this one thing, and you might as well recognize that you're as apt to fail at it as you are to succeed."

"I won't fail." Melody said this softly, through clenched teeth, but it marched out and stood in the air between them.

Willow's face went through a painful transformation. "Have a little humility," she said.

Melody shied back and shut her eyes. Humility? That was the one thing she had in spades. She had a supernatural excess of it. She thought so poorly of herself, in fact, that she would have to climb several rungs up the ladder just to get to the elevated position of humility. Whereas Willow—

Melody opened her eyes, ready to fire away. But there was something terrible there.

"Willow," she said softly.

Willow shook her head and waved her hand dismissively. "I'm fine," she said. "Disregard this."

Melody looked away and felt a wave of guilt prickle her scalp and rest in the pit of her stomach. "I didn't mean—"

"Of course not," Willow said. She blotted her face with her hands and made an effort to smile. "Melody," she said, her voice dropping a notch. "He's a tough kid. You don't know what he's been through. You don't know what he'll—"

"I know that. I know it."

"I don't want to see you get hurt."

"I know you don't." Melody studied her hands. Her face folded with the weight of her thought, and when she started again her voice was small. "I want him, Willow. I don't know if that's enough. But I'm asking you to let him start over. Let him start fresh, start now, and be welcome here."

"Melody," Willow murmured. "He has a mother."

"She let go of him."

"She *lost* him," Willow said sharply.

"All right! But it amounts to the same thing for Wrecker, doesn't it?" Melody struggled with her voice. There was a word for what she planned to do, but it would take fearlessness to use it. She was consumed with fear. Still, she brought her hands together and said, her words barely more than a squeak, "I'm his mother now."

"You're *what*?" Willow laughed.

Melody turned to face Willow directly. She might never have the guts to be able to say it again, and she needed Willow to hear.

"That woman? She had him, she raised him—but she let go of him. And the only way he's going to make it through is if there's somebody who stands up and says, I'm all in. I'm not just looking after you, I'm *for* you. You're mine." She hesitated. "From here on out? He's my son." There was a long pause. Melody could hear her own teeth rattle as she shivered. She knew Willow thought she was making a big mistake, and maybe she was. But *she* was making it, and she would go on making it with every breath she had.

Willow's fingers were awkward as she buttoned her sweater. She kept her head down. "I see," she said, nodding, studying something on the ground beneath her. Her voice was muted and she worked her jaw as though trying to exorcise an old pain. A shadow covered her face, but did not obscure the grief that stumbled across it. What *happened* to you, Willow? Melody almost asked.

But she did not. And when Willow raised her head again, it was the friend Melody knew; the Willow who could do anything, who conveyed flint and grace and attitude in every move she made. "Okay," Willow said. She cleared her throat and willed her voice to come out smoother. "All right, then. I'll help you however I can."

Melody, wary, waited for the but.

Willow gazed at her tenderly. She nodded once more, and then she stepped into the night.

CHAPTER FIVE

And then Wrecker was eight. He climbed atop a stack of produce crates in the back room of the Mercantile and ate dried apricots one sticky fruit at a time. He was waiting for Melody to finish work. The knees of his jeans were white with wear but as yet un-breached, and he was wearing red Keds whose rubber heels bounced impatiently off the wooden sides of the crates. It was always *One more thing, Wrecker, just let me finish this* and *Are you ready? Where's your jacket?*—and then someone else would poke his head through the stockroom door and call her name. Wrecker tapped his head against the wall behind him to the beat of the song on the radio. He sat chewing and tapping and bouncing his sneaker against the crate when DF Al the stock boy burst in.

"Sport!" Al said. He could make his face physically larger with his expressions, as though his skin had a special expansiveness that spread his hairline back and his ears farther to the sides. He stopped, stared diffusely, listened for the tune. Then he picked up a head of celery and played air guitar, mouthing the words.

Wrecker liked Al. Al walked with verve and carried food. "I have apricots," Wrecker told him. He extended a sticky hand with two flat fruits. "Want to trade?" The apricots looked like dried ears. Wrecker would not have thought of this on his own, but Al had taped two to the sides of his head over his own ears and walked around like that for one whole day.

Al lifted the dried disks carefully from Wrecker's grimy palm and sniffed them, ogled them, reached out the tip of his tongue to taste them. He squinted suspiciously at the boy. "Genuine?" Before Wrecker could answer Al popped them both in his mouth and glanced around furtively. Then he shut his eyes and faced beatifically toward the ceiling. Al was weird. Melody thought he smoked too much dope but Wrecker just figured he was probably born this way. He chewed and winked at Wrecker and reached into his pocket. He passed the boy a small handful of the cinnamon redhots they both liked. "You going to school?"

"Soon as Deedee's ready." Wednesdays he had the morning off and spent it helping Melody at the Mercantile. Wrecker slid down off the crates and crouched to extract the dry sponge they used as a soccer ball from between the wheels of the shopping cart. "Want to play?"

"I have to work."

"Yeah." Wrecker laughed. "Right." He faked to the left. Then he tapped the sponge forward with the toe of his sneaker, dribbled past the mop bucket, advanced toward the opposing defender, and slapped it with the inside of his left foot toward the goal. DF Al shot his leg out to block and deflected it into the open carton of soaps he was supposed to be pricing. Wrecker lunged for the sponge just as Al flung his foot out to bar his path and the boy was knocked off his feet while propelling forward toward the brooms that lay in a tangled mess in the corner.

The door flapped open and Melody entered. She was jotting something on a clipboard and didn't look up. "Wrecker," she said absently, "Got your jacket? We should go," checked a note she had pinned to the corkboard by the clock, registered the information, and swung back out.

Wrecker extracted himself from the brooms. He glanced at DF Al, who had snatched up the pricing gun and was waving it in front of himself. His black glasses sat crooked on his face and his hair was wild. "Easy, now, boy," Wrecker said. "Don't shoot."

DF Al leaned over, clicked the trigger, and rubbed the tag onto the sleeve of Wrecker's shirt. "Seventy-nine cents," he said. "This week only. Limit one per customer."

Melody poked her head through the door again. She had tied her blonde hair up in a bun but half of the strands had already defected. "You ready, son?" she said. She looked at Al. "You done pricing those soaps yet? Jesus, Al. Get a move on. I need you on the register while I'm gone." She let her gaze stray around the stockroom. "This place is a mess." She squinted at them. "What the hell's been going on back here?"

"Monsters," Al replied, and nodded his head solemnly. "Intergalactic. Had to fend 'em off with my long range hypno-gamma ray tommy gun. They won't give you no more trouble, ma'am," and he blew on the business end of his price tagger and made to reholster it.

A grin played at the corner of her mouth but gained no lasting purchase. "Can the bullshit, DF. You don't get your work done Dreyfus is going to—"

"Right, right. All work and no play."

"Find your jacket, Wrecker," Melody said, and a customer called to her and she ducked back out the doors.

DF Al beamed at her retreating back. He tilted his head toward Wrecker and sighed. "Women love me."

Wrecker nodded. The women he knew joked about Al when he wasn't there, called him Dope Fiend Al or Dumb Fuck Al or worse. Wrecker thought he should act more normal around other people, but he didn't know if Al could pull it off. "Seen my jacket?"

"Yeah. A penguin waltzed in here, asked if he could have it. Said it's cold at the South Pole. I told him sure, you were a generous guy."

Wrecker spied the blue sleeve of the parka on the floor by the meat locker. He pushed himself to his feet. "See you tomorrow," he said.

"Not if I see you first, brother."

Melody was in a huff. She had to get the produce order in by 3:30 and do the payroll and file the something and do the something something for Wrecker's school and still catch Ruth before five o'clock at the salvage yard with some kind of information. Wrecker yawned. His stomach hurt from too many apricots. The day was bright and cold. One kid from school had off to go hunting. He wanted to go hunting. Why couldn't he go hunting.

Melody tapped the steering wheel of the bus with her index finger while she drove. It was a nervous habit. "When you're older."

"How old?"

"Old enough to know better than to want to do that," she said, flicking her turn signal and flooring the gas pedal to urge the old bus past a lumbering pickup loaded with trash for the landfill. The motor made its cheery jingling VW sound. The little engine that could. On Tuesday, Wednesday, or Saturday, at least. The rest of the time was a toss up. She wished she could shoot the poor thing and put it out of its misery. She alternated between feeling nostalgic about its years of magical service and disgusted by its current unreliability. Disgust was weighing in heavily, but it wasn't like she could run down to the local dealership and pick up a new one. If she skimmed the top off what she took home each week, if she made payments, maybe she could spring for a skateboard. Maybe. She and Wrecker could take turns riding and running alongside. It would take them—oh—a day and a half each way to commute into town.

Why couldn't she have been born rich?

Oh yeah. She had been born rich. It just hadn't worked out.

Wrecker made a face. "Too many apricots," he said.

"Go easy on them, buddy. They sneak up on you." She cut a quick glance at his face and then swung the bus back into the proper lane. He was changing so fast. One week his face was all baby fat and foolishness and the next it had slimmed down, had an eight-year-old's skepticism and resolve. Well, not resolve. He'd always had that. They'd just labeled it stubbornness. Stubborn fit in with ornery and immature, but resolve?

He sure hadn't picked that up from her.

"What time is it, Wrecker?"

He lifted his wrist to check. She watched his lips move as he counted by fives. He was okay to thirty or so, but after that it started to break up. She had bought him a watch so he could practice. At school they played cooperative games and learned number theory with manipulatives; at home, guiltily, it was flash cards and torn sheets from the cheap pulp workbooks she picked up at the supermarket. "Eleven ten."

"Let me see."

Jesus, it was five to two. She was supposed to have him there by one fifteen. By two she was supposed to—oh, well, great. They were out in the open, three minutes from Wrecker's school, and a cop was dogging the van with lights flashing and the siren making its stupid little whoops. A cop? Out here? She pulled to the side of the road and shut her eyes. She rolled down the window. "Yes?"

"Holy mackerel, lady!" The cop had a beefy face that appeared red from internal combustion and not from any exposure to the elements. "You know how fast you were going?"

Speeding? No. Not speeding. She couldn't keep a small smirk from staining her face. "Not exactly, officer. But I can tell you this old bus"—her index finger flicked rapidly against the steering wheel—"she just hasn't got it in her to speed. I'm lucky if I can coax her up the hills."

"Up, maybe," he said. He looked earnestly affronted. He looked *personally* offended. "But coming down that hill I clocked you at sixty in a forty-five zone. That's—that's—"

Fifteen.

"—that's fifteen miles over the speed limit. I'll have to ticket you for that." He rearranged his features to express paternal disapproval. "Where are you in such a rush to get to?"

Melody rubbed her face with her hands. She was going to have to grovel. "I'm taking my son—" She tipped her head toward Wrecker and the words died in her mouth. His face was ashen and he had made himself as small as he could in the seat. His hands gripped the frayed piping of the upholstery edge.

The cop bent sideways to get more of his face in the open window. "Something wrong?"

Melody turned in the seat and put her hand on Wrecker's cheek. "Hey," she said softly. "You okay?"

The kid wouldn't look at her. He kept his head down and his eyes fixed on the white rounds of his pant knees. She leaned closer to him. Whispered in his ear, "You need the bathroom?" He didn't look up, but he freed one hand from the car seat and took hold of the sleeve of her sweater. He gripped it hard, his small hand kneading the fabric. He gathered more and started to twist. "Ow," she breathed out. "That hurts. You're pinching my skin."

"Miss? Is everything all right?"

The boy kept an iron grip on the sweater sleeve. He drew back so he wouldn't hurt her, but he wouldn't let go.

"Miss!"

Melody swung her head toward the cop. "Look," she said. "My son—I don't know what. I think he needs to get to a bathroom.

His school's just a few miles ahead. I'm going to have to talk to you later. Okay?" Her voice cracked. "Will you just—okay?"

"Oh," he said. His wedding ring clinked on the metal of the car door before he backed away. "Sure. Just slow down on the hills, lady. You need an escort or something? I could go ahead of you with the siren."

Wrecker gripped tighter and it sent a volt of pain to the root of Melody's brain. "No siren," she gasped. "I'll slow down." She remembered to say thank you and the cop climbed into his cruiser and pulled away.

Melody moved to extract her right arm from Wrecker's grip so she could start the engine. "Wrecker, let go." She kept her voice as calm and low as she could. "I can't drive with you hanging on." She studied his face. His eyes weren't closed but he kept them turned from her. He was as white as a sheet. What was this? Even his lips were pale. His hair had darkened with each year to a dirty blond but it looked brown against his skin. Slowly he eased up until his hand was open and resting on her forearm. She started to move her arm away but a thread caught on his fingernail and he gave a short, sharp cry of pain. "What!" she shouted, jangled to the quick. Trembling, she extracted the thread from his nail and took his hand in both of hers and held it to her cheek. "I'm sorry, Wrecker. I am. I'm so sorry."

She could tell from the slight quiver that ran down his arm that he was holding himself as still as he could to keep from crying. He kept his head turned and all the misery in the world seemed trapped in the twist of that stiff neck.

Melody was desperate to say the right thing. She racked her brain for the exact words. Maybe his real mother would know what to say. His real—she fit the key in the ignition and waited for the engine to even out before pulling onto the road. As if it weren't hard enough already, being a mother. No. Willow had to make it harder. She had to go and dig up that other one, turn her from the ghost who loitered around the edges of Melody's fear into a flesh-and-blood human being sitting in a prison cell while another woman mothered her son.

My son, Melody thought savagely. He's *my* son.

She looked straight out the windshield and kept the speed just below the limit until they arrived at the school. Melody halted the bus beside a spindly madrone. Wrecker stumbled out of his door, and she trotted around the front of the bus to catch up to him. "Does your stomach hurt?" She reached to adjust the shoulder strap of his knapsack. "Need the bathroom?" He pulled away from her touch and continued toward the front steps. "Wrecker," she called softly. His back was turned but she thought she saw him hesitate. Even softer, she called, "You okay, buddy?"

The boy glanced over his shoulder toward her, and Melody caught his eye like a bird on the wing. She felt her own heart pumping like a bird's heart, pulsing in her throat. She could haul him back or she could lose him for good and she stood paralyzed, afraid that any move she made would be the wrong move. But Wrecker slowed, and turned to face her. For a moment he seemed to waver. And then he started back in her direction.

Thank God. She opened her arms to him.

But he lowered his head and collided with her, butting her to the ground.

Wrecker's arms swung like windmills. It was all Melody could do to dodge the blows, and when she rolled away she somehow—half by accident—got behind him, got her arms around his to stop their flailing. She held on tight. Dropped her head to gasp in his ear, "What? In the hell? Are you doing?"

He had froth around the corners of his mouth and she could barely understand his bellow. Until, suddenly, she could.

"Fuck, no! I would never," she yelled, and squeezed hard.

104

Wrecker paused in his thrashing. Melody roughly spun the boy to face her. He dropped his chin and she reached out and lifted it until his eyes were forced to meet hers. "I would never let him take you. Never. Not him and nobody else. Do you understand me? *Never.*" He watched her and she thought, Oh God let it be true. Forget everything else I have ever asked of you and give me the strength for this one thing.

She felt him reach his gaze behind her eyes and grope around for the shape of her prayer.

For today. Okay.

His body relaxed some under her grip and she eased off a bit. Melody glanced over her shoulder and saw that they'd attracted an audience. She dragged her shoulder across her cheek to wipe the sweat and elbowed toward the school. "You going in?" He barely blinked but she understood him. "Then get in the car," she muttered, and released him.

Wrecker did as he was told. Melody stood and faced the small crowd that had assembled. Their faces were aghast. "Well," she said. She tugged on the hem of her jacket and cleared her throat. "I guess we'll see you on Monday," and she managed a wave before bolting for the bus and pulling away.

Wrecker was laughing softly. The color had come back into his face. "Did you see them, Deedee?" he asked. "Did you? They looked like—"

Melody brought the bus to a screeching, shuddering stop in the middle of the road. "Wrecker," she said, her voice trembling. "I swear to God I will not give you away. But *do not* hit me again. Understand? Because—"

"Okay."

"Because—"

"O-*kay.*"

"Okay?"

"Okay."

"Okay," she muttered, and shifted into gear and started forward again. They were as real as it could possibly get for each other. That woman in jail—"Okay," she said. She started to laugh. It tasted like salt and lilacs, like snot and pine needles and a torn heart. "Okay," she said again. Wrecker was laughing hard. He was starting to hoot. "Okay." Torn but still functioning. Okay. It would have to be.

Melody maneuvered the bus fitfully up and down the small hills and around the bends as the road traversed the valley and headed for the sea. Wrecker hummed to himself beside her. He seemed pleased to have the afternoon off. Melody squinted at him. He bounced back fast, but for her? It had been weeks and still she couldn't shake the scare of Willow's trip to the prison. It had flattened her confidence and left her second-guessing every move she made with the boy, looking over her shoulder for the long arm of judgment to snatch him away.

All this, because of that damned check. It had come in the mail without warning, a piddling inheritance that was the scant remainder of Meg's parents' estate once the banks and the creditors and the government and the lawyers got through taking their cut. It was laughably small, but Len was adamant. It wasn't right for one daughter to inherit everything. He didn't care what the will specified; as Meg's guardian, he wouldn't let her accept it. He would locate Lisa Fay and deliver her half.

He would not, Willow said. She was due for a trip to the city. She would take the money.

When Melody caught wind of the plan it raised every hair on her body. Len had launched some bad ideas before, but this one was terrible. Rotten as a fetid fish and just as dangerous, and Melody had not had a single stinking say in the matter. When she'd tried, both Len and Willow had gazed at her—gently, affectionately, entirely blankly—and then went back to debating the best way to handle the situation. When she'd shouted with exasperation that *she* was the one raising the kid and should therefore be party to this decision, they had finally paused and paid attention.

"Melody," Willow said, somewhat quizzically. "This is not about you."

"It's about Wrecker!"

Len and Willow looked at each other, considering, and then back at Melody. "No," Willow said, "it isn't, actually." It was about Meg, she explained, and Meg's sister. And their parents. It was a small part about Len, who wouldn't cash the check unless he could split it with Lisa Fay. "None of it is about me. That's why I'm the obvious person to bring it down to her." And Len, determined though he was, couldn't talk her out of it.

Willow was gone for a week. She took the Greyhound down to San Francisco, did some sleuthing, and tracked Meg's sister down at Chino, the giant prison east of L.A. Willow was gaunt and exhausted when she returned. She had visited the prison twice. They had spoken for a long time. Lisa Fay wouldn't take the money.

"She wants you to have it," Willow told Melody.

"Me," Melody scoffed. "She doesn't know me." Her face suddenly blanched. "No." She watched Willow's face closely. "You didn't," she said, shaking her head. "No, Willow. You couldn't have."

Lisa Fay needed to know that her son was safe, Willow explained. Was that so hard to understand? And so Willow—Willow had told her. Where Wrecker was, who was raising him in her absence, what he looked like at eight, which foods he liked and which he could not abide. Willow told Lisa Fay how Meg had

107

suffered in the dental surgery, she told her that her parents had died—but at length, and in as much detail as she could muster, she described the boy's life at Bow Farm. In exchange, Lisa Fay told Willow everything: who had fathered the boy, what happened in Wrecker's first years, the whole sordid story of her arrest and trial and incarceration.

"I don't want to know," Melody cried bitterly. "None of it." She glanced at Willow and away, her eyes flashing with anger and pain. "And don't you tell Wrecker." She glared at Willow. "Promise me that. Not a word."

"He should know, Melody. It's his history."

"*This* is his history!" She swung her arms stiffly. "Bow Farm. The Mattole. You, Ruth, Johnny, me. The rest is dead weight, Willow. You want to remind him of that? Whatever happened to him, you want to bring that back?"

Willow looked at her steadily. "You're making a mistake. Someday—"

"Someday I'll explain it to him." Melody felt her breath scour her insides. It was no lie, what they'd told him—and no secret. Someone Len knew had given the boy up for adoption. With Meg ill, Melody had stepped in to raise him. Len signed the important papers, but Melody was his mother. It was as close to legal as things got in the Mattole, and it had been working just fine. "But not now. It would just confuse him. He doesn't remember any of that, anyway."

"There's a photograph."

Melody felt Willow's soft voice seep in to stain her heart. "No." Her lips closed in a tight line and she worked her hands, squeezing the knuckles. "Absolutely not."

"It's his history."

"And this is his present," Melody snapped back. "This is his reality, Willow. Don't you realize how vulnerable he is? If she

108

wanted to take him back—" Melody stopped and tore her gaze away. Only Len, skinny Len, stood between her and losing Wrecker—and he was no protection at all.

Melody felt panic grip her throat. Her brother Jack was a lawyer. Could she count on him to help her? Maybe she should take Wrecker and run. But—leave the Mattole? Where would they go? She forced herself to turn back to Willow. "No." Melody lifted her eyes to confront Willow's steady, penetrating stare. "That's my decision."

The corners of Willow's mouth turned down. There was a long pause, and then she nodded slowly, as if deciding something. "All right," she said, her voice low and measured. "I'll hold it for him. You tell me when it's okay."

Melody shot a sidelong glance at the boy, now. He was gazing out the window at a trio of horses in a green pasture. Wrecker liked horses, but they made him sneeze.

Did his mother sneeze at horses, too?

It would never be okay, Melody knew. But that didn't mean she could keep it from him forever.

The boy rode shotgun for Melody all the rest of the afternoon. They took care of business at the post office, making copies at the only Xerox machine for miles, and Wrecker filled up on free popcorn at the counter while Melody struggled with paper jams and a defunct stapler. They doubled back to the Mercantile to check produce inventory and phone in the order by the supplier's deadline. Wrecker went looking for Al. Melody sussed the situation with the cantaloupe and kale; she was getting it down out of Eureka and it was looking a little shabby. The Ukiah distributor was more professional and had higher-quality stock but charged too much to bring it this far north. Nine tenths of this job was aggravation, and now she had to tell the others payday wouldn't happen until Monday. Dreyfus needed the weekend receipts to keep the checks fluid. Why were these apples stacked so poorly? DF Al was supposed to take care of that. Where the hell was he, anyway?

Wrecker reappeared. "I can't find him." He had shed his jacket.

"Where'd you look?" Melody was tallying: two crates of apples, an assortment of squash, spinach if it looked any good, low on citrus. Bad time of the year to buy citrus. Plenty of onions.

"In the stockroom, in the bathroom, out back by the trash bins. And I asked Sheila."

"What'd she say?" Melody glanced at the short redheaded girl in the velvet shirt running the cash register. Sheila was a slut. It was her most likable quality. Melody suspected her of under-reporting her drawer, but she had been there longer than anyone else and this gave her a kind of mystical protection. Besides, Drey-fus needed her. Everybody knew the Merc couldn't stay afloat on the business it did; Dreyfus had a more lucrative side gig hooking up the Mattole growers with his city connections, and Sheila's farm grew better bud than any of the others. Not even Johnny Appleseed's forest crop could match her quality.

Wrecker shrugged. "Said he had to go. Can I have a licorice?" He preferred real candy, but the Mercantile only stocked the healthy kind.

"No. Had to go where?"

"Fix his car or something. Why not?"

Melody had lifted the phone to call in the produce order but she put it down to look at him. "What'd you have so far today? Dried apricots, popcorn, and whatever candy Al gave you? Don't shake your head. I *know* he gave you candy." She lifted the phone to her ear again but kept talking to him. "He's in deep shit, your friend. He's supposed to be working today." She held the phone with her shoulder and dialed the number on the sheet. "He's this far away from—" She held her thumb and index finger barely apart. "Hello? Yeah, hi. This is Melody? Lost Coast Mercantile? I've got my produce order." She muffled the mouthpiece with one hand while she gestured to Wrecker to come closer. "What?" she said, turning her attention back to the phone. "No, nobody told me that. I know. I just don't think— Okay. All right. Monday, then." And she hung up the handset with a crash.

Sheila twisted her neck to look over toward them. "What?" Melody challenged. She looked down at Wrecker. "Where's your coat?"

"Just one licorice?" he bargained.

"One, then. And find your coat. We'll be late to meet Ruth." She fished a dime out of her pocket and gave it to him for the candy. "Get an egg, too. Something to keep you anchored down." She added a quarter to the dime. The Mercantile sold them hard-boiled. "Meet you in the bus. I've got to run next door and talk to the mechanic."

Wrecker nodded. He walked to the checkout counter and watched Sheila dig an egg out of the glass jar for him. He gave her the licorice and the coins.

"You could get another one with the money you've got," she said.

"I can only have one."

She yawned. At the end she patted her mouth delicately with her fingers. "Just doing the math for you."

Wrecker nodded. He walked back to the candy counter and strung another black shoelace from its mates. Already the shadows were getting long. He walked to the bus and climbed in. A moment later Melody jumped in the driver's side and fired the engine. Wrecker brought both black strings out from the bag.

"I thought—"

111

"It's okay, Deedee." Wrecker handed her one. "I got this one for you."

The main gate to the salvage yard was shut by the time they got there, but everyone knew that meant go around to the door in the chain link fence that flanked the office. Melody waved to the stout man who ran the yard from the desk. He never stepped out of the office until he was ready to leave for the day, but he had a photographic memory of the layout of the lot. He didn't need to step out. He could tell you which parts were still on which vehicle in the whole sixteen-acre spread. Melody marveled at a brain like that.

"Ruth still here?" she shouted.

He didn't look up. "Northeast corner '66 blue Ford one ton. Close in half an hour." The words ran together out of the side of his mouth. The first time she met him, Melody thought he spoke a foreign language. It took some experience to parse the meaning of his utterances. "Half an hour I ain't waiting," he warned. "I put the dogs in and I go home."

She and Wrecker took off at a trot. The lanes were wide enough between the rows of junked cars to tow them in and out. The place smelled of engine oil and the damp rot of car seats exposed to months of rain. It didn't help Melody to realize that half the cars she passed looked in better shape than her van. She tossed a look of longing at a black Studebaker coupe. Now, *that* was styling. She shook off the thought. That wasn't styling, it was stupid. More stupid. If she ever had the chance to replace the bus she'd probably get another just like it. Only one that worked.

She looked down at Wrecker, gliding effortlessly beside her while she puffed and strained. Maybe she should get a station wagon. Didn't mothers drive station wagons? Maybe that was the trick to it all. Get the station wagon and there, in the operator's manual, were all the little tips that made you successful not just as a driver but as a proper *carpooler*, as a fully accepted hostess and caretaker of other mothers' children, as a just disciplinarian, as a sympathetic listener, as a solver of problems (mathematical and otherwise), as a pillar of the community and an unshakeable source of confidence and protection for her own child's growing self-esteem—

All right. So that was a lot to ask of a car.

She looked down at the kid again. Good stride. Quirky sense of humor. Ten fingers ten toes. Deeply, unreasonably adored. That thing this afternoon—

So not everything could be anticipated. Not everything could be warded off. Not everything—oh, God! Where was the justice in this?

She crossed her fingers. She caught his eye and he smiled.

They found Ruth just where the desk man had said she'd be. They found her boots, anyway. The rest of her was banging away under the chassis of the blue Ford.

"Hey, girl," Melody said. "You almost done? They're closing in"—she lifted Wrecker's wrist to check his watch—"in twenty minutes."

Ruth's voice was muffled by the truck body. "You bring that number?"

"Got it right here." Melody reached into her pocket for the scrap with the information Ruth needed. The farm truck was down again. Ruthie had hitched a ride to the junkyard and called Melody at the Mercantile to ask for a ride home and to bring her a part number and a price from the book at the Napa counter. It would come in handy, Ruthie told her, when it came time to pay. The desk man was a genius, everybody knew it, but he was as tight as a man could get and stay in business.

Slowly, incrementally, Ruth started to work her way out from under the truck. Each movement radiated pain. Melody watched the legs of her grease-streaked jeans emerge first, then the broad belt with the fist-sized buckle that encircled her wide waist, then the faded plaid of her flannel shirt. Ruth's head arrived last, round and watch-capped. She grinned at Wrecker. "Hey, you little fart. Bring me anything good to eat?"

Like a magic trick, Wrecker pulled the egg, unbroken, from his pocket and held it like a diamond in the light. It glowed golden in the last rays of the sun.

Ruth guffawed. She still lay on her back. Melody knew it would be a lengthy process to get her unkinked and ambulatory. "You eat it," Ruth said. "I eat one more egg I'll turn into a chicken." They were all sick of them. Johnny Appleseed's hens laid the cheapest packets of protein they could access and there was some discussion at the farm over whether they would sprout wings or feathers first.

"Br-br-br-br-BAWK," Wrecker crowed. He cracked the shell and slipped the whole egg in his mouth. It made Melody shudder.

"You get the part?"

"I got it." Ruth handed Melody a cruddy lump of metal. "Wasn't easy."

"Think it'll work?"

"Damn well better," she grumbled. "After all this. Help me with my tools." She reached back under the truck for wrenches, for drifts, for a ball-peen hammer, and Melody took them as she passed them out, put them in their slots in the canvas tool wrap.

"Where's this go?" Melody held up a small sledge and Ruthie gestured to the bucket. "Wrecker saved me from a speeding ticket."

"How'd he do that?"

Melody flushed and looked up. The boy was several vehicles

away, climbing onto the running board of an old pickup. She watched him for a minute and turned back to Ruth. "I'm an asshole." She pulled her jacket tighter around her.

The older woman struggled onto an elbow. She wore a streak of grease across her face like war paint. "Well, I won't argue with you about that. What happened?"

"Damn cop." Melody shook her head. "Pulled me over at the bottom on Thompson Creek Hill. A cop there, on the Mattole Road. Can you believe it?"

"Your lucky day."

"Something like that." She gave a short, bitter laugh. "So I'm talking to him, and when I glance over at Wrecker he looks like he's going to throw up. I told the cop I needed to go ahead and get Wrecker to his school, that it was an emergency."

"He let you go?" Ruth was sitting up by now.

Melody nodded. "I got to the school and Wrecker went berserk." She glanced at Ruth. "I didn't realize it until then."

"The cop." Melody's face twisted in a thin smile and Ruth shook her head, looked down at the dirt. "Poor kid must have freaked," Ruth murmured. "Probably hasn't been that close to a cop since they picked him up under the bridge, all those years ago." She rubbed her hand across her face and the grease smeared onto her chin. "Sweet mother of God. If I could just wash all that—"

"Dream on."

Ruthie glanced at her sharply. "Oh. You giving up now?"

"Shut up, Ruth." Melody scowled and bunched her shirt cuffs into her fists. "I'm just saying. Those first three years? I thought we'd gotten past that. I thought that was over."

"So we quit on him?"

"You know that's not—"

"Well then, what?" Ruth struggled to her feet.

115

"Christ, Ruth!" Melody's voice rose into a yelp. "Back off." She shoved her hands into the pockets of her jeans and shook her head to fend off tears. "It's just hard." Harder than anything she'd ever done, already. Hard enough *before* Willow went and told that woman, that Lisa Fay, where to find him. What if she got out early? Wasn't anybody else as scared they'd lose him? She dropped her volume, tried to even out her voice. "It's a hard time, now. That's all I'm saying."

But Ruth wouldn't budge. "Hard for him?" Her voice was sharper than Melody had ever heard it. "Or hard for you?"

Melody felt it like the sting of a slap, and stalked away.

Wrecker was standing on the hood of the old pickup when he saw Melody storm off. He watched her back and then he slid down the left fender and walked over to Ruth.

"Where's Deedee going?"

Ruth wiped her hands on the rag she kept in her back pocket. She looked down at the boy and shrugged. "Taking the long way, I guess," she said. "We'll meet her at the gate. I've got to pay for this part before the Desk Man closes shop. Go on and grab that bucket and come with me." Wrecker hesitated and Ruthie laid her hand on the back of his neck. "Leave her be," she said. "She's just getting some air. Aren't you cold? Where's your jacket?"

Wrecker flushed. His jacket. He looked up at her. "I'm not cold."

"Left it at the Merc? Fair enough, then. Get it tomorrow."

They walked together past the rows of cars. Wrecker peered down each intersection.

Ruthie said, "She's coming."

They could see the office ahead. The Desk Man was standing outside with someone else. It could be Melody. But they got closer and saw that it wasn't. It was a man.

"Uh-oh," Ruth said. "Better hurry." But she couldn't go a lot faster than she already was. Faster for her meant a determined look on her face and a more exaggerated limp. When they got closer the other man came toward them. He reached to take the U-joint and tool roll from her hands. He was a young man with a friendly, almost goofy smile.

"DF Al!" Wrecker exclaimed.

"Hey, buddy!" He clocked the boy on the shoulder. "You out fixing your ride?"

"Where's Deedee?"

"Lady," the Desk Man grumbled. "I'm closed up."

"Not for me you're not," Ruth warned. "Let's talk about price."

"I said I'm closed."

"You quoted me six bucks over new. Forget that! I'll give you half."

"Did you see her?"

DF Al looked at Wrecker. "Is this your aunt?"

"Give me twenty bucks and get out of here. You're wasting my time."

"Al. She go out already?"

Ruth wasn't happy, Wrecker could tell from the red on her cheeks. But she pulled a crumpled bill from her pocket and handed it to the man. "This doesn't work, I'm bringing it back."

"I'm late," he grumbled. "Past closing." He gestured toward his truck or the setting sun, it wasn't clear. "Go on, now. I'm letting out the dogs."

Wrecker said loudly, "Where's Deedee?"

They all turned to look at him.

Melody reclined with the Studebaker seat pushed all the way back and her legs stretched out in front of her, her ankles crossed and her arms folded across her chest. The sun was a lump of red in the rear-view mirror. She had quit crying and was just listening to the breath whistle in and out through her nose. The sound was oddly comforting. She knew she should be getting back but felt that she had discovered a pristine, unrecycled pocket of calm that couldn't last, and that it would be sinful to turn her back on it. She gave it six breaths. She gave it ten and then opened the car door and got out.

Ambling up the lane was a thin man with a shuffling walk, a dark apostrophe that resolved, as he got closer, into DF Al.

"You," she said.

He stopped a few yards from her and shifted his weight from foot to foot. He reached a hand to scratch the back of his neck and then ran it over the beard growth on his chin. "I guess so."

She laughed. It surprised her and she put her hand to her mouth. She had been exposed, as—as what?

He didn't seem to care. He just stood there and let the evening air spill over him.

"You know what I'd like, Al?" Melody felt emotion swell again in her throat and had to talk just to keep it from spilling out. "For a little while? I'd like everything just to stop. Just for a bit. So I could stand here and smoke a joint with you." Her voice wobbled, but she kept going. "We could talk about nothing. Bullshit. Whatever." She took a deep breath and leaned back against the car door. "Then I'd like to smoke another one. And then—" She glanced at him and almost said it. Because it was true, he looked good, standing there like that. And the truth hurt.

It had been so goddamned long.

He didn't look embarrassed. He just nodded, his head gently bobbing, his body moving slowly forward with each dip of his chin until he stood close enough for one more nod to bring the rough scratch of his beard gently onto the crown of her head. His arms had somehow taken up positions around hers to circle her rib cage. He kept his body close but tilted his chin back and to the side to gaze at her. "Aw," he said. She watched him smile and then he leaned forward and let his breath ruffle the whorls of her ear. "I gave up weed a long time ago."

Melody felt a sob disguised as a warble of laughter escape.

Al shuffled into the opening it made and reached beside her to unlatch the back door. He made a formal gesture with his hand, but his eyes, warm behind the black-framed glasses, held her steady as Melody let herself sink onto the horsehair bench. Her heart was bruised and her confidence torn to ribbons, but when Al squeezed in beside her, bumping a bony knee against her hip and releasing a cloud of dust from the seatback, she could feel it start to mend. As long as he kept doing that. And that. As long as he didn't stop with any of that.

It was nearly dark when they made their way back to join the others. The Desk Man was agitated in a damped-down, church-whispering way. "Don't come back," he said, but not to anybody in particular. He led the dogs, two sleepy Dobermans who stretched and yawned and slobbered on Wrecker's hand, out of the office. He released them into the yard and then herded everyone outside the gate. "Don't you come back," he muttered again, and got in his truck and revved the engine and drove away.

"Ruthie," Melody said. She felt as though someone had scraped away the top layer of her skin and left everything internal—blood vessels, organs, emotions—horrendously exposed. "This is DF Al."

Ruth looked from her face to his and down to take in Wrecker. The boy was watching Melody carefully. Ruthie reached for his hand and pulled him closer to her, but he wouldn't be drawn in. It wasn't an angry resistance; he was simply magnetized in a different direction. "Right," she said. She turned her gaze back to Melody. "What's the DF part?"

119

Melody flushed. She had come up with many derogatory tags. She had not been discreet about it, either. She winced and offered, "Damn Fine?"

Wrecker kept watching her. He said, his voice soft, "Deedee's Friend."

The man stepped forward. He took Ruth's hand in both of his and shook it. "Douglas Franklin Albert Rice," he said. "And the pleasure is all mine."

CHAPTER SIX

Lisa Fay woke in the harsh half-light that doubled for night in prison. They dimmed the lights on the cellblock after ten, but real dark was as distant a memory as the feel of rain on her face or grass under her bare feet. Was that grass at her feet? Lisa Fay jerked her knees close to her chest and scanned the room. Delfine's bunk was empty. That would be Delfine, reaching out her spidery hand to stroke the sole of her foot. Delfine had nightmares; she woke up in the night convinced she was dead and had to lay a hand on something living to disprove the notion. "Quit it," Lisa Fay muttered roughly. "Get away from me."

Delfine's voice was a trilling whisper from the foot of the bed. "If you saw what I just saw," she said, "you wouldn't be saying that."

Lisa Fay gave a quick kick and Delfine backed off. She drifted in a slow circuit of the cell, wraithlike, and slipped beneath the blanket on her bed. Lisa Fay turned to face the wall. Dark, rain, grass—nothing was real here. She'd been fed fake so long she'd started to forget what real felt like. Even Delfine's nightmares lacked substance. Lisa Fay had asked her, once. *Nowhere*, Delfine answered, a quick giggle churning the air. *Nobody. Just dead as a doorknob*, and made a sound like a ghost might make, or a short gust of wind forced into the eaves. Lisa Fay waited a few beats and then called softly, "You awake?"

"Ain't no sense sleeping when they come for you in the night," Delfine answered. Sense was the last thing Delfine could claim but she called on it anyway. Sense and mother Mary, baby Jesus, Saint Anthony when she lost something, Saint Francis to keep the mice at bay, Saint Peter–open-your-pearly-gates-and-let-this-poor-soul-free. She'd been saved at an early age by an old priest who relied heavily on the laying-on of hands to rescue Delfine from the fires of hell. Now Delfine laid her own hands on things that didn't belong to her, hoarded them in a drawer until their rightful owners came to retrieve them. It was a miracle she survived the beatings that followed. "They aren't coming for me," Lisa Fay retorted, "they're coming for you. Let me get some sleep."

"You're the one asking," Delfine replied.

Delfine was damaged, with a brain that had buckled somewhere along the line and a crippled leg that dragged behind her like an afterthought. She had a fine spray of freckles across skin the color of weak tea, hair that sprang in tight curls from her scalp. Her mother was Creole. Her daddy—her daddy was Irish, Delfine's mother claimed. Or Estonian. Or Icelandic. She was a connoisseur of geography, Delfine's mama was, a collector of men from diverse corners of the earth. She told Delfine to keep an eye out for him and the girl did. Her left eye, the pale blue murky one that watered without relief. Her right eye—the one she called her good eye—was the stout gray-brown of swamp bark and saw things that weren't there. She wasn't clairvoyant; she was acquisitive. Saw things through that eye that she wanted to possess, saw them as real as though they were laying there before her, and she went hunting for them each day. Found them and stole them.

Like she'd steal my foot if it weren't bound to the rest of me,

Lisa Fay thought. Steal my eyelashes. Steal my thoughts. My worthless time. Ah, she thought, when she heard Delfine's breathing even into a snuffling drone. Steal my sleep, too.

Delfine was right, of course. They were coming for Lisa Fay. Marching like a ragged column of soldiers across the landscape of her past. Her mother, silently ironing the wind ruffles out of lakes and oceans. Her father, blustery, callused, his hands thrust deep into soil that would disappoint him with every season's yield. Jerry Skink, oh, and he could rot in hell for all the sympathy she'd extend to him. Arlyn? Lost at sea or land, lost to a seething city or a looping highway that never brought him home.

And herself. Young enough then to get caught up in it all, stupid enough now still to be waiting.

Lisa Fay lay in her bunk and let the memories slowly unfurl. Herself, not quite ten years before. Her father's angry roar and how, that time, that was all. Right then. No more. And how she had turned on the doorstep—turned once to get a good look at the two-story, clapboard sided structure she had for twenty-one years called home—and turned again toward the future and made her way to the city.

And wasn't she a rube, then, yeah! That girl who hovered at the back table at Spec's and listened to the men play jazz, listened to them fill the room with their booming voices, the poetry of their sex. Lisa Fay had never heard a person use the word *fuck* until she went to the city and then she heard it every day, casually, earnestly, in question and response, as part of people's names, in the soft unanswerable exhalations of working women on the bus after a long day. She practiced using it herself on her solitary daylong perambulations through the streets. She was a rawboned kid, flatter-chested than she could forgive God for, and her hair frizzed when the fog rolled up Broadway and muscled the blue sky out of its path. Her skin was rough from working the dirt that nurtured her father's garlic bulbs. She spent long intervals at the public sinks, trying to erase that stain from her hands.

And Arlyn. Oh, Arlyn. Arlyn "The Hook" Feyshon had an Old World face and hair that galloped in waves across his head. He wore the white cap and blue-and-white-striped ticking shirt of the longshoreman, his muscles bulging beneath it; he carried the trademark pair of gloves and grappling hook of the union brotherhood in the back pocket of his black Ben Davis jeans. He smelled of copra: coconut flesh and dusty vegetal hair and the musty hold of the ship where with twelve other stevedores he worked in hour shifts. He'd whispered details to her when she lay snug in the protection of his arms. Twenty minutes with a pick, hacking the dried, packed meat into manageable hunks. Twenty minutes with a shovel, pitching the pieces toward the vacuum that would blow it into the warehouse. Twenty minutes with a cigarette, leaning against a piling with the wind in his face and the best horn riffs from last night's session drifting through his mind. And then he'd stretch and flick the fag end into the oily harbor water and lift the pick to start again, hour after hour until the whistle blew on the shift.

The Cargill plant ran without stopping. Arlyn and his mates shuffled off and a new crew came on to replace them and the coconut kept its steady journey toward the vats that stewed it down to its golden essence: no more rat, no more sea salt, just pure, slick, edible oil, ready to be bottled and shipped to every kitchen in America. The Hook cared about food. Every day shift at noon he sat on the pier with his legs dangling over the dirty water and he unwrapped his lunch. Six hard-boiled eggs and a key-open can of sardines, the heel from the loaf of bread he ate the night before, a pair of chocolate Ho Hos in their delicate foil wrapping, a warm Anchor Steam to wash it all down. He liked boiled turnips. He liked cabbage and cauliflower, potatoes mashed with plenty of butter, pickled herring in sour cream, and cherries. He liked the idea of exotic flavors but in practice stayed away from them. Spicy foods gave him gas and tropical fruits made him break out in a misery of hives.

Swing shift called for a different routine. He brought his horn and a fresh change of clothes so he could leave directly from work to catch the late set. Those days he started early in Red's Java House on the waterfront and feasted on three, four, five of the foot-long wieners Red sold for a quarter apiece. He drank his joe and disagreed with the newspaper. He brought a ballpoint and scrawled poems on the back of Red's napkins. He was in the middle of a blunt paean to seagulls and soft winds when someone—she told herself this story slowly, as he had told it, and her heart raced a little as it always did—the someone who was Lisa Fay approached his table.

"Hey, mister. You through with that paper?"

Arlyn looked up. "I've seen you before," he said to the bony girl who stood so closely composed beside his booth.

She squinted at him. Then her eyes lit on the hardshell horn case resting on the bench beside him and she brightened with recognition. "You're The Hook," she said. "Aren't you? You play at Spec's."

Arlyn reddened. "Not professional or nothing." He peered down at the bottom of his empty coffee cup. "Sometimes they let me sit in."

She nodded. Stood there an awkward minute longer. "So," she said. "Can I have that paper?"

Arlyn stumbled over himself passing it to her. An uneaten hot dog lay on its paper plate beside his elbow. Arlyn watched her gaze flick toward the food and he nudged the plate closer to her. "Go ahead."

Lisa Fay looked dubious. "Aren't you going to eat it?"

"Please," Arlyn said. He gestured to the other bench. "Have a seat."

She lowered herself gingerly to the vinyl. She kept her gaze on the food. "It's my birthday," she said.

And with great formality and magnanimity and what could only be the most noble and generous of thoughts, The Hook said, "Happy birthday."

Lisa Fay blinked in her bunk. What was the opposite of celebration? Today marked a bitter anniversary. Five years to the day since her catastrophe and she could remember the smell of the grass in the park as she lay there, her hands roughly cuffed behind her and her sobs unanswered. That grass was real, all right. The dirt under it was real. She had tried to stuff her mouth with it.

Five years ago, she had started the day a mother. By the end of the day she was not.

Lisa Fay sat up stiffly, careful not to wake Delfine. She eased her feet to the floor. It was a familiar routine, rising before her cellmate, before any of the others awoke. She felt under her bunk for the Bible and slid the Bic pen from the book's cracked spine. Lisa Fay plucked the plastic plug from the rear of the pen, unclasped the safety pin she kept clipped to her tunic, and plunged the sharp end of the pin into the tube of ink.

The row of dots started on top of the big toe of her right foot, just before the nail. One dot. Two dots. Three dots, each composed of dozens of pinpricks saturated with ink, a tattoo to keep track of the time. On and on the dots wound, a row of refugees ejected from their homes and sent wandering. The line continued, each dot a rough quarter inch from its neighbor, across the sensitive skin on the top of her foot. Dipped beneath the anklebone, circled the ankle itself, and continued, a spiral, up her calf. It circled her knee. Made four revolutions about her thigh. Crossed her hip, circled her waist.

They made her body a calendar. The dot with a circle around it, that meant one month. A circle blackened with short rays that sprung from its perimeter—a symbol that looked like a bomb, exploding—that meant a year had passed. Lisa Fay had one of those on the ridge of her shin. Another behind her knee. A third on her creamy inside thigh. The last just below her hip.

And now, today, a fifth. Five years to the day since she'd touched his skin, watched his smile gape across his face.

The line of dots had arrived now at the stretch-marked skin of her belly. That was fitting, she thought. Five years. And here, where she'd held him. She wedged the ink tube upright with the pin in it into the narrow gap where the mattress met the bed frame, and then she opened the bible and lifted a photograph from its pages. It was the only precious thing Lisa Fay owned. A gift, of sorts. An exchange.

The boy in the photograph had the same slope to his cheek and his brow as her son. He was squatting on the hood of a broken-down car, raising a hand to something in the distance, his mouth shaped mid-speech, his body coiled as though ready to spring. The tail of a dog waved a blurry smudge through the corner of the shot. Sunlight struck a path through the photo, glinted off the car's windshield, glowed on the boy's tanned chest, caught in his shaggy mop of hair.

Wrecker, the woman had said, handing it to her across the table. He's eight.

It sounded strange to hear her son's name spoken by this stranger. I can have this?

It's for you.

And Lisa Fay had hesitated. The photo from Belle had sustained her through these years. But she drew it from the pocket of her smock and slid the dog-eared square across the table. Will you give this to him? Willow? You'll make sure he gets this?

There was a long pause. If you want me to, the woman said, I will.

Even so, Lisa Fay almost reached to snatch it back. She wasn't sure how she could bear to be without it. Belle had come to the trial; she had sat through the sentencing; she had made the long trip by bus to visit Lisa Fay monthly in prison. Yolanda would have nothing to do with her friend once Jerry Skink weaseled his way between them, but Yolanda's mother had not abandoned Lisa Fay. Belle had noted the delinquence that crept under her fingernails, the self-doubt that dulled her skin and jaundiced the clear white of her eyes, and she sought to challenge it out of the girl. She smuggled in chocolate cake and fed her grandiose ideas. When she got out of there, Belle insisted, she would hit the ground running. Fifteen years was fifteen years; if Caesar stole them that was plainly the fact of it, but to give him a second more of her time was a sin and a worse crime. No. She must study. Read. Learn to type. Teach herself some skill that had currency outside the clanging gates of prison, or when she got out she'd be no less vulnerable to the scoundrels and scammers who put her there in the first place.

But Belle would not speak to Lisa Fay of her son. It was as if the pain of losing the boy was doubled for her, first when Lisa Fay stopped bringing him to her flat to look after while she worked, then when he was whisked off by police to some other household. Let Wrecker have his own life, she counseled his mother, if she mentioned him at all. Let him *survive*. Lisa Fay could picture Belle. She could still see the way her lower lip trembled slightly when she added, else those tentacles you stretch out will bring you both down.

And then, on the third Saturday of the ninth month in Lisa Fay's second year of incarceration, she waited for the summons that meant she had a visitor, and it never came. A month from that she waited again. Felt the gnaw of loss and worry, and the day passed. On the third month, when Lisa Fay was called to the visitors' room, she found Yolanda, her eyes red-rimmed and her hands clutched in a nervous ball before her. Lisa Fay sank opposite her at the table. She looked at Yolanda and waited.

Mama Belle passed on, Yoli said.

Lisa Fay forgot to breathe. When she began again the air chased out of her lungs in a ragged huff. They sat together and let the fact settle between them.

In time, Lisa Fay said, Will you come again?

Yolanda turned away. I can't come often, she said. The little ones.

But you're here now.

I can't stay. She pushed her chair back and stood up from the table. She shared her mother's habit of canting her weight forward onto an elbow before pushing herself up to standing. Mama had a sweet spot for you, she said. Even after you did what you did.

Lisa Fay dropped her eyes. They did it to me.

Yolanda snorted. You did it to your own self, she said harshly. You did it to your son, who needed you. She let the accusation hang in the air and then she opened her purse. I found this in her special things. Seemed to me you should have it.

Lisa Fay glanced at the photograph and laid her trembling hand across it. She steadied her voice. And how are your boys? How is Ton-Ton?

Anton is in trouble all the time, Yolanda answered. The ghost of a familiar smile flitted across her face. He is an incorrigible child. Belle said he has the devil inside him.

He's fine, then.

They're all fine, yeah. She lifted her eyelashes and Lisa Fay saw the old Yolanda—the Yolanda who had been her friend—flicker briefly toward her. Belle said Wrecker's fine, too, she said softly. Said she could just feel it.

My sister took him in.

Yes, Yolanda said. She stepped away from the table. Be strong, girl. She glanced at the guard and then back at Lisa Fay. I'll see you when I see you.

Vaya con whatever.

Yeah. She laughed. You too.

And Yolanda had left, and Lisa Fay had sat for a while and stared at the photograph. She remembered the day Belle snapped it. She took out that little Brownie camera for special occasions. There was everything special about this day. It was her son's third birthday. Lisa Fay and Wrecker sat side by side on Belle's stoop, the sun falling over them. It was before Jerry Skink came into their lives. Her son's face a little blurry and his mouth circled with ice cream. Chocolate ice cream, his favorite. His eyes said as much. His hair was a lion's mane, an unruly mass that resisted her brush and sprang in all directions under the baseball cap she'd bought him. Hers was hardly neater. She wore a long skirt and a tank top that made her look fat. Blueberry ice cream cone in one hand and the other wrapped around her boy and a feeling in her heart she can call up still, and does. Every morning.

Sitting on her bunk now in the eerie half-light that passed for night at Chino, she gazed at her boy, alone, and older.

Be well, she whispered softly, and brought the photo gently, briefly, to her forehead.

She returned it to the Bible. Then she began to work on the mark. Five years. One thousand, five hundred, thirty-six days.

This one would scab before it would heal.

The lights banged on and the guard began his morning walk down the cell block, his stick clanging against the bars. Lisa Fay finished hastily and hid her gear. "Get up, Delfine," she called to the wisp in the other bunk. "Time to rise and shine."

It was pest control day. The rats and roaches had gotten out of hand and they were bombing them back to the Stone Age, the guards guffawed. That meant an extra hour in the yard for the inmates. A privilege, the warden called it. Before they returned to the block to breathe in the acrid fumes and sweep up the bodies of the fallen soldiers.

About time, Lisa Fay thought. She had to watch her back for guards and inmates and now she was sleeping with one eye open to make sure her bunk stayed clear of crawling things. They were everywhere. Just the day before she'd pulled work duty in the kitchen and was cutting thin pieces of processed ham on the meat slicer, paying attention to the sharp glide of the blade. "Bunkie?" A familiar voice giggled softly, and Lisa Fay's heart sunk. She glanced around warily. Delfine risked seg just for being in the kitchen, and they'd both catch shit if anyone saw her sneak the skinny woman an extra lump of food. In one fluid motion Lisa Fay slapped a mound of sliced ham onto a sheet of butcher paper and held it behind her. "Take it and go," she muttered roughly, and felt Delfine's dry and wrinkled hands lift the parcel from her own.

Suddenly, eerily, Lisa Fay felt eyes on her. She jerked her head toward the sink. It wasn't the matron, back from the pantry; it was a large, fat, fearless rat sitting on the drainboard, pinning her in its beady gaze. Without thinking, Lisa Fay reached for the two-pronged butcher's fork beside her, balanced it in her hand, and flung it at him.

The fork rattled against the stainless steel backsplash and Lisa Fay darted toward it. A trace of blood smeared the sink board— she must have nicked him, at least—but the rat was gone.

The matron thundered in—"The hell was that?"—and though

Lisa Fay explained, described the rat's size, his audacity, the challenge he flung at her, standing there amid the drying pots and pans, the matron would not hear it.

"If there's trouble, you call me," she threatened. Lisa Fay breathed out. That meant Delfine had slipped away unseen. But the injured rat was on the loose, too.

With any luck they'd be nuking him now, Lisa Fay thought. She paced the back wall of the yard, ran her tongue across her teeth, picked up grit. It was a professional wind, here. No puny breeze ruffled the air at the women's penitentiary. This wind gathered speed and the odor of steer manure from the feed lots south of the prison and swept up every variety of dust on its way before ripping through the yard. Lisa Fay faced into it as she headed west, turned her back to it as she returned. She stifled a hankering for a whiff of sweet air. City air, even, with its pungent neighborhood mix of coffee and cabbage and hot asphalt, all of it freshened by bay salt and bus exhaust, its edges softened by the rolling Caribbean lilt of ladies who sent money to their own children back home while they pushed strollers full of rich babies through the eucalyptus groves of Golden Gate Park.

Lisa Fay wondered what it smelled like, up there where Wrecker lived. Meg had been the bit of brightness she could count on to turn to. Meg, her champion and protector, her model and cautionary figure, eleven years older and gone gone gone. Took up with that quiet man, the timber faller from Tennessee who moved her clear to the top of the state before she'd passed her twentieth birthday. They'd married in a fever, Meg and Len; cleared out before the father ever knew what hit him, gave him a full year to calm down before they came back down to visit. Lisa Fay couldn't help but shiver, remembering. They'd sat around the dinner table in a tense silence, their father so angry he could barely open his thin lips and cram the pot roast into his cheeks; he'd chewed rapidly, spitefully, swallowed too early and got the meat wedged in his windpipe. Len had motioned them aside. He pushed up the sleeves of his good shirt and squatted behind her daddy, hoisted him up to sitting, wrapped his arms around his belly and gave one sharp squeeze to his midsection that propelled that piece of meat halfway across the room. Daddy didn't even bother to thank Len. He lit into Momma, let loose a string of curses—trying to kill him, was she?—and Lisa Fay had huddled next to Meg and prayed she'd take her with them when she left. We'll visit again, Meg had whispered, but they hadn't. She'd sent a real letter once with photographs of a little house and big trees and a pet goose who stalked the yard. She sent Christmas cards for a few years. And then even those fell off.

Now her boy was there. The lawyer fellow had told her that, at least. Came to court smelling of whiskey, a rumpled shirt and a stain on the knee of his trousers, and bungled her case so badly the judge had wondered—aloud!—whether he had truly passed the bar or had just wandered in off the street. He had a ratlike face and a loose thread that dangled from the side seam of his suit jacket. Lisa Fay pinned her attention to the single charcoal thread that threatened to unravel the man, reduce him to a tangle of threads too haphazard to ever find their way back to whole cloth. And with them her chances.

And so they had. The judge was a short, dark-haired older lady who didn't have much regard for a mother who would endanger her own child by exposing him not just to drugs but to guns and to a *morally compromised*—she caught Lisa Fay's eye as if to say you know exactly what I mean—*living situation*. No, some cases had to be taken on their own merits. This defendant, found guilty of aiding and abetting the attempted murder of a police officer, guilty of possessing a concealed weapon, guilty of accessory to unlawful distribution of controlled substances, was likewise guilty of child neglect. She was unfit to mother her child, who would remain in the custody of the state until a suitable home could be found for him. And the defendant was hereby remanded to the care of the criminal justice system for a period of thirty years. Eligible for parole—she added this as an afterthought—eligible for parole in fifteen years. Young lady, she'd said sternly, we take none of this lightly.

In the prison yard, Lisa Fay's pace slowed nearly to a crawl. She caught herself and forced herself forward, made her wooden legs march at a brisk, defiant rate. She'd served five years. Five years done. Ten to go—ten only, if she kept her head down, showed none of the pain, groveled at their feet—ten if they kept their word, that is. All of the power rested with them. Ten only. Ten still? Was it possible that she could last through that? Was there skin enough on her body to sustain?

The lawyer had visited her in jail when she'd been there a year. She almost refused to see him but held just a glimmer of hope, the faintest thought that maybe the judge had changed her mind, was ready to set her free.

He wore casual clothes this time, a pair of khaki pants and a buttoned shirt with no tie, and his hair flopped over his collar. He'd decided to leave the law, he told her. He'd never had a real calling. He'd entered to please his parents and now his parents had abandoned their faith in the status quo and bought a sailboat and were on their way to Polynesia, and he—well, he'd always harbored a wish to paint.

Lisa Fay stared at him, dumbfounded. Had he come this far to tell her this?

I thought you might want to know, he said. He looked around guiltily. He had the face of a rat, long and sharp, but none of a rat's cunning or resourcefulness. Lisa Fay wondered how he could function in the world. I'm not supposed to tell you this, he warned. Once the courts terminate your parental rights you're not entitled to any information about your child's whereabouts. The lawyer shrugged. I've been disbarred, he said. So what can they do to me? He tipped forward, leaned close to her ear, put his ratlike lips to it. He's been adopted up to Humboldt County, he whispered. Your sister and her husband. Then he sank back into his chair and watched her. Hey, you're a nice kid, he said. Look me up when you get out of this joint. And he slunk his way out of the folding chair and shambled across the ugly tiles to the door.

And just last month that woman, Willow, there to tell her Meg's mind was harmed, her parents dead, her son in someone else's charge.

The question trembled on her lips but went unasked. Does he recall—

She had sent her boy the photograph. It was all she could think to do.

Lisa Fay pulled up short at the end of the yard. She lifted her hands to her hips and waited for her heart to still.

One hundred laps, forward and back. The wind had slowed to a dawdle and the other women clustered in casual groups, talking, laughing, complaining, harassing one another, braiding hair, dozing in the sun. She caught a glimpse of Delfine lurking behind a trashcan chained to its stand, trying to pass unnoticed. A group of women had clearly noticed her. Others parted to the side as they advanced.

The Mountain had been looking for Delfine. Now that she had her in her sights, she could afford to take her time. The Mountain—aptly named, Lisa Fay thought, with her small peaked head and that solid hunk of a body so broad it required custom clothes—turned her back to Delfine and said something to Pearlie and Little Red that made them laugh. Even if it weren't funny, those two would laugh on cue. The Mountain could tell them to drop

135

their drawers and piss in the middle of a crowd and they would do it. But when they sang, the three of them, it could quiet the whole yard. It brought tears to the warden's eye, and the guards had been instructed to overlook The Mountain's occasional, minor infractions of the rules. Delfine had not the slightest chance of escape.

Delfine caught her eye before Lisa Fay could look away, and the scrap of a woman scurried across the yard toward her.

Lisa Fay groaned. "What have you done, now."

"What!" Delfine said, and gave a small, happy squeal.

Lisa Fay looked closer. There was gray in Delfine's hair. She had never noticed that before. How old could she be, this woman who behaved like a backward child? "Delfine," she warned. "Don't mix me up in this."

"In nothing," Delfine scoffed. "Miss Mountain!" she chirped, as the group came close. She curtsied.

The Mountain surveyed her blandly, without prejudice, as though she were considering an unexceptional piece of furniture. But when she turned her gaze to Lisa Fay her eyes were backed by malice. "I believe," she said slowly, "you have something of mine."

Lisa Fay took an involuntary step back. She glanced warily at the three of them. Then her eyes glazed softly and she gazed past them toward a bird who sat perched on the ugly wire atop the yard wall. A mockingbird, was it? It opened its mouth and let a complicated stream of nonsense flow. There were mockingbirds in her father's yard in Watsonville, good-sized birds who could snatch a song out of the air and run with it, riff on a melody like a man with a saxophone. Her boy had that in his blood, too. Not just the backyard in Watsonville but the music that motivated Arlyn to pick up his horn and flesh out a tender melody. He had it all, everything she could remember, everything that had happened to her up to his birth, everything Arlyn had given him, all of it running unheard beneath the steady pumping whoosh of his blood as he grew, unaware.

What she would give to see her child.

She turned back to The Mountain. Here's what she would give: her preference. Until she was released to see him, she would not care what happened to her. She would not let it spawn a reaction, anything the parole board could latch on to as evidence of flawed remorse. She would offer no resistance to their program—their shitty, abominable program of systematic degradation—and they would have no choice but to set her free. That's all she sought. Earlier, rather than later. Early enough to have some time with her son before he was grown. Lisa Fay sighed. She dropped her shoulders. She said, "No. I don't believe I do." And as she watched the dark pupils widen in The Mountain's eyes, she thought, Go ahead and kill me. I'll be out of here that much faster.

The Mountain slowly advanced upon her.

"Hey hey hey hey hey!" Delfine aspirated. "This one? She don't give a flying fork what you believe!" And she insinuated her scrawny little edge-bitten body into the group until she stood just inches from The Mountain. She squared her flimsy shoulders and puffed her little chest.

"Uh," The Mountain said, a volcanic rumble.

There was a long moment of held breath. No one stood up to The Mountain. She had the power to crush anything in her path. She was large and solid and fatally smart and relentless in her need to subordinate others. She leaned forward slowly, incrementally, toward Delfine. She leaned, Lisa Fay thought stupidly, like an ox that had been bludgeoned but whose bulk has not fully registered the blow. "A flying *fork*?"

"Yeah," Delfine whispered. "That too."

Lisa Fay shut her eyes. The rumble grew. Little Red and Pearlie chimed in with tentative laughter.

Lisa Fay forced herself to look. The Mountain had bent forward far enough to clap her mighty paws around Delfine. She was squeezing her. Delfine was almost absorbed into the bulk of The Mountain's voluminous breast. And then The Mountain opened her arms and Delfine popped free. The Mountain held something in her hand. She opened her mouth and situated her custom bridgework snug against her gums.

"Me neither," The Mountain rumbled. Laughter was a seismic event. "Do you, Little Red? Do you, Pearlie?"

No, they answered in tandem, they didn't give a flying fork either.

Psycho. Freak show. Delfine, you crazy bitch, Lisa Fay thought. You stole her *teeth*?

She would smuggle Delfine more food tomorrow. She would let her use the toilet first.

But the foot? Not in a million years, Lisa Fay thought. Never again would she let Delfine touch any part of her body, attached or not.

CHAPTER SEVEN

Willow stood with one hand on the back door to the farmhouse and listened to the sounds coming out of the kitchen. It was a Saturday morning in January, the sky was a preposterous blue, and Ruth was singing like a cat in heat. She made up raunchy lyrics to accompany the popular tunes she remembered from her youth, and the boy kept time with kitchen utensils. Not quite music, Willow thought. The song ended and she pulled open the door and stepped inside. More like—cheerful noise.

"Hello, radio listeners." Ruth grabbed a banana and purred into the makeshift microphone. She winked at Willow over the boy's head. "That was Methyl Ethyl and the Ketones, doing 'Get Your Hand Out of My Oven.'"

Willow snorted. She looked around at the cloud of dust that engulfed them. "What happened?"

It wasn't dust, it was flour; and Wrecker was poised at the center of it. He knelt on the stool to be tall enough to lean his weight into the sourdough Ruth had flipped onto the counter. He dug his elbows in and pummeled it with his fists. His eyes flashed blue in a sea of white. Flour ghosted his hair, his exposed skin, the counter, and a good patch of the floor beneath him. He wore a long-sleeved pullover hanging out of a pair of Wrangler dungarees, and a leather belt with cowboy emblems burned into it. They were dusted white, too. "What's it look like?" he crowed. He was raucous with happiness. "We're making bread."

"Mind your manners." Ruth's silvery scruff was flour-sprinkled, and a white blaze powdered her ruddy cheekbone.

"Bread," Willow echoed. "Of course. Need a little more flour, maybe?"

Ruth ignored her sarcasm and shook the paper sack to release a new cloud of white by the boy. Wrecker slapped his hand into the pile and quickly planted a white handprint on the back of her jersey. "You're it, now."

"You don't know the half of it. Keep kneading." She wheezed her way into a chair and nodded for Willow to pull up another. "He's a maniac baker, that boy. Better keep your distance."

"I'll do that." Willow wore old work clothes and still managed to look elegant. "I hope you washed your hands," she called, and his grin showed his front teeth, square and bright and still sharply serrated and enormous in his face. Willow had described them to Lisa Fay. It was a trademark of eight-year-olds, she explained. They looked comical, but they outgrew it. Same way the soft, rubbery flexibility of the boy had turned into compact muscle. Little-animal muscle. Not stretched long like an adolescent's or bulked up like a man's, but articulated and vigorous—he was strong, Willow told her. Always had been, Lisa Fay said, her eyes softening with her smile. And, right then, Willow had made up her mind, and handed her the photograph.

She hadn't been certain she would. Watching the woman's hungry eyes soak in the sight of her son, she was sure she'd done the right thing. Willow had had to turn away to allow Lisa Fay the privacy of her emotion. It was only later, describing the visit to Melody, that she found herself rethinking her decision. Melody had used words like *betrayed*. Words like *endangered*. She had made her sentiments clear.

140

"Knead that good," Ruth threatened. Wrecker tore a small section off the dough, rolled it into a lump, and lobbed it at her. She caught it one-handed. "Oh!" She creaked out of her chair and advanced on him. "You are *so* going to regret that," and she grabbed him before he could escape. "Bad, bad, bad! And love you for it," she shouted over his giggles, as she tried to make him eat the dough. It was her steady refrain. The others had leaned on her to choose something more constructive, but Ruth would not be swayed.

Willow had long given up trying. Ruth was on the far side of sixty and was likely to break something if she didn't quit roughhousing, but nothing would persuade her to change that, either. Her energy with the boy was boundless and deviant and driven by a heart of gold. Not just the clichéd heart, Willow thought, although she was that, too—she was kind, and sympathetic, and a bit of a pushover. But Ruth's heart was made of something rawer. Something molten and enflamed. The stunts it inspired were epic. The spud gun? An old can of hair spray, a length of vacuum cleaner pipe, a deafening explosion, and a splotch of smashed potato on the side of the tool shed you could still see, five years later, when the sun shone right. The Eliminizer . . . Jesus. That one nearly brought in the FBI. These were not escapades dreamed up by a person who ran on ordinary octane. Ruth ran hot where she, Willow, ran cool. Willow understood that. Crank the BTUs up to Ruth's temperature in Willow's body and you'd have a shimmering oil spot on the sidewalk where Willow had been standing. Willow reached for the bag at her feet. "By the way," she said drily. "I forgot to give you this. It's from my trip."

The two stopped tussling and watched her draw a brand-new baseball cap from the bag. "Man," Wrecker muttered, drawing out the syllable. A Giants cap. He reached for it, but Willow tugged it away before he could touch it.

"You're covered in flour," she said. "Let me do it." Willow

situated the cap on his head and compressed his hair—thick, unruly hanks of it, buzzed by Ruthie each spring and fall and left to tangle and fall in his eyes the rest of the time—into the woolen dome. She watched him closely for his reaction, but caught nothing more than simple pleasure at the gift. She brushed the white powder from his cheeks with the sleeve of her shirt and stood back to take a look. "Hey, batter, batter. Best-looking player in the lineup."

"Go get your mitt, hot shot," Ruthie said, and he slid from the stool and ran to find it. She glanced at Willow. "What's up for today?"

"Len needs help with something. Wrecker can come with me."

Ruthie nodded. Unless Johnny Appleseed was around, the boy spent his Saturdays with them. Melody couldn't get out of her Saturday shift at the Mercantile, and Dreyfus had eighty-sixed Wrecker from the place on days when he didn't go to school. Too much time on his hands led to trouble, and there'd been witnesses to his misadventures.

The screen door banged shut behind the boy. "It wasn't there." He was breathing hard.

"Where?" Ruthie asked.

His eyes shifted to the side. "Where it was supposed to be."

She yawned. "Oh," she said. "You mean out in the middle of the yard where the rain would have soaked it?" She tossed her head toward the wobbly sideboard that stood in the corner of the kitchen. "Check the junk drawer. Next time put it where it belongs." They watched him yank the drawer open and fit the glove to his hand. Secondhand, broken-in dark leather that reeked of neatsfoot oil—Melody'd found it for him at a yard sale the summer before. Wrecker pulled the hardball from its pocket and started driving the ball back into the webbing. He could do it for hours. *Thwap, thwap*—it drove them insane.

Still, Willow had to admit, he was a good boy. Noisy, messy, smelly, as eight-year-olds were made to be, but with a goodness that was particular to him. He cried hard when the smallest of Sitka's pups picked a fight with a wolverine and couldn't be mended. He was some kind of physical freak, climbing and leaping and lifting like a kid twice his age. And he was smart, although that wasn't always easy to see. Willow had identified extraordinary strengths in spatial reasoning, in relational thinking, that overshadowed his weaknesses in more traditional fields of study. He could improve in those if he ever got interested. He wasn't the dunce his teacher thought he was.

Willow liked him, even. It was a terrible feeling. She couldn't get over the thought that this made her at least in some part responsible for his unexpected childhood. Not that there was anything *bad* about the life he had happened into. It was odd, but odd was no crime. He was safe, he was loved, he was well cared for. Melody saw to it that he had everything a kid could need and a hefty portion of the things he simply wanted. There was even a way that you could look at his life and think: the perfect childhood. Rousseauian—if Rousseau's noble savage had a pirate manqué for an aunt, an abandoned Willys Jeep for a rocket ship, and the run of the forest.

And still there seemed to be something unforgivable, something almost reprehensible, about condoning the way things had worked out. He'd been deprived of a past. That was it, wasn't it? His mother pined for him in a cell six hundred miles away—and it might as well have been the moon. She might as well not have been, Willow thought with a chill, for all he knew of her. Sure, she'd made mistakes. She had failed him, even. But Lisa Fay had conceived him, bore him, raised him as well as she could for as long as she could—and that was worth something, Willow thought. Surely it was.

The boy resembled his mother, and now Willow could not get the face of that woman to leave her mind.

"Willow?" Ruth looked at her funny.

"I said thanks," Wrecker said, peering at her.

"You're welcome, buddy. Let's go shell some beans." Willow glanced at Ruth. "That crop of Jacob's Cattle beans Len put in last summer? He hung the plants to dry in his sauna. Hasn't used it in years, but now he's got the itch to get it going again and he has to get them down, first." Len planned to move a wringer-washer into the small room and run the plants through it. "I guess you run them through the rollers and that pops the dry beans from the pods. It's new to me."

"That's the old way." Ruth nodded. "Bring me a handful when you come back. I'll plant a row in the garden this spring." She tugged on the brim of Wrecker's cap. "You? Come back hungry. There'll be fresh bread waiting for you."

He had changed quite a bit since he'd arrived. He could read, write, tie his shoes, choose his clothes, button his shirts. He was too big to pick up (unless it was urgent, and then it took two of them), and too old to send to bed before dark. He showered on his own. He had learned to swim. He could use logic as a tool of argument and he asked more sophisticated questions. Walking to Len's, passing Willow's yurt, he gestured to the small wooden shed that housed her power generator. "I get how cars run," he said offhandedly, and Willow smiled, thinking there might still be some distance to go on that subject. "But how exactly does gas make an engine go?"

Combustion, she told him, and described in detail the interaction between gas and oxygen in the presence of a spark, and the role that process played in driving pistons and, when properly geared, propelling a shaft.

He listened closely. There was a period of silence when she finished. And then he asked how he could get himself some gasoline.

He had changed considerably, Willow thought, but he still harbored that same dangerous mix of curiosity and enthusiasm and utter lack of caution that he'd come with.

"Len," he said, when they arrived. "I need some gasoline."

Willow tipped her head toward Len and walked over and crouched beside Meg to greet her.

"Hello, Wrecker," Len said. He grinned at the boy, but his gaze followed Willow.

"Do you have any?"

"Gasoline? I keep that under lock and key." He tapped the boy's head. "Nice hat."

"Willow got it for me," Wrecker said. "Come on, Len. Gas?"

"None today," Len said, and the boy drifted away toward Meg.

Willow looked up at the mention of her name. Len caught her eye and she moved to stand beside him. They watched Wrecker and Meg play together in a small rivulet of mud. That was a change, too. Meg adored the boy, followed him around the yard, batted her eyes at him, brought him little gifts of pine needles or spare buttons or the lemon drops Len carried around in his pockets. Wrecker spoke softly to Meg, and she seemed to understand him. He let her put her arm around him and warble in his ear, and he answered her with sympathetic noises of his own. Even Meg's goose treated him with deference, honking and flapping its wings when he got too close but never opening its beak to bite.

He was a good boy, Wrecker was. He had a sweetness Willow couldn't deny, and an innate sympathy for creatures smaller or weaker than himself. It made him furious to see them mistreated. But he was a big boy, extraordinarily strong, and when he took matters into his own hands all hell broke loose. A few months

145

back he'd beaten the bejesus out of another boy, a ten-year-old he had accused of removing the legs of a frog at the banks of the creek behind the schoolyard. A live frog? Serves him right, Len murmured, when Willow told him. Maybe, she said. Only the boy had spent two days in the hospital with a detached retina and another week recovering at home before his parents packed up and moved down to Mendocino. Melody was lucky they didn't press charges, they said. Willow agreed. If her son had been hurt that badly—no matter what he did to cause it—she would have dragged the other boy's parents straight to hell by their hair.

Bet that boy won't be bothering frogs any more, Len had said, and chuckled softly.

He's a loose cannon, she'd told Len.

He answered, He's a kid. He'll outgrow it. Len relied on time to cure everything wrong with Wrecker, Willow thought. He treated the boy with a kind of affectionate bemusement, as if the very fact of his presence was something surprising and delightful and at the same time too thorny to address in any but the most formal way.

They all treated him as though he had descended from the heavens. As though his life had begun, day one, when he arrived at Bow Farm. Only Johnny Appleseed understood the danger of that. Johnny, whose own past was a mystery to her—and who kept his present largely under wraps, as well. He had begun to speak out for the trees, for preserving the forest, in a way that set Len off. It had forced a wedge between them, and Willow could feel Johnny begin to drift away from Bow Farm, leaving for long periods, reappearing unexpectedly, leaving again. There were rumors about what he did while he was gone.

Len's hand took light hold of her elbow, now. "You hungry yet? I've got lunch on." He steered her to the small fire he had banked in a rock-lined pit. Several foil-wrapped lumps roasted in the coals.

"Potatoes?"

"And onions and carrots and turnips. And lamb chops in the kitchen." He looked both abashed and secretly pleased with himself. "I'll go get them." Willow watched him jump the steps to the porch two at a time. Blue jeans and a chambray shirt today. And yesterday, and most likely tomorrow—Len kept a drawer full of them, washed and pressed and identical so he wouldn't waste time in the morning choosing what to wear. True, he was a rough, chapped, stubbly, angular, dense, and stringy man, but even when he was covered in forest dirt and chain saw oil he was the most tucked-in man she knew. Len returned with a plate full of tiny chops and tenderly arranged them on a grate he placed close to the coals. He glanced up at her. Tucked in physically, Willow corrected herself. Emotionally he still had some loose flags flapping in the breeze.

Willow hadn't felt hungry, but the smell of seared meat made her suddenly eager to eat. Meg and Wrecker had edged close, and they all waited for Len to declare the chops done. A wood fire for a kitchen, some splintered porch steps to dine on—she'd come a long way from Bellingham, where every night she'd laid real silver for the family dinner and made a serious effort to teach her kids good manners. For one fleet second she wondered how much further she'd be willing to go. She glanced at Len and quickly looked away. No. She'd shut that thought away years ago.

Len filled the plates and passed them out and the four of them sat in a line on the second step and tore into the food with their fingers. Len helped Meg open the foil wraps and used his pocketknife to divide her vegetables. He let Wrecker cut his own. Willow watched with concern, but the boy managed well enough and then handed the knife to her. Len looked on approvingly. Wrecker had turned the knife to offer her the handle, the way Len had passed it to him.

Willow chewed slowly. The chops were tiny—two bites each—and unbearably succulent. "Oh my God," she said. A dribble of meat juice ran down the side of her mouth, and she stopped its escape with the back of her hand. "You could be arrested for this."

"Good?" Len grinned.

"*Good* doesn't come close." She felt half drunk with the meat and its savor.

Forget Bellingham. There were moments in this life that more than made up for all of its hardness and rough edges. The clarity of a blue sky in January after weeks of rain. The dense flavor of vegetables grown in local gardens, the smell of young lamb chops fresh off the grill. Every August, Willow waited for the sheer ambrosial sweetness of wild blackberries, sun-warmed and ripe to bursting. It took effort to collect them, to pluck the berries from the brambles while steering clear of the thorns. She'd learned to value patience. It had not come easily to her.

When Willow first arrived, she'd been overcome by the physical bounty of the place. Len was a part of that. He was exotic to her then, a man who made his living from the land, who muscled his way with sweat and skill toward the things he wanted—he was the opposite of Ross, and attractive to her in a way that had nothing to do with ambition or social standing. And she'd taken right away to Meg, who was matter-of-fact and funny and shyly offered friendship. They had made her feel at home when her heart was broken. It was painful to see how Meg had been damaged by the surgery, to see how it had changed things between them. Still, Willow reminded herself. They were married. And she was not the kind of woman to take their marriage lightly.

Willow finished her plate and leaned back to rest against an upper step. Wrecker showed no signs of slowing down. He devoured the two remaining chops and polished off the rest of the vegetables. When Len let him know there was a slice of squash pie

148

waiting for him on the table inside, he got up and went in and returned a few moments later, dragging the sleeve of his shirt across his mouth.

"Sure can eat," Len murmured.

It was no stretch for Willow to remember back to her own sons at that age. Not just the size of their appetites, but their intensity. When hunger struck she'd had a small window to satisfy it, and if she failed that they fell apart, turned from fairly reasonable human beings to beasts out of control, raging, accusing, carrying on until a critical mass of calories had been processed. Kids that age were as biological as slime molds. Kids only? People just learned to cover it better as they aged. Willow glanced sideways at Meg, tipped over on the step and snoring lightly. Meg was as subject to her body's demands now as any kid. Len had related the time—it happened a few years back—when he'd brought Meg along to run some errands in Eureka. Nothing unusual about that, he said; not until she grew tired and needed to lie down. *Right then.* Len's voice was quietly jocular, but the wrinkles around his eyes had deepened. In the shampoo aisle of the Fred Meyer supermarket Meg fell supine to the floor, and no manner of beseeching would convince her to sit back up until she'd napped for half an hour. A sympathetic checkout girl sent a stock boy with a blanket to cover her and a folding chair for Len to perch on while he waited for her to rise.

"If you can't beat 'em . . . ," Len said now, and tipped the brim of his cap to shade his eyes while he napped.

Willow hadn't meant to sleep, but when she opened her eyes next she found that the sun had moved a noticeable distance in the sky and that Len's arm had shifted in his sleep to lie pressed against her thigh. She blinked and sat up. She moved away from him, worked a kink out of her neck, and smoothed her hair back into place. "Len," she said brusquely. "If we're doing this, let's do it."

Len rose quickly and stretched. Meg and Wrecker squatted

together a short distance away, building a small city out of twigs. He called to them, and together the four of them walked to the back of the cabin, where Len had dragged the wringer-washer onto the back porch. "Here," he said, guiding Willow's hand to the best place to grasp the galvanized frame. "Heavy son of a gun. If we can get it down the stairs, we can use the hand truck to move it toward the sauna. Then we have to haul it up into there."

"I can do it," Wrecker insisted.

"You're strong, but you're short, my friend."

Willow edged the disgruntled boy away from the machine and gripped the rolled edge. "Tell me again why we don't do the beans outside? It would be a lot easier."

"You'll see." Len grinned. "They fly everywhere. We'd lose them all and end up with a bean patch there in the spring."

Down wasn't so bad. Len wrestled the machine onto the cart and wheeled the wringer along the short path from the cabin. He stopped before a tiny redwood cube. A stovepipe jutted from its roof and the entrance threshold sat two feet above the ground. "You've never been inside?" Len wiped the thin sheen of sweat from his forehead and pulled open the plank door. "Let me give you the tour."

Wrecker rested his hands on the floor and leaned his torso in. "Dark in here," he reported. "Dusty."

Len grabbed him about the waist and swung him in. He handled Meg with greater care, helping her situate her foot on the high step and then getting behind to boost her up. He turned to Willow. "Ma'am?"

She could manage, she said, but she took his hand to support her up the step and felt the palm of his other strong on the small of her back.

It was tightly packed. Hundreds of plants hung by their roots from the rafters and littered the floor with their dry leaves. The

150

beans rattled in the pods when Willow ran a hand through them. She waited for her eyes to adjust to the murky light. Len kept a running commentary. He had milled the redwood, sanded it butter-soft, pegged it so there'd be no hot metal to burn skin. "Every stick of it's from a single tree, so they'll all expand the same. Should hold up." He patted the woodstove. "This one cranks, too. Warm as you want. You should come try it some time."

"Maybe," Willow said thinly. It was hard to picture the sauna in action. It was a dark box with perimeter benches, a musty, vegetal smell, and a small, high window that let in a little light— but Willow knew it meant something, something good, that Len had decided to use it again. "How do you want to do this?"

They hauled it inside in one big heave that broke a nail on Willow's left hand and almost pinned her against a bench. With the wringer inside there was barely room for them to stand. Len was delighted by their success. He reached up and unhooked a few of the dried stalks. The leaves crumbled into a dust that floated in the air and tickled their lungs. "Let's try this. Close the door," he instructed, and when Willow reluctantly pulled the door shut they were thrust into a dusky silence. Len gave Meg's shoulders a reassuring squeeze and climbed around her to position himself in front of the machine. Willow maintained her post by the door. She wanted to be able to exit quickly, if it came to that.

Len showed Wrecker how to spin the handle of the wringer. Then he carefully fed the plant into its rollers.

The machine spit dry beans like little pieces of shrapnel in every direction. Meg and Wrecker burst out laughing as the beans ricocheted off their skin. They cackled and hooted and Len joined in, casting a shy glance at Willow. "Victory," she proclaimed, and laughed because he was laughing, and it happened so rarely. And then the boy started to sneeze. "You all right, sport?" Len asked casually after the third or fourth explosion. But the sneezes continued, and Wrecker abandoned his post to stumble past Willow to the door and out. Meg slipped out with him. He'd had enough, he said, when the sneezes slowed enough to let him speak. He wasn't going in there again. Meg planted herself by his side in solidarity.

Len agreed. It was a good start. He glanced wistfully at the machine. Willow could take a sauna here any time, he said. He guessed she'd earned it.

"Nobody's taking a sauna as long as you've got these things hanging in here." Willow rubbed her itchy nose. "We could see what we could get done." She gestured to the door. "Meg's fine with Wrecker, isn't she?"

Len's eyes widened, and he laughed. He stuck his head out the open door. "Meg, honey. Will you stay with Wrecker?" He had a swimmer's build from behind, with muscular shoulders and a narrow waist.

"Stay," Meg said.

He looked from her to the boy. "You're sure, now?"

"Sure." It sounded like *shore*, but it was a miracle that Meg had come so far with her speech.

"I'll stay with her," Wrecker promised. "We'll work on the fort."

Len looked at him closely and nodded. "You know where we are. Come get me if you need anything," he said, and he pulled the door softly shut and turned to Willow in the dim light.

There was a rhythm to the work. As they went along they fine-tuned the motions, Len reaching up for a plant with one hand as he fed another through the rollers with the other, Willow adjusting the speed of the crank to match his movements. The beans caromed about, bouncing from the walls, the ceiling, the floor, their bodies. The temperature rose from their body heat. Len paused and fingered the buttons of his shirt. "Getting warm," he said.

Willow stopped turning the crank and fanned herself. "Hot."

"We can quit." Len glanced at her with concern. He reached a hand to lift the collar of his shirt. It was glued to his neck. Large patches of sweat darkened his blue shirt to navy.

"Go ahead, Len," Willow said. Len looked startled. "It's too hot to leave it on." Willow peeled off her sweat-spotted work shirt. Beneath it she wore an opaque camisole. It was modest enough, and the light was low. She stood up. She wanted to try feeding, she said.

Len moved awkwardly around the machine to let her switch places.

They began again. The beans—creamy white, kidney shaped, with maroon splotches that made them look like the coat of an Appaloosa horse—sprung from their pods and covered the floor in shallow drifts. Willow liked the rough scratch of the plants against her skin. There was something satisfying about working in tandem at this. They were making good progress. If they kept at it, they would finish well before dusk.

Len raised a hand to get her to wait. He moved to the high window and grinned. "Meg's got Wrecker cooking with mud," he said. With his back turned to Willow, he removed his shirt and folded it and set it on the bench behind him. Stiffly, without looking at her, he returned to his task.

His modesty amused her. As if Willow had never seen a man's bare chest before. She kept the plants steadily entering the rollers. He had small tight curls that spread beneath his collarbone like decoration, and the hair on his back was a delicate downy stream that followed his spine into the waistband of his jeans. She glanced up at the hanging plants. "Halfway through, you think?"

"Would've taken me five times as long, working by myself." He glanced at her. "I'll bring you a bag."

Ruth would like that, Willow said.

Len stopped turning and eased back onto the bench. His eyes were the color of rich dirt, loamy and reliable. He kept his gaze on her.

"What?"

After a moment Len said, "That cap. That you gave the kid."

Willow cleared herself a spot to sit amid the beans. "I figured you'd notice."

"Did he?"

"He didn't seem to." She flexed and fisted her hands, stretching them. "I don't know. Do you think he remembers any of that?" And when Len shrugged, "What I guess I mean is," she said slowly, "don't you think he ought to?"

Len removed his cap and ran his hand through his thin hair. "If he remembers, that's one thing." Willow had shown him the photo Lisa Fay had given her for Wrecker: the boy, barely three, wearing a Giants jersey and cap. Melody hadn't wanted to see it. They figured it best just to hold it for Wrecker; wait until he got older. Len tilted his head to the side and frowned. "But if he doesn't? I don't see how it can help to push him that way. We're his family, now."

"It could prepare him for later."

Len gazed at her steadily. "What later."

It was dangerous to ignore the truth, Willow thought. "The later," she said carefully, "when Lisa Fay comes up to get him."

"If." Len held her gaze. "Not when."

But Len hadn't been to the prison. He hadn't seen what she saw. The look in Wrecker's mother's eyes as she drank in the sight of her son. It was part of Willow, now, the afternoon she sat beside Lisa Fay and handed her the photograph and spoke to her of her son. Willow hadn't told Len about that photo. She hadn't told any of them. It might have been—she wasn't sure, any longer. But maybe she'd made a mistake.

Willow and Len stood and switched places, careful to keep a safe distance from each other as they passed, and went back to work. There was something hypnotic about labor like this; something soothing, unexpectedly sensual, that reminded Willow of the clack and slide of the loom as she worked the shuttle over the yarn. They worked without talking and let the swish and crackle of dry leaves stand in for speech. An hour later, only a few plants remained to be hulled. Willow could feel her body weary with the effort. It was a good kind of tired and she noticed it in him as well, his body slowing slightly. "I can finish," she said, sinking onto the bench. "Just let me take a break."

Len nodded. He retrieved the last plants from the rafters and stacked them on the bench. When Willow started to stand, Len waved her away. She eased down the bench a bit and watched him feed them in, one plant at a time, as he turned the handle. Each revolution sent the mildest breeze in Willow's direction. She tipped her head back and let it play against her skin.

The last plant emerged, its pods exhausted of its beans, and Len sent it to lie with its fellows on a tall stack that covered the opposite bench. He got up and gazed out the tiny window. A smile broke across his face. Willow rose to see. Wrecker and Meg were lying on their backs in the cleared dirt in the front of the house, laughing as the goose waddled in circles around them. When he turned to consider the beans that carpeted the floor, Len's shoulder brushed hers. He didn't move away. Tired, she thought. "Look at that," he said, his voice rich with content. "Not bad."

"Not bad, nothing," she said, flushed with accomplishment and the feel of him close. "We did it."

Len turned toward her and an amused smile tilted the corners of his mouth. He reached forward and brushed away a scrap of bean pod she had stuck above her eyebrow. "There," he said. "You couldn't go out in public like that." But he held her gaze, and

Willow saw something unexpected enter his eyes as he smoothed her hair behind her ear and let the palm of his hand glide down her cheek.

Oh, she thought. There was a pang—a pain, almost—of clarity, a sharp note rising through a pool of warm water.

Willow reached up and laid her own hand over his. With the lightest pressure she guided its path over the planes of her face. When his fingers grazed her lips she let them fall open. The rough tip of his first finger fell between her teeth, and her tongue rose to cradle its callused pad. She felt the shock of it surge through them both.

If they didn't look at each other, Willow thought, it was possible they were imagining this. Imagining that she slid from the bench to kneel on the floor. That when she faced away from him and stretched forward on her knees like a cat to scoop the beans toward her, stretched and scooped, that's all it was, gathering the shelled beans into a pile before her. That when he dropped to his knees behind her, leaned over her to stretch, to scoop, one arm supporting himself and the other snug around her belly, her ass drawn hard to his hips and his hand reaching toward the warm center of herself, he was helping her collect them, mound them into a hill beneath her.

Willow rolled to face him.

Len looked terrified. She wondered if she looked that way, too. Her legs in the soft wool trousers lay gripped between his. Len's chest was bare and he was trembling. Willow laid her spread hand against his breastbone and felt his breath swell against it. Slowly she ran her fingers down his chest. When the bottom of her hand rested on the waistband of his jeans, Willow curled her fingers against the tight muscles of his belly.

The muscles pulsed and he drew a sharp breath and tore his gaze from hers.

156

Willow placed both hands on the knobby bones of Len's hips and drew him toward her as she lay back into the beans. The pile rustled and gave as they surrendered their weight to it. So they were going into this, Willow thought. They were crossing the line they had stumbled close to and withdrawn from a hundred times since Willow first arrived at Bow Farm. Willow felt Len press against her and wanted him then with something close to fury. She did not give a damn about any line. She reached down for his belt buckle, slid the leather from the keeper. Her fingers fought the button of his jeans as her hips arched hard toward his.

A sound outside startled them.

Len's head jerked forward. They heard the rapid slap of foot-falls approaching.

Len leapt from her, banging his elbow hard against the wringer-washer. Willow felt her body shudder at his sudden absence. She scrambled awkwardly from the floor, her face hot, and reached for her shirt. Len grabbed his own, thrust his arms into the sleeves, and threw open the door.

The late-afternoon sun flooded in. "Len!" Wrecker said. He pulled up short and looked at the man.

"What is it, son?" Len said. His voice shook.

The boy sounded casual. Meg's foot was stuck, he said. He couldn't get her loose. He glanced back and forth between them when Willow appeared at the door.

Len stepped down and put a hand on Wrecker's shoulder. "Let's go see about that," he said, and the two of them walked together. Willow waited long enough to catch her breath, waited for the heat to recede from her face, and followed behind.

Meg wasn't far. She lay on the ground amid blackberry bram-bles and made small whimpering noises. Willow felt her heart sink. Somehow Meg had crossed into middle age while they'd had their backs turned. Her cardigan was twisted and her dress

157

had a tear Willow knew she would offer to mend. On her feet were sturdy brogans that laced up and tied, and Willow was sure that her socks matched—Len would have seen to that. She sounded like a frightened child. One foot was trapped in a tangle of berry canes. Len squatted beside Meg, and Willow watched the easy way he talked with her, calmed her, gently worked her foot free of the brambles. He reached and adjusted her spectacles to sit comfortably on her nose and smoothed the errant hairs away from her face. He leaned in and whispered something in her ear. She stopped whimpering and Len rocked back on his heels and smiled. He ran his hand expertly down her calf, flexed her ankle, made sure nothing was broken, and then he carefully untied the shoe and removed it and massaged her foot. He said something to her that made her laugh. Then he replaced the shoe and tied it firmly, and the two of them sat there with their knees pulled up to their chests and their arms wrapped around them, their heads inclined toward each other, and on Len's face that look he reserved for Meg, a look so open and intimate Willow had never seen him turn it to another person.

He didn't even look back at me, Willow thought, stunned.

Wrecker sidled up beside her. He looked unsettled. Willow reached down and took his hand to stop herself from shaking.

"Let's go see about that bread," she said.

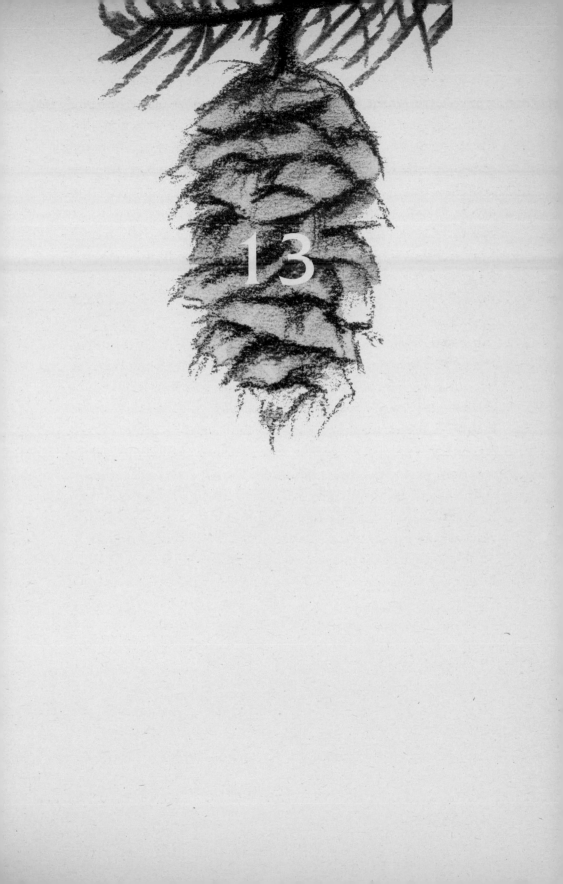

13

CHAPTER EIGHT

They discussed and conferred and argued and flat-out fought and then they broke down and bought him a motorbike. He was thirteen. A kid up at the college in Arcata was selling a 250 Enduro, good on gas, not licensed for the road but then neither was Wrecker. It could get him up and down the mountain. It could get him to the grange hall where the other kids hung out on weekends. It might get him to school on time. Wrecker exulted. The bike was his ticket out. He lay in bed and planned trips to Tierra del Fuego. Okay, he would wear a helmet. They made him. Ruthie made it plain. She would disassemble the bike bolt by bolt and throw all the pieces into the river if he didn't. Did he understand this? Sure, he understood. Helmet. Okay.

He would mount a coon tail on the handlebars and tear up every trail between here and Fort Bragg.

But he damaged the front fork going over a rugged jump the day he got it and the bike was holed up all that winter in the shed, catching dust, and he was back to riding to school with Melody, who only sometimes let him drive. It rained all winter, anyway. When spring came the rain slowed and Melody said, Kid? Why don't you see if Len could help you fix that bike? She said maybe Wrecker could work for Len in trade. Like maybe he could—she flicked her hands in that funny way she had—stack firewood or something.

Wrecker found Len in the tool shed. He was swapping out the crankcase oil in the big splitter. Wrecker hovered in the doorway until Len looked up.

"You're blocking the light," the man said. His voice was softer than gravel but stiffer than wood chips. "Either come in or go out, but get clear of the sun."

Wrecker slipped inside. "Listen. You got any work for me?"

Len wiped his oily hands on a rag. "What kind of work?"

"Any kind." Wrecker rolled his shoulder in a shrug that looked like he was working a kink in the muscle at the same time. "I got to get the fork fixed on the bike and I can't pay you to do it."

"What'd you do to the fork?"

"Broke it on a jump last fall."

"You ought not to be jumping that cycle," Len said.

"Jumping wasn't the problem. It was the landing that whacked it."

Len flashed him a look and fiddled with the oil plug. "I've got plenty of work," he said, lifting his chin and meaning more than Wrecker could figure. "Bring it by. I'll give it a look. It wheel okay?"

"Wheels fine. I'll bring it."

Len nodded and looked down and tried to keep the wobble off his face until the boy disappeared.

Len had him sweep, first. Wrecker was thorough. He didn't let dust build up in the corners and he hefted the heavy sacks of trash like they were filled with cotton fluff. He was strong for his age.

The next Saturday Len had him move the cement sacks out of the root cellar where they'd hardened and lay them along the cut bank of the ditch for flood control. Thirteen? He was very strong for his age.

Then Len showed him how to cut and nail the wood siding for

the tractor shed he was finishing up. "Whoa," Len said, running the sleeve of his shirt across his sweaty face. The boy stopped the handsaw mid-stroke and looked over at him. Len paused to take it in. His stance, his level of concentration, the strength he exhibited, the way his hands seemed to fall naturally to the task—the boy was a goddamned dynamo. He kept his face turned to Len. It was open and direct.

"Yes?"

Len stumbled. "You don't want to cut too many boards," he said. "Might go over what we need. Be a waste."

Wrecker nodded slightly. "I measured and counted. Six more and I'll start nailing them up."

"Oh," Len said, and Wrecker grinned and went back to the final strokes.

Len shook his head. He thought, God help us when he discovers power tools.

There was nothing for Len to complain about, in how they raised the boy. He was grateful to them for rising to the task, and over the years he offered what he could: money sometimes, all the firewood they could burn, he brought meat and kept the road passable and repaired the gates and ran errands if they asked him to, though they rarely did. He was in a kind of permanent and thus forgotten debt to them. Melody had gone along to the courthouse to finalize the boy's papers and sat beside him in solidarity when he'd signed his name. She'd trembled all the drive up, but they'd had to wait so damn long in the courthouse hallway that by the time they actually saw the judge they were both exhausted and dulled into terminal boredom. But it was simple and it was done and from then on Melody and the others did the rest. And a good thing. Meg was steering down a steady decline, and it was all he could do to set the brake and lean his weight against the inevitable. Willow was a help. Len blushed. She was more than a help. She was an inspiration.

The boy had his hair pulled back and the face shield covered to beneath his chin. He gestured to a section of the beam they were sawing. He'd been working with Len for six months now. Wrecker had paid off the bike fix in the first few days but kept coming to work, and Len found he liked his quiet company. Still, Len could not get past the hair. When he turned thirteen Wrecker quit letting Ruthie buzz his head and now, a year later, he resembled the Breck Girl with a dirty lip in a lumberjack's plaid CPO. Why didn't they say something to him about that? And this whole messy business with school: they should just *make* him go and close the door on backtalk. Len didn't go in for this declaration-of-independence modern method of child rearing. Fourteen years old? You didn't get to make up your own mind. Your father made it up for you.

Or—whoever.

He looked down at the knot the boy was pointing to. It wasn't a knot. It was a shiny sliver of metal the saw had just exposed, a dark iris of tannin staining the pale wood. He caught Wrecker's eye through the scratched plastic, and the boy nodded.

Len walked again to the front of the saw and shut off the motor. It faded to quiet. He'd heard of a man who went down like that, the spike spit backward when the blade caught it, pitched a neat fastball to the strike zone. His mate dug it out of his chest and his blood ran out before he got to the hospital. He watched the boy flip up his shield and look for his reaction. Len turned aside. He despised the activists—their righteousness, their cowardly methods. What kind of fool risks a man's life to save a tree? But he forced himself to shrug and smile.

"Why don't we call it a day," Len said.

Wrecker raised his eyebrows. They were broad and wispy, an

undisciplined smudge that softened his steady gaze. "Still light out."

"What do you say we go to the river?"

Wrecker opened his mouth in a lopsided smile that Len had to look away from. He had a crazy grin. You had to watch out or it was catching.

"I'll get Meg in the truck. You mind picking up here?" he asked the boy, and it was as good as done.

Len hadn't even shut the engine when Wrecker was out of the truck bed and halfway to the water, his shirt wrenched off in one fluid motion and flung backward to catch in the blackberry thorns. He paused briefly to yank the boots from his feet and step out of his jeans, left his shorts on in deference to Meg, and used the giant boulder as a springboard into the fat dry August air. It held him suspended. Fourteen. Broad-shouldered. Stringy from sudden growth. And then he raised his knees to his chest and wrapped his arms around them and made himself a compact bullet, a musket ball swallowed with enormous splash and spray by the shining sheet of river below him—down, down, bubbles of zany laughter escaping—pushed off the soft muck of river bottom to twist and torpedo up and break the surface with a whoop, his sun-bleached hair water slicked and slung sideways with that quick flick of the neck—"Len!" he shouted, his voice lurching up the register, "Get on in here!"

Len finished helping Meg struggle out of the loose clothes she wore over her swimsuit and watched her waddle toward the water. He squatted on his heels at the riverbank. "Fine the way I am," he called back. "I'll stay dry." He could see in his mind's eye the look Meg wore on the faded palimpsest of her face. Her head was oddly shaped. Flat in the back, and her forehead a perfect reclining rectangle lined in creases almost straight across and crosshatched lightly: it had been written once and then erased. But she would be happy now, and shining the broad flat beam of her glee at the boy. She shrieked as her toes got wet. He watched Wrecker tread water, his arms extended to sit on the river surface, palms cupped like hydroplanes ready for takeoff and the water streaming from his hair and glistening on his shoulders. His skin was a darker gold than his mane and his chest was still smooth, hairless. He could work like a man—like the best of men—but he was still a boy. Melody's boy. Ruthie's boy. Even Meg's boy. But not Willow's. And somehow, through something that felt to Len like failure and loss, not his either. Len heard the sudden unencumbered peal of Meg's clear laughter. And then Wrecker surfaced, smiled, and swam toward her.

Wrecker did his growing in bed. When he turned eleven and Johnny Appleseed went away—for good, it seemed, although they'd still receive reports from the tree huggers who came by (Johnny in Alaska, Johnny doing time for resisting arrest, Johnny Appleseed busted loose and living in the broad arms of the trees, vowing never to touch ground again)—Wrecker moved from the sunny space Melody had carved out for him in the barn back to the ramshackle cabin. To celebrate his independence Willow pieced him a quilt. It was navy blue and white, with sails and waves in alternating blocks, and he fell asleep under it to the soft snores of Sitka and her pups. Then Sitka died and the pups themselves got old and slow, and Wrecker stitched them up some fluffy pillows to ease their arthritic bones. Evenings Ruth cooked and Wrecker helped and the four of them—Ruth and Wrecker and Melody and Willow—gathered in the farmhouse to eat. Melody took up the oboe. Willow bought a TV. Wrecker studied algebra and Greek mythology and the comparative ecosystems of tundra and steppe through the flimsy pamphlets the home-school company provided.

166

They all tried to help him learn to spell, and they failed miserably; still he passed eighth grade. He passed ninth. He studied with
them and ate and laughed and told stories of his days with Len
and argued over which programs to watch and suffered through
Melody's interminable practice sessions and washed dishes and
did something that really fouled up the washing machine that
Ruth had to fix. In the summers he grew cabbage and cauliflower
in Ruth's garden. He let the screen door slam every time and
clattered like an elephant when he bounded down the porch stairs
and plucked an armload of wildflowers, guiltily, the week after
Mother's Day and argued unsuccessfully for permission to ride his
motorbike into town after dark. But he grew at night, alone, in
his bed.

And he dreamed.

Sometimes he dreamed of cutting the wood, just that, and the
sweet intoxicating odor that rose up to greet him. His body
added inches in length and girth, and muscles swelled onto his
bones, and the texture of his skin changed as he grew hair places
it had never grown before. He dreamed of speeding through the
forest, his face whipped by twigs as he dodged trees and his body
a forward hurtle faster than the bike could ever take him. He
dreamed of dog faces and half-caught conversations; his fingers
stretched along their callused lengths and the bones of his face asserted themselves more ardently, and he dreamed of the dark-haired
girl who camped on the banks of the Mattole every summer. His
body went looking for her in his sleep and found itself, and he
woke laughing.

Also he dreamed that dark disorienting dream. He felt something inside himself shrink. He felt part of himself leaving and was
afraid of that. Sometimes the future felt like something he could
wrap his arms around and lift with ease and sometimes it was a
shape he couldn't quite make out that waited for him in burned-out

167

buildings in distant cities he found himself lost in. The ropy muscles of his trunk felt puny then, and his hands reached to catch himself. Always the fall was faster than he could stop.

He grew a downy mustache, sparse but insistent. His skin rebelled. An Adam's apple rose in the flatland of his throat. His voice was husky to begin with, and though it tumbled two notches, it held on to the sweet color that distinguished it.

Wrecker knew there were parts to himself he would never retrieve.

One night he lay awake and was still. He heard the door open and felt the draft of cool night air cross his face. He listened for the dogs to stir. Heard the thump of a tail and the sandpaper scratch of wet tongue on skin. He listened for footfall but heard none. The night was dark. He waited for the flare of a match. "Johnny Appleseed?"

"Sshhhh."

He shifted onto his elbows. His shoulders and chest were clear of the quilt. "What are you doing here?"

"I forgot something." Wrecker heard his friend rustle through the piles of dirty laundry and stacks of odds and ends that cluttered the floor. Johnny was a vague shape at the end of the bed. And then the squeak of wood being pried up, resisting a nail. Something down there caught the light and shone but was quickly covered. And then the dull thud of Johnny's fist pressing the wood back into place. He turned to Wrecker and there was just enough light for the boy to make out the familiar face, those bright eyes and that beard, a dense mat that covered nearly all his skin. He was smiling. "Don't ask," Johnny Appleseed warned.

Wrecker sat up with the quilt clumped around his waist. He shifted his legs to make room on the edge of the bed. "Where you been all this time?"

168

"Ah, you know. Places to go, people to see." He squinted at the boy. "You got big. What are they feeding you?"

Wrecker felt a sharp pang. He hadn't realized how much he'd missed him. "Stick around and find out," he said. "Ruth'll put meat on your bones. You're looking kind of thin."

"Got to travel light." Johnny paused. "Hey, Wrecker?" The corner of his mouth turned down, and then up, and then down again. "Keep this a secret, will you?" He watched the boy to gauge his response. "Don't tell anybody I was here."

Wrecker nodded. "You a fugitive from justice?"

Johnny Appleseed laughed. "A fugitive *for* justice, better. But probably both."

Wrecker hesitated, and then he reached over to lift his friend's shirttail. The polished stock of a pistol stuck up from the waistband of his pants. So it was true. People whispered that Johnny had turned Guardian. Whatever it took to stop the logging, they'd do it. Crazy-ass fools, Len called them. The worst kind of outlaws. "Who you planning to shoot?"

Johnny met his gaze. "I might have to scare some people to keep them away from the places they shouldn't go."

"I'm working with Len," Wrecker blurted.

Johnny Appleseed nodded. Even in the dark, Wrecker could see a wave of sadness cascade down his face. "I know that," Johnny said. "Len's not the worst. Just tell him to leave the wildest ones be." He walked around to the dogs, knelt down to stroke each one. He turned to the boy. "Sitka?"

"Last year," Wrecker said. He still got a lump in his throat.

Johnny Appleseed nodded. "Take good care of yourself, kid," he said, and walked outside and left the door open.

There was a sliver of moon that barely lit the grass. Wrecker dropped his feet to the floor and stood in the doorway with his quilt wrapped around him like a toga. "Johnny Appleseed!"

Johnny looked over his shoulder and lifted his hand to still the boy. Wrecker stood frozen. He had the terrible, wrenching feeling that this was the last he'd see of Johnny and he wanted to run at him, bring him down, force him to stay. But he couldn't move. Johnny was going and his hand, raised like that, meant Wrecker had to stay.

Meant good-bye.

There was the barest shimmer in the shadows. There, again: a dark shape distinguished itself from the trees and approached the small man. From every direction, dark smudges resolved into men moving silently, stealthily, toward Wrecker's friend and surrounding him. Guardians. If Johnny went with them he would never find his way back.

Johnny stood patiently in the moonlight. He made the men wait. They waited until, at last, Wrecker lifted his own hand, and waved good-bye. And then, once more, they were absorbed into the trees.

Meg loved the water. She loved it for hours in a pan she could sit beside and stir with a wooden spoon; she loved it coming down day after night after interminable winter day to flood the yard and sop Len's canvas tarps left hanging on the line. She delighted in the river, in the sea, in the brackish standing swamp of a lagoon where Len mucked about in waders and collected tubers for a feast. Anyplace wet was where she wanted to be. Especially in the bath, with Len's lean economical body a prop for her own soft flesh. "The water lapped over her belly," he sang, stitching his own words to the tune of "My Bonnie." "The water lapped over her thighs. The water lapped over her ninnies," Len's voice a scratch more satisfying than the loofah he coursed over Meg's shoulders and back, "which grew to incredible size."

Every night they followed the same routine. Len came in from the yard or from town or dragged his weary bones home from the forest after felling trees with Wrecker and he stood at the stove and put together some concoction that would satisfy their need to eat. He flicked the switch on the propane boiler to heat the water for their bath. He unscrewed the faucet clamps he'd had to install; Meg was safe at home, days, so long as he kept her from emptying the cistern and flooding the place while he was gone. He whistled and sometimes he played the radio. Meg rearranged the lumber scraps he brought her. Some evenings she liked to lie under the table and peer up at the rough side of the planks. They ate together and Len scrubbed the dishes while Meg stood beside him with her hands in the soapy water and chased bubbles. And then they took their bath.

That morning Wrecker had found the gas tank empty on the motorbike and had to hike over to work. He was fifteen, now, and starting to fill out. Taller than Len by an inch or two and wide in the shoulders, not too narrow in the hips but every ounce of it muscle and more under his control than it had been in his gangly days. He could shoulder a wet log and walk with it, his footfalls thunderous under the weight. He swung an ax—tick, tock—like it was the second hand on the clock of the world: Paul Bunyan with a sharp blade and Len's aging International, winch-outfitted, for his Blue Ox. Len handled the chain saw. All it would take was for the chain to break and the kid would be ribbons. Len shuddered to think of it. Wrecker was too young to work the woods, his focus not fully honed and the dangers too profound, but he was too good already to turn down. And God knows too bullheaded to boss around. He wouldn't take no for an answer. He'd go ahead and find some straightforward way to do what he wanted.

Straightforward: that's how he'd asked Len for a ride to the dance the high school in Fortuna was throwing that evening. Len gave him credit for that. The boy had worked through every detail. Melody couldn't take him; the hatchback she'd bought to replace the VW when it finally expired was turning out to be no more reliable than the van it had supplanted, but she was happy to come sit with Meg for the evening. Meg took a keen interest in the oboe and would listen, mesmerized, as Melody practiced her simple pieces. And for Len's time, Wrecker pledged in return as many hours of work as he took Len away from his place. He planned to leave that night at seven. A few hours at the dance, the good hour and a quarter ride home—Len could be home by midnight. That meant five hours' labor exchange. Would Len consider?

"Sure, I'll take you," Len said gruffly. "Forget about the rest." He owed the boy at least this. With Johnny Appleseed gone there was no other man around to guide Wrecker and he was changing so fast, giving off a man's odor, building muscle mass and sure enough bulking up in other ways, too. He showed a keen interest in the girls his age who gathered in occasional gaggles at the post office and general store. A keen interest and dubious social skills, from what Len could tell. Not that Len was expert in the field. He'd been nearly thirty and a virgin to love, if not to sex, when he'd fallen hard for Meg. He was certain Wrecker was a virgin on both counts. Ruth would have squeezed the information out of him and passed it on to them in subtle ways, but instead Ruth gazed at the boy with an expression that joined mirth with intense pity and a sense of impending doom. Len grinned, thinking of it. Poor sod, he thought. Not one of them could soften the blow, when it came. But Len could give him a lift to where the girls were. He could kick in his share to give Wrecker half a chance. And then his expression sobered. He was fifty-seven, himself. Old enough to be through with that kind of foolishness. And deep in the throes of the worst kind of want.

They'd worked hard all day and when the sun tilted toward four o'clock Len had quit early, run the boy home to get cleaned up for his evening out. Len had a parcel Willow had asked him to pick up at the p.o. in town and he wanted to deliver that, too. He drove in as far as the road would allow. Wrecker mumbled his thanks and slipped away. Len found Willow gathering her laundry from the line and he opened his mouth to shout across the meadow to her—but his mouth shut of its own accord. He stood and watched her free and fold the billowing sheets. All at once his insides lurched as though they had tired of him and decided to make a sudden break for freedom. He turned abruptly and hurried to the main house. He left the parcel with Ruthie. He got back in the truck and drove swiftly home.

In the tub, Meg splashed water onto her face. She chortled tunelessly. Len scrubbed a dirt spot above her elbow. He scrubbed harder and she slapped the water with the flat of her palm and moaned and he eased off. He looked closer. It was a mole he was trying to scrub off. The same mole that had always lived in that spot. He leaned against the tub back and slipped lower in the water.

His eyes shut, the water warm around him, Len's mind lit with his memory of the afternoon. The line was strung high and Willow had reached above her head to unpin the sheet and carry its edge down to join the other. She'd stretched her arms wide to flatten the fold and then brought them together and halved the rectangle and smoothed the sheet against her body with her spread hand and then halved it again. And smoothed again. And folded again.

Len had never seen anything as breathtaking. It terrified him. *He* terrified him. He sat straight in the bath and he forced himself to forget what he'd seen. His hand found the plastic cup they kept on the tub edge. He gently touched Meg's chin to persuade her to tilt back, and poured the water in a stream over her long hair. He kept one hand cupped at her hairline to protect her eyes. When her hair was fully wet he poured the shampoo into his hands and softly kneaded her scalp. He combed the suds tenderly through the long strands. He ran a delicate finger inside her ear and around its fleshy lobes to soap it clean and she giggled. He rinsed her hair and soaped her skin and rinsed that too and hurriedly scrubbed himself and stood for a towel and eased Meg from the tub and into the looped cotton. She hummed in his arms as he dried her, and he helped her into her flannel nightgown and robe to be ready for bed before dressing himself.

There was a knock at the front door and Len shouted from the bedroom for Wrecker to come in. The boy entered. Behind him sauntered Melody, her arms wrapped around the oblong leatherette case that housed her oboe. And behind her Willow.

Len glimpsed her through the half-open door to the bedroom and felt his heart jump. His cheeks flushed. He yanked his right arm from the sleeve of the threadbare chambray shirt he'd thoughtlessly chosen. The striped dress shirt was still folded in the bottom of the drawer; he shook that one free of its creases and awkwardly pulled it on. He stuffed the shirttails into the waistband of his jeans and forced his feet into his boots. He glanced at Meg. And then Len combed his hair.

"Hello," he said, stepping into the room.

Willow wore the faintest curl of a smile. "I need to get out for an evening. Mind some company?"

"A bit tight in the cab," Len said, to his instant regret. He coughed into his hand.

Wrecker came to the rescue. "We'll fit," he said briskly. It was October and the air was cool but he was stepping out in threadbare jeans and a T-shirt with a Black Sabbath graphic on its front and a couple of quarter-sized holes gaping in the side seam. "Let's go. I don't want to be late."

Meg had opened Melody's oboe case and was reverently stroking the polished instrument. "We'll be fine, here," Melody assured Len. She turned to her son. "Behave yourself," she said fiercely. The boy blushed and she reached up and tucked the tag of his T-shirt under the collar. He was taller than her by a head. "Have fun." Her eyebrows knit together as she reconsidered. "Not *too* much fun." She glanced at Willow. "You'll be sure he gets home fine?"

"I'll tuck him in and turn out the light."

"Good." She tossed her sleeping bag onto the couch. "I'm no good at staying up late. Try not to wake me when you come in, Len."

Wrecker gave a short huff like a bear rooting in downed timber for grubs. He tilted toward Melody and suffered a kiss, and then crossed to Meg and planted one on the crown of her head. "Let's go, already," he growled, and they did.

Wrecker, usually quiet, chattered endlessly on the ride to Fortuna. About football, which he followed only sporadically, and television shows—reception at the farm still subject to the vagaries of the weather, in spite of the antenna he had rigged on the roof of the farmhouse—and about the weather itself, which had held steady all month but about which the farmer's almanac (but could you really trust that? they were wrong as often as they were right) predicted a severe season of storms, so Len had best clear out the bar ditch that was supposed to carry the water off his road but which had clogged the year before. He was thinking of learning to play electric guitar. There was this guy who had tried to jump his motorcycle all the way across the Snake River Gorge and dang but he wished he had seen that. When they got to the high school and Wrecker slouched off, Len nearly fell out of the truck, frazzled by the unexpected onslaught of language. He turned to Willow. "Is he on drugs?"

"Better than that," she laughed. "Endorphins. They're free."

Len shook his head. Most of the time the boy was calm, level-headed, and immensely competent. "He sounded like a—"

"A teenager?" Willow offered.

Len had been thinking more along the lines of used car salesman.

It was remarkable, really, she said. Teenagers, observed in the wild, had been known to sustain that level of acoustic barrage for hours at a time. They'd been observed sleeping past noon and had the documented ability to consume in a single sitting the accumulated caloric stores of an entire social group for a week.

"Oh, really." Len chuckled. She was mocking him, now. He liked the way it made him feel. "Wasn't there that special on them? Mutual of Omaha's *Wild Kingdom*. They talk, they sleep, they eat."

"My boys did."

Len glanced sharply at her. A streetlamp spilled its light into the dark cab and limned her profile. She was gazing dreamily down. Then she lifted her eyes and looked frankly at him. "I could stand something to drink right now."

Len nodded and shifted into gear. He stared straight ahead. Something had just changed between them. There was a little bar he knew—it was a workingman's bar but women went there, too; not her kind of woman maybe, but it was all he could think of, on the spot like this—and he piloted the truck to its lot. His mouth was dry. "Think this'll do?"

"It's perfect." As Willow slid across the bench seat to reach the far door her dress gave static sparks that made Len look away, dizzy. Lovestruck. There. He might as well admit it. He stole a glance at her as he held the heavy door to the bar. Something had changed in *her*, and the crazy buoyant feeling he had fought for so long—the one that started lower than the pit of his stomach and

176

left him breathless and ready to rise—was set loose. His shoulders lifted. He didn't know where he was going and he made himself believe he didn't care.

The theme of the dance was Fall Harvest and the Fortuna High School gym was decorated with pumpkins—real pumpkins as well as some leaf-stuffed orange trash bags made to look like giant, malicious jack-o-lanterns—and a motley assortment of party streamers and hangings and a mirror ball that cast its little pebbles of light in a dizzying stream across the faces of the teenagers. Wrecker stood among them, paralyzed. He'd spent hours anticipating this evening and had finally decided that if he could just get himself here there was a reasonable chance he could fake the rest. But something had gone wrong. He'd been shuffled by the small crowd into a corner of the gym with other gawky, singular boys. Their defects were relatively apparent. Were his?

Len had taught him: identify, then remedy. Name the problem and then solve it. The problem was that he was trapped in hell and there was no way out. He'd been thrust into freakdom before he even had a chance to— Whoa there, now. Wrecker struggled to keep the terror from creeping into his expression. Steady, boy. That was the kiss of death, that look that told the world you'd piss your pants if you got close to a girl. And a few yards away a girl stood, for a brief moment, alone. Wrecker recognized the look that flitted across her face. He wasn't the only one suffering. His shoulders cranked down a quarter of a notch and he forced himself to move closer to her.

"Hey," he said.

She could have glanced at him and turned her back. For a second he thought she would. Then she tipped her head a little to the side and considered him. She was halfway pretty. He had his hands jammed in his pockets but if he were to extract one and extend it she was actually close enough to touch. The music was loud and Wrecker felt a sudden surge of possibility.

"What," she said.

It was a start.

Len and Willow sat in a booth in the dark bar with a broad table between them and what looked like instruments of torture—Willow identified them as nautical objects—decorating the wall adjacent. They were talking. Mainly Willow was talking. Whatever had infected Wrecker on the drive over seemed to have been contagious. Willow noticed Len's stifled surprise and apologized. It was just, she said, that if she stopped—if she didn't get it all out—she was afraid that what was left unsaid would knot itself around her windpipe and squeeze it shut.

Len had the opposite problem. He was sure that if he said what he was resisting saying he would be finished in thirty seconds and his world would implode. If he told her, if she knew, there'd be no turning back. Either she felt the same way or she didn't, and either option charted a future he couldn't live with.

It was her work, partly, Willow explained. The carpet restoration had tapered down to a trickle. Of her best clients, three had died of old age and another two had largely curtailed their collecting. She'd tried to drum up new business, but her heart wasn't in it and her close eyesight had grown blurred, making the work harder. Besides, now all she could focus on was stories.

"Stories?"

Len wrinkled his forehead and Willow took another stiff swallow of scotch. She drank it neat and Len noticed she was drinking it fast. Stories, she repeated. Epics, adventures, folktales. Why did people do the things they do? The—she sputtered a little as the scotch burned her throat—stupid things they do? She was obsessed with stories. She'd always loved them. Had told her children stories every night, half of them drawn from the borders of the rugs she handled.

There, again.

"Willow," Len said gently. He set his beer down and tenderly reached across the table to cup his hand around hers. "That's twice."

"I'm sorry," she said, a flush rising in her face. Len couldn't tell if it was the alcohol or the warm air in the bar or something else. The something else he was bringing up or the something else he was trying not to. "Am I repeating myself?"

"That's twice you mentioned your children. Do you . . ." He cleared his throat. "Did you . . ." He didn't know how to phrase the question. "I'm listening," he settled on.

He watched her face. He wished he could commit it to memory, each fold and crease and stretch of luminous skin, each freckle, the way her lips parted slightly and quivered, the few stray hairs she tamed against her temples, the way her gaze dropped and darkened and resisted, calling a kind of interior light, and then darkened further; the way her neck bent like a swan's to bring her lovely head forward, first, and then down close to the table.

"Ah," she said, her voice softly upbeat and only slightly ironic. "Look at that. I guess I've had too much to drink." She raised her head again and looked directly at Len. "You and Meg. You didn't want children?"

Len opened his hand in a small, helpless gesture. "They never came." He smiled weakly. "Meg got the goose."

"And you got Wrecker."

It surprised Len, the quick flush of emotion that flooded him. He had to look away quickly. He opened his mouth but said nothing.

"You've done fine, Len." Willow kept her gaze on his face. "Come on." She slid out of the booth and reached for his hand. "It's time. Let's get the boy."

It was still early when they arrived again at the parking lot outside the high school gym. A few other vehicles sat scattered across the asphalt. Some were occupied. Len tried not to look. There was a fair amount of activity evident in two or three of them and it was hard to ignore. Willow had scooted to the middle of the bench seat to make room for Wrecker and she was close enough to Len that when he turned his head to face her he could breathe in the scent of her shampoo. Delicate, complex. Some kind of flower he had no name for. He leaned past her to switch on the radio for distraction but his upper arm inadvertently brushed the side of her breast. He froze. Then he retreated stiffly to the far edge of the seat.

"Len."

Some kind of flower—he reached again to turn the music up and this time she shifted with him. Opening, somehow. Widening in a way that made him gasp.

Willow took Len's hand from the radio knob and placed it so the callused tips of his fingers straddled the arching dome of her knee. The heel of his hand slumped into the warm hollow between that knee and the other.

Len made an involuntary sound—a deep sound, almost a moan—that appalled him. He held his breath to try to wrestle back control. He couldn't retrieve his hand from its home between Willow's thighs but he kept an iron grip on the door handle with the other. If he held tight he couldn't reach over and lay it on Willow's breast. He couldn't shift closer to her on the seat or—

"Oh, Len, no," Willow exhaled.

Len's head jerked up and he yanked his hand clear, his knuckles rapping hard against the dash. The sudden pain pierced him. He looked around wildly. "There," Willow said, tipping her head toward the gymnasium door while she smoothed her skirt. "The children," Willow clarified. They were both breathing rapidly and some moisture had condensed on the windshield. Through the foggy glass Len could make out the shapes of hulking boys exiting the gym and heading for trucks. The girls could be identified by their smaller size and the snug fit to their jeans. Both Len and Willow scanned anxiously for Wrecker. They didn't dare look at each other.

His eyes trained on the windshield and his voice no higher than a whisper, Len said, "It's no, then?"

Willow cast a furtive glance his way. Her eyebrows lifted. A small hiccup of laughter slid out from under her control, and then one more.

Len felt surprise and relief spread like a mantle of warmth throughout his chest and arms. He let his head fall back against the seat back. His own laughter escaped to join hers. They laughed tentatively at first but their joined laughter grew bolder, more full-throated, edged toward giddy. Len didn't know why he was laughing. He wondered briefly if they would be able to stop. He reached over and gave her a quick hug, a hug of comfort and collusion, and Willow returned it. And as they sat apart recovering, making little gasps and sighs and exclamations, Len realized that he had been deeply mistaken. Everything was suddenly so clear.

Willow tapped his wrist. "There he is," she said, and pointed.

Wrecker was dressed like all the other boys. The shoulder-length hair that fell in his eyes, the torn T-shirt, the ragged jeans—it could have been a uniform. But something distinguished their boy from the others. Something—

He was happy.

"Oh," Willow said.

It was palpable. His happiness was a shine that transformed the darkness about him. He was alone but the glow he gave off suggested he hadn't been alone recently. They saw him catch sight of the truck and tip his chin toward them, head their way.

"He's beautiful," Willow murmured.

Len glanced at her. It was funny to hear her say it, but it was true.

The boy reached the truck and opened the door and swung himself in, and in a moment the air in the cab changed from the charged intimacy Len and Willow had created to a wild, swirling, circus brew of hot breath and pheromones.

"Wow," Willow remarked.

"Huh?" Wrecker settled himself on the bench. He was all thigh and shoulder spread and strong deodorant and Len could detect, mixed in with the boy's own personal aroma, a distinctly girl smell. "Okay," Wrecker said. "Let's go."

Len fired the engine and shifted the truck into gear. The driving gave him something to do, an action to steady his legs and focus his mind. Willow's body was pressed close to his and she was trembling slightly. Every breath she took vibrated against him. Len reached for a blanket he kept stored behind the seat. His hand trailed against the nape of Willow's neck as he drew it forward. "Are you cold?"

Willow opened the spread across her legs and his. "Just a little." She straightened the blanket from beneath and let her hand linger in his lap.

Len swerved into the opposite lane.

"Easy!" Wrecker's eyes widened. "Len! I can drive if you're tired."

"Sorry," Len muttered.

"Good dance?" Willow ventured. With her head turned toward the boy, Len glimpsed the long line of her neck. He wanted to follow it deep into her blouse.

"It was okay."

"Anybody you knew?"

"Not many." He gazed dreamily out the window. "A few."

Len drove with an acute concentration. He kept the truck steadily in its lane as the road wove up the narrow mountain pass. The headlights splashed over the broad leaves of shrubs and shone in brief flashes on fir trunks. Streaks of moonlight stuttered briefly through the canopy, but when Len climbed out of the trees and crested the ridge the moon suddenly appeared, swollen and luminous, before them, spilling its milky shine into the cab.

"Pull off, Len." Wrecker looked entranced. "You ever seen it like this, before?"

Len parked the truck by the roadside and the three of them piled out. The fog had moved off the ocean and the moonlight spread across the waves. Out in the distance, the rest of the world waited.

"Pretty decent day," Wrecker declared softly.

He dozed the rest of the way, his big head leaning first against the window glass and then shifting to fall to Willow's shoulder. Len and Willow stayed silent and solemn for the steep descent to the water. One sharp turn after another swayed them back and forth against each other. They rode without speaking as the road hugged the beach and turned inland at the river's mouth, and when they turned at last onto the dirt road they woke Wrecker to open the gates. Len stopped above the farmhouse and Wrecker spilled out of the cab. He shook himself like a newborn colt. "No work tomorrow?"

"No work, buddy."

"See you later, then." He trotted off into the darkness toward his cabin.

They watched his dark back disappear. The moonlight flooded in and lit Willow's face. She kept it slanted slightly from him. Len's throat was tight. "Willow?"

"Drive up a little farther, Len."

He released the brake and backed the truck onto the road again.

"Just ahead. On the edge of the meadow."

Len eased the truck to a stop and shut the engine. Willow slid away from him and opened the door and got down.

Len pushed his way out and walked around to stand in front of her. He draped the blanket over her shoulders and rested his hands on her waist. Her chin tilted toward him now and he paused because he wanted to remember all of this: the shine of her eyes, the thrum of his body, the softness of her skin, and that first day, too, how fragile she'd seemed, cracked in half from whatever she'd come from but gorgeous, terribly and irresistibly and unreachably beautiful. It clobbered him. It drove him out to the privacy of his woodlot for solace. He was in love with his wife and still every cell in his body had turned toward Willow with a kind of magnetic conviction that had never let up. Len dipped toward her now and let his lips brush lightly from her forehead down the line of her profile to her lips. If she wanted him to, he would stop there. He would let that be enough. That single, tentative kiss.

Willow reached a hand behind Len's head and brought him close and kissed him hard. He felt her lips open to him and her body tremble against his own. "Come with me," she said hoarsely, breaking for air. "I can't wait anymore."

She led him across the moonlit meadow to her yurt. He was barely in the door when she was rushing through the buttons of his shirt, fighting his belt buckle, running her hands wherever they would reach. He kicked off his boots and struggled out of his jeans. "Hey!" He laughed a little. "Whoa!" He'd wanted this for so long and he was afraid for it to be over before he registered what was happening.

"I know, Len." He couldn't tell if Willow was laughing or crying as she dragged him toward the bed. Somehow she had slid out of her clothes and her naked body stunned him. "I know." She reached for him and he didn't resist and he heard her gasp, saw her eyes widen and shift focus as they moved together. Len let his head sink to her neck, felt her lips move lightly along his ear. "We'll slow down later." Small, delicate cries finding their way into words. "Next time, Len." He felt himself fall into his body as he listened. "Next time," she whispered. Softly, in his ear. "I promise."

CHAPTER NINE

It was a giant tree, the trunk misshapen by fire and encrusted with lichens, and it dominated the slope with its girth and the broad circle of shade cast by its canopy. It was a mammoth, a monster, a dinosaur even, a relict fir left standing when its regiment fell to loggers a hundred years before. Noises flattened beneath it. Its hollow had housed bear and cat and bird and the occasional juvenile delinquent escaped from the boys' reformatory in Lassen. In a storm it waved its limbs and threatened to uproot and roll itself and half the hillside down to dam the creek and block the county road below. It was a public hazard, the owners declared. It was an insurance spike. And it was square in the intended footprint of their new house, a modern extravagance planned to poise on the hillside and command a view of the sea.

It would have to go.

The contractor was a youngish guy with a bulbous nose and pants that sagged under a lazy gut. He was paying on his equipment like he couldn't believe and his naturally generous impulses were constrained by the red that showed up in his checkbook too often for comfort. It had crossed his mind more than once, recently, that success in the construction business might require more than a strong back and an unfettered delight in the orderly repetition of milled lumber. This house was a chance to make a name for himself and put some change in the bank—or at least keep his machines on the job and out of hock. He was itching to start. And the first item of business was the tree.

Too wet, Len said.

So the contractor fussed and fretted and set his crew to work on a kitchen remodel where they tripped over one another and on an otherwise uneventful Thursday started a fracas that left one guy fired and another sidelined on workers' comp. The contractor drummed his fingers. He had four solid guys left and a deadline for completion that would cost him a hundred bucks for every day he went over. Probably dry enough now, he told Len.

Maybe, Len said. But then it rained again for one full week and they had to wait that out.

And then suddenly it was springtime. Len went out in the morning and smelled the air. Wrecker came walking up the drive and saw him poised there, pensive, his chin lifted and his gaze taking in the surroundings, and knew something was up.

"What?"

"Good morning to you, too," Len said. He looked at him appraisingly until Wrecker, uncomfortable, stood straighter. "What do you think. Is it time to cut that tree?"

Wrecker's face brightened a beat faster than he could shuffle and yawn to hide it. "Depends," he said, his voice still sleepy. "You figure the rains are over?"

"Window of opportunity. Help me load the gooseneck."

Together they tied on to the long trailer the saws and the big winch and the logging chains and everything they'd need to take the tree down and carry it back, in multiple loads of manageable pieces, to Len's yard for milling. They piled into the cab of the heavy diesel and started down the mountain. They stopped in Mattole for coffee and Len got on the telephone. Meet us out there, he told the contractor.

Thank you Jesus Mary and Joseph, the young man whispered.

He had the crew there to help. By the time Len and Wrecker arrived, there were half a dozen men milling around in eager anticipation. In a land of big trees, the only ones that rivaled this in size were sitting protected in the government groves. The grandfathers of these men had cut trees this big and bigger, thrown their brawn and hubris against the massive forests and held dances on the stumps. It was a lost era of plenty, of flapjack and ham breakfasts and untrimmed beards, of locomotives and mules. Len looked around drily. Styrofoam cups littered the roadside. "Just one tree," he said. "Won't take but the two of us to bring her down." The men shuffled their feet and looked around sheepishly, but they remained. Everyone wanted the moment of falling. Everyone wanted the thud as the trunk hit the ground.

Len and Wrecker set about their work. A tree this size—nearly two hundred feet tall by Len's estimation, with a trunk it would take three grown men to girdle, arms outstretched—ought by rights to come down in pieces, Len reminded the boy. Safer. Easier to control. Better all around. And impossible, in this case, with that landslide higher up that left no way to get the crane in above. The best they could do was to plan the fall, working the slope and the soil and the tree's shape, to lay her down as gently as they could. See, there? Len pointed and gestured and mapped his plan so the boy understood. Wrecker watched and nodded. Yes, he got it. Yes. And then Len watched him clamp the tree spikes to his boots, rig his ropes, and climb into the upper branches to trim selectively and fine-tune the weight.

Yes, Len said softly to himself. Like that. Exactly.

Felling any tree was a dance with gravity. No kind of science alone could predict which way a tree could twist, and Len knew to lay a hand on the bark, to listen to the roots. It wasn't magic, just common sense and a kind of intuition that developed after nearly forty years in the field. Anybody could muscle a tree down. All it took was a chain saw and enough gas in the can to keep its noisy little motor running. Of course, anybody could be crushed by a wayward fall, too. Anybody could be impaled by a sharp branch. Anybody—no matter how careful, how experienced—could hit a pocket of compressed twist in a limb that caused the saw to buck and twist its teeth into the operator's thigh. Len had the scars to prove it.

Anybody, Len thought as he watched Wrecker work his way back down, could have a moment of inattention and tumble from great height.

Len's breath came easier when the boy was safely grounded. "Nice," he told him. The boy nodded. A streak of pitch discolored his cheekbone. Len could swear he'd grown taller while aloft.

"Have at it, old man," Wrecker said, grinning. He pulled the cord start on the thirty-inch McCulloch and settled the engine, passed the saw to Len, and stood back.

Len eased its whirring blade into the thick bark of the tree. The motor pitch dipped and a stream of pale dust spewed from the cut. He lifted the blade back out, repositioned it over the first cut, and angled down until the two kerfs met. Then he removed the blade and stilled the saw. Wrecker passed him the small ax and Len set his feet again, his hands gripping the ash handle. He swung and the sharp head bit into the trunk. When he pulled it out again the wedge came with it.

"No turning back now," he said to the boy.

Len worked the trunk methodically, whittling chunks from it in strategic places and deepening the cut behind the direction of fall. The wind was still but it could come up at any time, and he worked steadily, aiming to ground the tree as quickly as he safely could. Down on the road came the murmur of idle conversation, someone's sharp laugh punctuating the hum. Len kept his mind focused on the tree. He ate what Wrecker brought him and never let the tree leave his sight. It was a wild card, standing, and he knew better than to turn his back on it. He sent the boy downslope for tools; he had him sharpen the chain and refuel the tank. When he got close to dropping it he sent Wrecker below with instructions to stay there. "And don't let nobody else close, neither." There was blood in his eye. "I don't care what they say. Until I yell the all-clear, you keep them on that pavement." He made the boy promise not to move from his post. Just because the tree was on the ground wouldn't mean it was safe, he warned him. Len's face was ruddy and his pale lips rode it like stripes of gristle in a tough cut of meat. "Could roll and crush you. A slope like this? Ugly. You want to know ugly? Ugly."

Len waited until the boy scrambled down to the road and made the others gather a good distance back. He felt the sweat cool on his back in the spring breeze. Then he lifted the saw and made the last few cuts and the great tree foundered and fell.

The saw stopped and for a moment there was silence and the held breath of every person watching. They couldn't see Len from where they stood. The sun was shining and dust motes rode the air currents. Then a growl, as though low in the throat, and a puff of breeze as the canopy swayed, and the growl rose to a grind and then a tearing, more like a shriek, as the massive tree began to fall and the men watching took another step back and a wind barreled toward them, the weight of the tree moving quickly through air, the trunk turning like a cat to correct, a split second of splinter as the remaining branches broke the fall and then a deafening crash, a tremendous thud, a tremor in the earth they felt in the soles of their feet as the giant came to earth.

The men rushed forward. Len was nowhere. They hastened up the slope.

Wrecker stumbled back when the tree began to fall. He planted his feet to steady himself and after some gaping seconds the shock waves galloped across the ground to climb his legs and rearrange his chest. He absorbed the blow into every cell of his body, felt it change the chemistry of his brain, shake into shape some amorphous category of soul. And after the noise abated still he stood and let the slow seep of warmth—the afterglow of destruction— feed his muscles and flush his face.

"Kid." The big nose and generous face of the contractor loomed into Wrecker's field of vision. "Better get up there. Your old man's a little tee'd off at the moment." He peered at the boy's dazed expression. "Kid? Something the matter with you?"

Wrecker shook his head clear. He brought his gaze to focus on the road, on the gravel, on the knees of the contractor's jeans. He looked up at the man's eyes. He shook his head again and let the tremor continue down his spine. Something enormous had fallen and he had been a part of bringing it down. He felt weirdly superhuman and insignificant at the same time and he wanted the feeling to last and when it wore off he wanted to destroy something else to get it back. A drug had entered his bloodstream and he was frantic for more of it.

For one brief moment he had let go of himself. Just for then, for that one violent, rending, concussive moment, he had not had to hold himself up.

"Boy?" The contractor reached out and grabbed Wrecker's arm. "Take it easy, there, son. Why don't you sit down for a minute. Get your breath."

Wrecker snarled and shrugged him off. Then he rushed up the slope toward Len.

CHAPTER TEN

Melody had laid down some rules. She'd had to. It wasn't an activity that came naturally to her, but at fifteen the kid was big and headstrong, and unless they came to an understanding about what she would allow and what she would not and what would happen if he overstepped those boundaries, the petty disagreements that arose frequently between them could turn into full-blown shouting matches. Shouting matches and—*whatever*, and, honestly, it was a territory she didn't want to explore. What*ever*. Like what? Like he'd take off? Join the army? Stop talking to her? Like she'd say something she didn't mean but would never be able to take back? One second he'd be sweet and funny and considerate and wise beyond his years and a second later he'd be a million miles away, sullen and unreachable, or he'd flare up in some hotheaded display of poor judgment, or sulk over some insult she hadn't even intended. Sometimes her hand itched just to reach out and smack him. Sometimes her hand itched to grab the front of his shirt and drag him close for a hug. Most of the time she couldn't do either, hug him *or* hit him—he moved too fast. Too fast away. Ruth blamed it on hormones but Melody suspected it was contagious. He'd got it from her. When she'd been that age? Pushing sixteen? She'd been a monster. Justified by circumstance, maybe, but still way beyond the pale.

There were two rules, and they were straightforward. The

first—BE NICE—was something they agreed would apply to both of them, and was subject to a margin of error of roughly fifteen percent. Either one of them could fuck up and be forgiven as long as it fell within the tolerance. So far, the rule was a success. Backing off just that little bit brought them closer. They were learning the arts of compromise and negotiation, and maybe even the hormone thing was smoothing out a little.

The second—PASS YOUR GRADE—was more complicated. Also more simple. Len got involved. Wrecker could pass tenth grade and continue to work for him, Len decreed, or he could not pass it and find some other line of work.

Melody got out of Wrecker's way, the day that news was delivered. The boy was out of his mind with fury. The next day he was ashamed, and that was even more brutal to watch, almost impossible for her to stay sidelined. On the third day he was morose. And then she very tentatively approached him with an offer of help, and he (bristling and insulted, and who could blame him?) rather ungraciously accepted, and together they struggled through the home-school segments he'd had trouble with.

He passed them.

Today was celebration, plain and simple. They had no need for rules today. Wrecker had finished his exams the month before and had been on a run of nice since then, with only a few fairly isolated shithead moments. She'd had a few herself and he'd forgiven her those. Today was a special day. June 30, 1981, his sixteenth birthday.

"Sweet sixteen," Jack said, and let out a long, low whistle. "Glad you called me."

Melody and her brother were slouched against a picnic table in the backyard behind the farmhouse. Every few years Jack would motor in unannounced, gunning his two-seater BMW over muddy washboard and ruts, half sliding down the abandoned drive to park as close as he could get to the farmhouse, and he and Wrecker would be inseparable for however many hours Jack had mysteriously allotted to the visit. Then he would disappear again. Sometimes gifts for the boy arrived in the mail. No card, no message. But who else would send a new set of handlebars to replace the mangled ones he'd destroyed in a jump?

Wrecker and his friends were building a fire in the barbecue pit, while Jack shouted random bits of bad advice from his bench seat. Jack could hardly move. He'd driven down from Seattle two days before with a bushel of oysters packed in ice in the trunk of his car and the bright idea to take Wrecker backpacking—bushwhacking, he figured—across the King Range and down to the coast. Melody found this hilarious. Jack was an urban boy whose tenting experience was limited to Boy Scout camp before they threw him out for bad behavior. He had a shiny new backpack and a bedroll still in the bag from Abercrombie & Fitch. Wrecker had done his best to protect him. As long as Jack stayed away from skunks, Wrecker had promised, he'd get his uncle home in one piece. If Jack got skunked, he was on his own.

Melody glanced at her brother. Crippled, but he'd recover. Jack got the family looks. Rangy, fine-boned—the Irish trumped everything else in him. Melody had hazel eyes, eyes the color of brackish water, but Jack's were as blue as Wrecker's. The skin around them was wrinkled from too many hours squinting at legalese, but even at thirty-five he had a boyish, devil-may-care expression, and a dimple in his chin that sealed the deal with women. He couldn't make love stick any better than she could, though. Two marriages that went up in flames and a guilty conscience that resulted in alimony for both women.

Jack's visits tended to correspond with his divorces. He'd come for the first time post-Amanda when Wrecker was ten, stayed a few days, took the boy on a wild spree in Eureka—arcades, movies, the batting cage, enough junk food to bring on gale-force vomiting and a headache that didn't abate until Jack was gone—and Wrecker loved it. They were well matched. Jack viewed a gap in any conversation as an opportunity to rebuild the world with words, and Wrecker was a quiet boy who paid attention. Melody wished Jack would spend more time with Wrecker, but her brother had no staying power. He looked good and talked a blue streak but it took a special combination of guilt and self-interest for him to stay in the game once his initial curiosity wore off. His relationships with women proved it. His first marriage lacked that combination; his second tanked when his wife discovered he'd been supplementing their marital bliss with visits to call girls when he went away on business and one time—once only, he swore, only that once—when they traveled together on vacation. He was fastidious about work, preparing his briefs diligently and following up on contacts and opportunities, but his personal life intruded in unsavory ways. He was busted for soliciting sex with an undercover policewoman in his office during working hours. He conducted an affair with his boss's wife. There weren't many bartenders in town who didn't recognize his mug, or welcome him by name when he sauntered through their doors. But there were no records of liaisons with underage girls (*good*, Ruth said crisply), no arrests for public drunkenness, no injuries attributed to his compromised condition. He coached a Little League team—the Tewksbury Tigers—and showed up sober. The kids loved him for his irreverence, his sense of fun, and for what they rightly felt was his acute interest in their well-being and sports prowess. He had good intentions and the wherewithal to follow through. But when the next season rolled around, the Tigers were looking for a new coach. Jack gave them one successful season and then pulled up stakes and moved across the country, an irate husband of one of the players' moms in hot pursuit. All of this, and more, he reported to anyone who would listen.

"Gentlemen, ignite!" Jack called. He lifted his mirrored sunglasses and added, "And lady. My apologies." He tilted his head toward Melody. "What'd you say her name was? The cute girl."

"Sarah." Melody found it hard to believe this girl—perky, good-hearted, dumb as a rock—would be sixteen in a few weeks, too.

"Oh!" Jack shouted, as the kindling caught and the fire roared. "Houston, we have blast-off!"

The buckeyes were small, still, the round nuts loading the branches of the backyard trees. The thermometer said 88. It hadn't rained in three weeks. That was normal for this time of year, the grass edging toward amber, the cows lowing over the washes, new fawns, still wearing their spots, scampering with their mothers through the pool of Melody's headlights when she drove home at night. Ruth had heard a mountain lion scream three nights in a row. A fox had made off with the last of Johnny Appleseed's elderly chickens. Melody's neighbors' crops ripened in their fields and under their grow lights. There was money to be made hand over fist in the bud market, and Melody wasn't tapped in to any of it. There was one main reason for that.

Willow was with Len and Meg at the other picnic table, fighting a breeze to lay down a tablecloth. Ruth had control of the kitchen and was running some kind of potato salad factory in there. Melody watched Willow grip the cloth edges and laugh as Len let the wind tickle his edge out of his hands. Willow was laughing more, lately. Meg laughed too, standing to one side, her fist clutched to her mouth. Meg was easy to love. Willow—she was harder. They were such opposites, Melody and Willow, stuck to each other by the shared bonds of respect and affection and property and history and antagonism. It rankled that Willow was so often *right*. But she'd been wrong about Wrecker, hadn't she? Maybe she was wrong about the cultivating, too. Willow had been adamant when they'd bought the place. She would associate neither her name nor her money with Bow Farm unless Melody could assure her that there would *never*—under *no* circumstances—be illegal plants grown on the acreage. Inside or out. Hither or yon, over hill or dale, *comme ci, comme ça*, Melody thought—and a good thing Johnny Appleseed kept his patch well hidden when he'd been financing his covert activities that way.

"Oh, Jesus, Jack. I didn't tell you about the time we got raided by the DEA." Melody leaned back and laughed, rueful. "That was *so* fucked up."

"You were growing pot?"

"No way." She nodded toward the wind-swelled tablecloth. "Willow wouldn't let us." It was just as well, though, maybe. Having Wrecker changed the way she looked at things.

Jack shifted to watch the others. His eyebrows rose and he gave a short, sharp bark of a laugh. He leaned closer to Melody. "Hey. When'd Willow and Len get together?"

"What?"

"Oh," he said, backing away. "Was it a secret?"

"No," Melody said. "What? No. Wait. What?"

"Oh," Jack said. "Sorry." He wrinkled his lip in amusement.

Melody snorted. Jack was full of shit. He was sure that any friendship between a man and a woman had to be sexual. Why not? he'd said. If you like somebody . . . and Melody had countered with the decency argument (Melody, of all people)—sanctity of marriage, blah blah—to which he nodded gravely and said, Oh. Thanks so much for setting me straight on that.

Jack, who'd made a play for Ruth when he first arrived. Out of respect, he insisted.

"You got raided?" Jack said politely. "Care to tell me about it?"

Melody looked closer. Willow and Len? Not possible.

"Uncle Jack!" That was Ryan, Wrecker's friend who, to his father's deep regret, stood only four-eleven at sixteen. He had the bottom-heavy look of a marsupial and a mind quick enough to outwit any adult he'd ever met.

"Yo!" Jack creaked his way up from the picnic bench and shielded his eyes from the sun.

"Tell Wrecker to go get his Frisbee."

"Get it yourself," Wrecker answered. He laid a shoulder into Ryan's midsection and lifted him off the ground. They were playing a kind of rugby, Wrecker and Ryan and the kid who drove the Corvette—what was his name?—and the girl Sarah. They lacked a ball and made up for it with Ryan.

"Where's it at?"

It was in Wrecker's cabin, Ryan sputtered, his voice muffled by the bodies that lay on him.

"Come with me," Jack said. "I want to hear about this raid. As your attorney, and all."

"Yeah, right," Melody retorted. "You'd let me rot in jail."

"No! I'd visit you to find out where you kept your stash. *Then* I'd let you rot in jail."

Melody untangled herself from the picnic bench and shouted to Wrecker. He should check with Ruth, she said. She might want him to put the oysters on soon.

Wrecker extracted himself from the scrum and faced her. He knew, he said. He was going to. His tone of voice said: You don't have to tell me.

Melody took an extra moment to look at him, standing there. "See?" she said to Jack. "See what a pain in the ass he is?"

Beautiful, he agreed. And her heart swelled to see her boy grown tall like that, strapping, independent, still here, mouthing off, catapulting toward his future but for the moment standing shining in her sight.

Wrecker's cabin smelled like peat with a hint of wet dog and motor oil.

"Jesus," Jack said, stepping inside. "Something die in here?"

Melody hovered outside. Better to let Jack negotiate the mess. She had too many battles running already with her son to want to take on the condition of his cabin. Her mother had forced her to keep her room clean, make her bed every morning and run the vacuum on the weekends, and look where that had gotten her: the crowned queen of mess. It was half that—the futility of it—and half that it took too damn much effort to hassle the kid into cleaning it up. Twice a year she went at the barn with a vengeance, cleaning it down to its bones, but the rest of the time she was content to sweep sporadically and straighten here and there, knock down the dust if it had laid up thick enough to write in with a finger. Her restoration efforts had petered out once she had a place dry enough and warm enough to satisfy her comfort levels. It was good enough for government work, she told Jack. Good enough for the girls I go with, he answered gleefully. "Smells like boy." Jack's voice sounded hollow. He was trying to avoid breathing. "Man. Mom would've killed us."

"Should I make him clean it up?"

"Hell, no." He flashed her a sardonic grin. "Wait'll he leaves home, then torch it."

That was the problem, Melody thought. Half the time she thought she was too strict, laying on chores, making him pull his weight around the farm, and the other half she was convinced she was letting him get away with murder in the name of freedom. It was exhausting, really. There was no reliable scale that let her know whether she was doing a decent job or screwing him up royally. It seemed like pure luck—better luck than she deserved, for sure—that he was (she crossed her fingers, here; she knocked on wood) turning out okay. More than okay. Turning out to be a person whose company she enjoyed. At the end of most days, it was Wrecker she wanted to hang out with.

Jack emerged into the waning light with a Frisbee in his hand. "Another minute and you'd have to go in after me with oxygen."

"That bad?"

"Pretty bad." Jack tossed the disk into the air and caught it. "He's a good kid, sis. How'd you manage that?"

"I had help," she said soberly. It was the truth of the matter. Without Ruth and Len and Willow, without Johnny Appleseed when he'd been around, Sitka and the pups—without even Jack—she'd have failed miserably. Well, and maybe with a different kid. Wrecker had some rough edges but they were nothing compared to what she'd been like, growing up.

Jack draped his arm over her shoulders and they walked the path back toward the farmhouse. "He said school's been a bitch for him."

"He talk much about that?"

"He doesn't talk much about anything. But I gather he's not exactly a scholar."

Melody shrugged. "He's smart. Anybody can see it. He'd just rather figure things out on his own, with his hands, than learn it in a book." She paused and ferreted a thorn from her sock. "Some of his friends board in Fortuna, go to the high school there."

"You think you could make him go?"

"Not really. Plus, there's no way in hell I could afford it."

Jack grinned noncommittally and looked off to the distance. That's how it was between them. Melody had to sweat and scrape each month to make ends meet and Jack went through life with his hand in the cookie jar. The car, the job, the house with the beach view—he had it all. Not that Melody would trade places. She'd decided early on it wasn't worth the price. She'd had help to buy Bow Farm; that was enough. Still, the difference between them was enough to throw a dose of awkwardness into any conversation where the topic came up.

"You could ask Dad."

Melody glanced at him sharply. "Right."

Jack stepped to the side and paused to scrutinize her. "You've got a great life here, Melody," he said. She snorted, and he shook his head. "You do. I respect it. But how are you going to send Wrecker to college? He's sixteen, Melody. How're you going to help him get started?"

Melody kept walking. There was a low roar in her head it was hard to think through. "He doesn't want to go to college."

"He might."

Melody stopped on the path and spun to face him. "You know what, Jack? Fuck you. Dad disowned me. So don't make it like I'm a bad mother for turning down some imaginary help for my son." She turned again and stalked ahead. The Frisbee sailed over her head and collided with a branch. She stooped to pick it up. Then she turned and spun it at him, hard.

Jack caught the disk and shook it at her. "That shit's in your head, sis. You think Dad gives a crap about twenty grand? The man's a fucking millionaire." He spun the toy on his finger. "They'd like to see you."

Melody laughed a short, surprised gasp. "For what?"

"Beats me. You're such a bitch." Jack caught up with her and nudged her in the ribs with the Frisbee. "But maybe they'd just like to help. I mean, why not? Let them be grandparents."

"You know the kind of help I could use? Spend a little more time with him yourself. Don't just show up and be the hero when it's convenient."

"*Moi*? I'm a hero? Oh, I like that." Jack flashed his roguish grin. No wonder women fell for him, Melody thought. It was hard to stay mad. "But listen, sis." His voice turned suddenly serious. "Don't count on me. You're the solid one." Jack walked a few fast paces ahead and then turned and walked backward. He crowed, "The solid one who got raided by the Drug Enforcement Agency."

"Yeah," she scoffed, and shook her head. "I'm just glad Wrecker wasn't there when they came."

Jack walked beside her, then, and she told him how she and Wrecker had spent the day in Eureka shopping for new basketball shoes. Size ten and a half—he was thirteen and growing out of everything, and she had the day off from the Mercantile. "We got back to the farmhouse and Ruth was a mess. Two guys with dark windbreakers and mirrored sunglasses came in and told her they had to search the place. They ransacked it. When I got back to the barn it was pretty clear they'd been there, first."

"They had a warrant?"

"They told Ruth they did, but when Willow showed up she demanded to see their badges, and they cleared out."

"Shit, Mel. That's scary."

"Maybe. But we don't grow, so they didn't find anything. Assholes took some cash from the barn, though."

"They weren't DEA."

"Then who were they?"

Jack shook his head. "Couple of thugs, sounds like. Why didn't you tell me about this when it happened?"

Melody brushed the stray hair out of her eyes. "I had bigger fish to fry. They took the bag of cash I was holding until Monday to deposit in the bank. The drawer from the Merc." She shook her head. "It wasn't a ton of money. Two fifty, three hundred bucks, maybe. But I was freaked. That was way more than I could cover. So I tried to get a hold of Dreyfus to tell him." She flashed a glance at Jack. "This is the fucked-up thing. Nobody saw Dreyfus again. I kept the Merc open for a couple of days until his business partners sent a truck and a carpenter up from Oakland to haul out the inventory and board up the place. Everything perishable, we just gave it away."

"And you were out of a job."

"After ten years." They were nearly to the farmhouse.

"They never found Dreyfus?"

"Nope." She shook her head. "I'm just glad Wrecker wasn't there when they came. He has a thing about cops."

"What kind of a thing?"

She glanced up at him briefly and then back down. "A pretty bad thing."

Jack tilted his head toward her. "Yeah. You know, you never told me the whole story about him. Before and all."

"What's to tell?" Melody shrugged. "Shit happened. His mother couldn't take care of him and Len knew her, so he adopted him. Meg was sick, so I got on board right after that."

"You adopted him."

Her brow wrinkled. "Sort of."

"What do you mean, 'sort of'?"

They could smell the smoke from the fire and see Ruth through the trees. "Well," Melody said, "I never, like, did any paperwork."

Jack stopped in his tracks. "So you have no legal rights."

Melody's eyes darkened and she looked away. "I've raised him all this time, Jack. He's my son."

"Yeah?" he said. "Says you. Says Wrecker. But what if something happened to Len?" They were back at the farmhouse. "Let's talk about this later." Jack stepped into the yard, lithe and power-ful, and sailed the plastic disk into the dusk.

The kids were playing chicken; Ryan riding the shoulders of Corvette Boy, Sarah perched atop Wrecker. The light was wan-ing. The fire in the pit crackled merrily. Meg and Ruth were standing beside a picnic table laden with potato salad and corn on the cob and baked beans and sliced tomatoes and the box of oys-ters ready to be grilled. Melody stood just outside the frame of it, taking the picture to preserve in her memory: her brother, her friends, her kid, his friends, on the day he turned sixteen in the place she loved more than any other in the world, perfect, per-fect, perfect, if Jack would just leave that shit alone, as the disk soared high and hovered for a moment and then turned on its trajectory and arced its way back to land.

It was headed for Wrecker. In one fluid motion he raised his arms and lifted Sarah over his head and placed her safely on the ground, and then, without a break, he dove—graceful as a por-poise, streamlined and in perfect accord with his body—to catch the disk. His hand sealed, sure, around it, and Wrecker continued his slow airborne descent to earth.

There was a boulder that wouldn't get out of the way.

There was the moment of impact, and the sudden damping of all sounds but the one crack, the sound of his bone breaking, and then—from this boy who never cried—the low-pitched *unh* of pain.

And then Melody was flying, was by his side.

The cast accomplished what poor grades had failed to do: it kept Wrecker unemployed that summer. He was in a foul mood. His body conspired to return to work and fired off signals that drove his brain berserk with their force and persistence. He couldn't walk, couldn't drive, but he could damn well crutch, and he wore out the rubber buttons on their bottoms racing the quarter mile to the road each day to collect the mail. He made Melody drive him to the sports store in Eureka so he could buy himself a training bench and a set of free weights. His shoulders bulked out while the muscles of his right leg languished. He grumbled bitterly. He had come upon his calling, and instead of being out in the woods felling timber, he was stuck at home watching reruns of *Mister Ed.*

He took up fishing.

It was Ruth's idea. Wrecker could mobilize well enough over rough ground to make his way down to the Mattole and back. Why not make himself useful once he got there? She liked fish. All of them did except Melody, who could go on eating her red beans and pumpkin seeds and pass up the nice poached steelhead with lemon butter. Ruth fashioned a creel out of an inner tube and a pair of old jeans. She bullied Len into providing a rod and reel. Every morning she made Wrecker a lunch and watched him hobble down the path toward the river. Some days he returned with a fish squirming in the creel, some days he didn't, but his mood improved noticeably. Ruth grew suspicious. Wrecker was an independent boy, but he was not solitary by nature. He was angling, she began to suspect, for something other than fish.

She cornered him one day when he slid a speckled trout into the kitchen sink. "Nice fish," she said. She reached into the sink and grasped the slippery body, stabilized it on the drainboard, and whacked it over the head with the wooden mallet she used to tenderize game. The fish's mouth gaped open and its eyes grew cloudy. One more whack and the body lay limp. She looked purposefully at Wrecker. "Something new down at the river?"

It was into the second half of August and Wrecker's hair had grown out thick and shaggy, sun-bleached, a shelf of it spilling into his eyes. Behind the hair his eyes sparkled. "New? Nah," he said, his voice gruff but his eyes laughing.

Ruth cocked an eyebrow and determined to sleuth it out. She gutted the fish, cleaned it, dredged it in flour. She lit the propane burner and heated oil in a pan and scalloped some potatoes and baked them while the fish sizzled on the stovetop. The next morning, a fine, fresh, August day, she packed his lunch, gave him a short head start along the path, and followed behind.

Ruth was huffing by the first bend in the trail. The crutches slowed him down, but not nearly enough for her to keep up. She stopped and used her apron to dab at the sweat that ran into her eyes. By the time she reached the base of the hill, her heart was pounding—*chug-ah chug-ah*—like a rickety steam engine, and the boy had vanished from sight.

Ruth rested with one pudgy forearm wedged into the crotch of a tan oak. Pain radiated up her right side and she heard an unfamiliar, faintly ominous wheezing sound come out of her rib cage that scared her enough to turn around and retreat slowly to the farmhouse. She didn't want to collapse there on the path where Wrecker could find her on his way back. The plan would need to be amended.

The next day she had her stealth on. Also a hat, a sturdy pair of walking shoes recycled from the free box at the Presbyterian church, a stripped stick that balanced her over rocky ground, and a pair of binoculars looped around her neck that she cursed every time they banged against her sternum. In her pocket she carried a *Peterson Field Guide to Birds of North America*. If anyone asked, she was birdwatching. She had borrowed the gear from Willow. There was nothing wrong with taking up a new hobby; she could use the exercise, and this time she paced herself, trudging along the path instead of trying to keep him in her sights. True, he might veer from the river route, head deep into the trees or cut toward the road, but she would take the risk on his destination. Didn't he bring back fish? There was something—something or someone— down at the river that had him hooked.

Exercise was overrated, Ruth decided, puffing even at the slower pace. She paused to let her racing heart slow. Every single thankless joint in her body squawked when she took them out on parade. She was sixty-eight years old and had the balance of a drunken sailor, a finicky ticker pulsing in her chest, and unreliable eyesight. There was a perfectly good chair in the kitchen of the farmhouse that offered a more sensible and comfortable place to locate her wide backside. It had to be said that bushwhacking miles through poison oak and blackberry bushes was no easy stroll. Ruth wrinkled her nose and sneezed pollen into her embroidered handkerchief. Then she shouldered her small satchel and continued along the trail.

She was sixty-eight, but she was a hell of a long way from decrepit. She still cooked and cleaned and handled the laundry, churning it in the wringer-washer and clipping it onto the line to dry. Her blunted fingers fumbled when she tried to thread a needle or repair the tiny tired guts of the vacuum motor, but she climbed ladders, weeded the garden, swore with abandon when the occasion warranted it. She surprised them all by praying. They shouldn't be alarmed, she said. It was a precautionary measure. She'd taken a few missteps in her life and just wanted to point out the mitigating factors.

It had been a while since she'd visited a church. Not since her mother was alive, bless her tender skinny little soul, and gently herded them all, scrubbed and freshly dressed, out the door on Sunday mornings. *We always have time to go to God's house*, in that voice so soft and quietly persuasive no one gave a thought to disagreeing. Even her father went along, his back bent with the weight of hauling in the nets and offloading the catch at the end of each day. He'd wink at Ruthie at the end of the pew, the tallest, the only girl in a sea of small boys. Ruth didn't mind church. It was quiet in there, and clean, and all they had to do was listen and pray. She'd considered the convent but there were too many things she'd grown to like that weren't allowed. Her father thought she'd stay home. And she might have, if Elizabeth hadn't shown up on the front steps of the library that day.

The river was slow this time of year, but Ruth cocked an ear and caught its whisper. It wasn't that bad a walk, really. Just the breakneck cliffside descent ahead of her which she'd be lucky to survive and luckier still to manage to haul her sorry butt up the face of when she was heading home. She should have just asked the boy again. Tickled him until he spit it out, or been content to stumble forward in darkness. Ha! As if there were any chance that he could keep anything important from her. From Ruth, who knew him better than she knew the nose on her own face. She creaked forward the last few paces until she had a clear view of the river beach. And then she steadied herself on the trunk of a tree that branched sideways before it climbed skyward.

Well. There was her answer.

Ruth slung the satchel from her weary shoulders and eased herself to the ground. The hot August sun baked a sweetness from the dust and pine duff, and a smile yawned across her face. Wide. Gap-toothed and sloppy and quivering and out of her control, and right behind it a clutch of unattended tears shoved and scrambled their way forward.

He was down there, all right. His blond mop shone in the sun and his plaster cast stiffened his leg straight out in front of him while he reclined on the sand, his arms bent sharply at the elbows to cradle his head. Pitched beside him like a loyal dog was a cheap nylon tent, blaze orange, staked and saddlebacked, its snout pointing toward the water. And coming out of the river was a girl. Skinny-dipped and dripping wet and headed right toward him.

Not all people were born into happiness, like Ruth was. Not all people grew up cherished and honored, as she had. Not everybody— not many at all, really—had the luck (what else could you call it? the undeserved blessing) to find the person who made them *more*. More themselves. More all right in themselves. Through what they shared. But Ruth was lucky. From that very first day, she had Elizabeth.

Not that Elizabeth knew it, then. Elizabeth thought this baby-faced girl—this *teenager*—on the library steps was no more than a distraction. Well, a *sweet* distraction. A confection. A surprisingly complex confection, a much richer-than-anticipated dessert, in fact a meal in herself, really, a nutritious, energizing, *luscious*, yes—and Ruth had her then, and for the rest of Elizabeth's life Ruth made sure she never went hungry.

This girl down in the river, climbing out of the river, swaying loose-limbed toward Wrecker—she might not be his Elizabeth, but Ruth was certain he had found a girl who was willing to enter-tain the possibility. The possibility of him. And what more could she wish for him than that? To have the chance to be seen, to be known—he was built for this, this boy, this blessing, this gift, this kid saturated with love. He'd been the apple of someone's eye. And then he'd been dealt a blow so severe he might have been made cruel by it. All these years Ruth had watched to see which way he would turn and there were times she'd held her heart in her throat, watching his anger explode. He wanted to blow up the world. He wanted to knock it all down, reduce it to smither-eens, and he could—with his fists, with a word, with each choice. It was for him to decide. He could throw himself into the sea as she had done. There was no choice but that, really—to throw himself in, into life, and see what became of him.

A peal of laughter sprang up from below and Ruth closed her eyes, yielded them their privacy. With her eyes closed her heart fluttered—a large leap and several smaller ones—and she was flooded without warning with Elizabeth: the color of her skin, the daredevil glint in her eye, her devotion to books and to justice and to Ruth, the way the sunlight fell across her hair when she slept in Sunday mornings. Ruth could hardly bear it. The feel of Lizzie's hands on Ruth's hips, coming up behind her at the bathroom sink as she brushed her teeth. The mash of lips, the taste of spearmint and blood where tooth grazed lip. The urgent drop to the rug. The furious reach and grope—*still to want*, after so many years, to want so fiercely what you deeply have—and then the wave that arched her from the floor and left her sweaty, gasping, newborn.

Ruth waited for her breath to still.

When Elizabeth died Ruth did as she'd desired: she let the funeral men take Lizzie's body away and deliver her ashes in return. And just as Elizabeth had asked, Ruth had packed them gently in the old car they shared, set them safely, comfortably, on the front seat, propped by pillows—and driven the long distance to the beach they once had loved. She'd parked the car in the lot, left the keys balanced atop a front tire.

Just shake 'em out, Lizzie had instructed, laughing. Just send 'em sailing. That way, wherever you go in this big world, I'll have already been there. To its beaches, anyway. Waiting for you.

Ruth hadn't meant to walk so far. She hadn't thought she'd walk through the night, wait until morning came to sit, weary, on a drift log. Or that she'd remain rooted there until the sun caught hold of the day and burned back the fog. But then she carefully removed the lid of the box, untwisted the tie that held the plastic bag closed, and reached her trembling hand in.

Soft. So soft.

When she finished, her clothes had come off and she had waded belly-deep into the frigid water. She set the box, a merry little boat, upon the swells. And surrendered herself to the waves.

Ruth lay on the bluff that broached the river, now, and felt that day tremble through her. Her hands opened and closed like bivalves on the soft duff. She felt a rumble in her belly and recognized it as laughter. Her own. Soft and quiet, far too still to carry, but joining the laughter below.

When she woke up that day to Willow's worried face hovering over her, she knew she'd lost her Liz. She knew she was gone. There was no following her. So she gave up then, at that. She gave up everything. Who she'd been. What she'd had. Even what she'd wished for. And then—more than a year later—Wrecker had come, with his face that switched from a fist to a shining star, and let her love him.

Sitting up now, the voices of the children rising from the river below, Ruth felt the chuckles spill painfully from the side of her mouth. Her ribs hurt. Her creaky aching muscles had tuned up their symphony of complaint. It took a ridiculously long time for her to stand up. Good Lord. She would need a week to recover from this crazy idea. *If* she made it home in one piece. She was still laughing. It made her side hurt worse. But she would never give that up. She would die laughing. It seemed a better way to go, all in all.

They all had secrets at Bow Farm. This was Wrecker's, and nothing could make her give it up.

18

CHAPTER ELEVEN

The bus squealed to a stop, opened its gassy maw, and belched its passengers onto the pavement.

Lisa Fay stumbled down the steps and took a long, deep breath. Was that what freedom smelled like? The diesel-tinged, soot-soaked air of San Francisco reeked of catastrophe. She swallowed hard. Behind her, passengers jostled for position by the Greyhound's luggage hatch and clambered about for their bags. They swarmed as one body and moved off in a mass and left her standing there, hardly able to breathe at all.

"This yours?"

The driver offered her a tattered suitcase belted with duct tape. He gripped the bag firmly and avoided her eyes.

She shook her head. Lisa Fay carried everything she owned in a paper shopping bag. They'd issued her a tote on discharge but she'd left that behind at a rest stop on the highway in Coalinga. As soon as she found a place to buy new clothes she'd get rid of the ones they'd provided, too. She wanted nothing of theirs.

"Terminal's that way." The driver flopped the suitcase on a cart alongside cardboard boxes and stepped briskly from the bus.

Lisa Fay watched his back recede. It was dusky in the parking garage. Motes of dirt rode the stale air and the buses huffed and whined as they eased into their slots and discharged their cargo. They were a clan of dull-witted creatures, and Lisa Fay was seized with the wish to live there among them, lumbering and dispirited, each day's demands mapped out in advance. The idea of stepping into the light of the city morning paralyzed her. But the bus driver paused with his luggage scow and fixed her with a suspicious squint. She understood. She was not a bus. She was a free woman, and this was no way for a free woman to act. She tightened her grip on the paper handles of her bag and aimed herself toward the door. It opened for her. She stepped into the Transbay Terminal and felt the air whoosh behind her as it shut.

Inside the terminal everyone moved swiftly. Lisa Fay let the energy propel her toward the ticket windows. She had planned it carefully: buy a bus ticket north, finagle a ride west, follow the map Willow had drawn to Meg's house. There were no buses into the Mattole Valley. They stopped at Garberville and then passed on to Fortuna, Eureka, up into Oregon—as far north as you wanted to go, but if you were headed west then good luck to you. She had a map of the state that showed the area as a hazy green blur. Lisa Fay knew there were roads where Meg lived. Willow had drawn them in, labeled them in her confident hand. But they were too small to show up on the map of the state; they weren't real enough, she suspected, to show up. That area, that whole knob of land, seemed like a new growth on the body of California, some untendered, nonnegotiable figment of the imagination, risky for visitors and subject to change without notice. She pictured it a Shangri-La that disappeared behind the mists once the rains started and only reemerged when the sun came back and baked it dry. Which is why she should go now, in October, in the dry time.

Or risk losing him for good. That land was so wild, her friend Alma had told her, a person could get lost in those mountains and never get found. Lisa Fay glanced down at the crumpled map she held. The creases were worn white from the hours she'd spent studying it. Her rib cage ached, her bones, those muscles, her heart—Wrecker *couldn't* be lost. There were big trees, weren't there? She calmed herself with that thought. Enormous trees. You can drive a car through one, Alma had told her. If the land could support giant trees surely it could hold on to one small boy. She screwed her courage and approached the ticket window.

"How much to Garberville?" Her voice was a whisper.

The clerk turned to face her. He had kind eyes, loose and watery, behind thick lenses, and a neck that rested in accommodating folds over a tight collar. "Speak up, dear." He tapped a bulbous device that wormed into his ear canal. "I can barely hear you."

"Garberville," she said, louder this time.

He nodded. His eyelids flickered rapidly, almost imperceptibly, but his gaze remained steady on her face. "Twice a day," he said. "You missed the first one. Next bus leaves at one fifty. Check back for the platform number. How many in your party?"

Her voice was so soft it barely puffed past her lips. "Only me."

"Three?" He tilted his head to thrust the listening device closer to her.

Lisa Fay shrank back from the window. His eyes were too friendly. The plastic aid was disturbing, and the next bus would not leave until one fifty. It was 1983, she was forty-one years old, and she'd been waiting fifteen long years to see her son. She could make her own decisions, now; wasn't that true? She could determine for herself who to smile at, how to move in the world, where to rest and when to move again. And still she would have to wait. Fifteen years. One fifty. Five hours. Five hours? Fifteen long years and for the moment she could remember none of it. Her mind was flooded with the image of his face as he had been, and she could barely stand. A small cry escaped her lips.

"Miss?" The clerk's eyes glistened with concern.

She turned her back on him and fled into the city.

Lisa Fay stood on the sidewalk and let the sunshine strike her eyelids and warm her cheeks. The city noises filled her ears. The city smells traveled in through her nose to reach that part of the brain that forgets nothing.

She'd meant to write a letter. She had started it a thousand times in her head; a dozen times she put pen to paper. *Dear Son.* And had gotten no further.

She'd written a letter to Meg, a long one, and heartfelt.

Dear Son.

There was so much to tell him.

A paper cup lay overturned in the gutter; a pigeon lit beside it and gave it an idle, exploratory peck. A bus rumbled by and the draft lifted the edge of Lisa Fay's untucked blouse. The air smelled better out here. There was salt from the bay and a sweet burnt odor from a coffee cart down the block. It was terrifying to be free and terrifying to be alive and look how that pigeon went on pecking, nonchalant, nearly indifferent to the traffic that sped past. Lisa Fay hoisted the weight of her life onto her shoulders and trudged toward the smell of the water. Remove that yoke and she would blow like a piece of trash in the wind.

The bay was still there, dirty and uplifting. The Ferry Building squatted beside the water and suffered its slosh against the dark timbers of its dock. Lisa Fay set her bag onto a concrete bench and eased herself down beside it. There was bustle but no real rush, and she could sit there in the shadow of the elevated freeway and sink into her thoughts. A young cop lounged like a hoodlum against the building's weathered marble face. He cupped his hands to light a cigarette and caught her eye, and she quickly looked away.

She wanted her son to know his father. But what could she offer him, to make that true? What, to weigh against the absence? Arlyn was big, and strong, and never once in all the time she'd known him had she seen him put his strength to anything but good. Well, or whimsy. He could lift her in one arm, he could hoist her to his shoulder like a circus girl—and they'd laughed, they'd laughed. He had not meant to leave. She was sure of it. Dear Son, she thought. She despaired. Words were small and Arlyn had been a large man, large hearted, and there was no way she could think to tell him that. Lisa Fay unwrapped the remains of a muffin she had purchased at a rest stop. It tasted grainy and dry, peppered with tiny blueberries that lent texture but no taste. She ate a few bites and then carefully rewrapped it for later.

Arlyn loved food. Cabbage and cauliflower mostly, but The Hook had a sweet tooth, and one time he had bought her a steak dinner, enormous, more than she could eat, and for the first time in her life she got up from the table and left something on her plate. Wrecker loved food, too. Did he still? Dear Son, she thought. And then she wrenched her thoughts back to the privacy of her grief. She didn't know why he left, or where he went. The concrete bench stored the sun's warmth. It felt good to her when clouds grayed the sky for moments before scudding on.

She glanced around at the solitaries and small groups moving along the waterfront. Ghosts peopled her life. She could be going along with her business and find herself hijacked by memories forcing themselves onto the shapes of strangers. There were too many who ought to have been there but no longer were. Lisa Fay's parents were dead. Arlyn had disappeared. That hazy shape of a woman waiting a block away for the bus—that was not Belle.

Lisa Fay closed her eyes; felt the sun return from behind the clouds. When she opened her eyes again, the young cop had moved on. The clock by the Ferry Building read 10:15. She had slept a bit and woke anxious and confused. Everything was different, now. Fifteen years since she'd been in San Francisco, and the city she'd known inside and out, up and down, forward and back, had developed yawning chasms between neighborhoods that wouldn't allow her to traverse them in her mind. She could walk along the Embarcadero and eventually she would arrive at the ocean; but if she walked in the other direction, would she know where to turn to reach the Greek grocery? The apartment they'd lived in, was it still up that ratty flight of stairs, sunny in the mornings and ripe with the smell of olives floating in their brine beneath? She pictured the park, the sprawling reach of green, the duck pond where Wrecker loved to play. Which streets should she take to reach it? Her mind preserved memories as sharp as shards floating in a damaged geography. Was heaven like this? Was hell?

Belle would know. But Belle was gone.

Lisa Fay stood. She could get to Belle's flat. She could picture the way. Belle was gone, but if her building was still there it was one part of Wrecker's history that wouldn't be lost. Dear Son, she thought, her legs carrying her urgently across the wide boulevard that hugged the waterfront. Do you remember Belle? Lisa Fay's eyes watered as she recalled Belle's mottled hands, her sharp wit and the strength of her love. She brushed away her tears and strode on. The ground inclined up and away from the Embarcadero; the streets narrowed, and the people who traveled them kept their heads tucked with the resolve of someplace to go. The shop signs crowded together and shouted their messages in Chinese. On that corner, there—twenty years ago, an old crone had needed help setting up her produce stand and offered a corner of a storeroom for Lisa Fay to sleep in in exchange. Not just the room but the spoils, too, and sometimes a sweaty, crumpled dollar bill pressed into her palm; and when the old lady's grandson took over her position Lisa Fay faded into the foliage, slept a few nights tucked unseen among tree roots and tall stands of pampas grass. Later, she'd traded those trafficked spots for her cozy camp behind the DeYoung. Lisa Fay sighed and walked on, slower now, and the sun rose higher. She detoured up Vallejo in search of stairs she knew were there and felt the old familiar pull in her calves as her muscles strained to climb the hill. Back then she'd bounded up these slopes; later, with Wrecker tied like a twenty-pound barnacle to her back, she climbed them more cautiously. It winded her, now. She paused at its crest to gaze at the water.

It was exhausting, being there. All of her senses were on high alert, navigating, watching for danger, noting changes, grasping at all of the faces, hundreds and hundreds of them. At Leavenworth the number 27 bus pulled up beside her and she climbed aboard. People pushed past her to board the bus; they parted on the sidewalks to flow around her. At Chino they were packed like rats in the hold of a ship, but they were familiar rats. The fear tightened her scalp and lifted the roots of her hair. The sounds assaulted her. Chino had been loud with ugly noise, but it was predictable, regular. Everyone here moved with a head start past her. The enormity of the city confronted her. She could enter that door and sit at a table and look at a menu and someone would bring her food from a country she'd never heard of before. She could enter that door and it would be cupcakes, thirty different kinds in a pert lineup. Everyone was going somewhere, meeting someone, checking their watches or daydreaming at a bus stop.

Lisa Fay had no watch to consult. Her daydreams were memories, too full to escape from. They felt like floodwater she strained to hold back.

But it was clear, now: she had created an imaginary city in her head, a city composed of only those places that had meaning for her and none of the rest, and the city she crossed now was a brand-new city, shiny and charged and rife with land mines, memories that exploded in her as she turned a corner, blank spaces that overwhelmed her as she peered into neighborhoods she'd once known. She had to choose where to go. That side street? That alley? Toward the ocean, or away from it? To Belle's flat? To the park that last day?

Not there. Lisa Fay gripped the rail and turned to look out the window of the bus. The woman it mirrored back was obvious, exposed, an open book anyone could read. Her hair capped her head in a short pale helmet that made the lines on her face stand out more starkly. They were deep lines, marks a clawed animal will leave in fear and frantic effort. The bus paused at a stop and Lisa Fay hurried down the steps. She held her bag close to her chest and tucked her chin to hide her face. The blocks disappeared underfoot. Through the Tenderloin—she looked up to see a pair of lovers, their torsos entwined, wave to her from a window high above the street. She looked around, and then she raised one arm in a cautious salute.

There was more than what had been lost. What she had gained, what the city had brought to her, was written on her body as well. She moved on with an animal frenzy now, barely registering street names, crossing against the light, her feet pounding the concrete as though only motion could keep her from blowing apart. Dear Son. Lisa Fay looked up, startled by the sound of her voice as she spoke aloud. This city brought me heartbreak, but it brought me you.

The day Wrecker had been born, the pains had caught her by surprise. She was homeless once more. The building's owner had discovered the basement squat and booted them onto the street. Lisa Fay had shared the space with others—a blond bearded man, a girl who covered her mouth when she spoke, couples who came and went—and they scattered like raindrops when the man padlocked the door. Sadly she made her way off. Without her friends, life alone would be lonely. But then she felt the baby stir inside her and corrected her thoughts: life would never again be lonely. She had a little crocheted hat pushed down in the bottom of her bag for when her baby was born. She felt another kick, and then a flutter, and then lower down . . . she stumbled to her knees as the first contraction seized her like a field mouse caught in the tines of the thresher. Lisa Fay forced herself to standing. The sun fell bright over her like the raiments of a saint. She gripped the handles of her bag with all the ferociousness of fear and suddenly had to pee and just as suddenly felt the gush of warm water slide down the skin of her leg, bare beneath her skirt, and drench her rolled sock and pool in her canvas sneaker and turn the light gray of the sidewalk a deep, polished color and she stood there a minute, stunned.

She had planned to have her baby at home. That's what she told them all, proudly: "I'll be birthing him here," there in the basement squat with the long-haired girl to boil water and, after, the blond bearded man to score joints and pass them around like cigars, slapping the others on the back. But now this. And another set of contractions like a wrecking ball knocking down a row of buildings, each one crashing into the next with the force of the one behind. Lisa Fay waited until the pain slid back and stood again to get her bearings. She was closer to General Hospital than to the jaunty newness of St. Luke's. She plotted her route and started to walk.

It was early evening, then. It was late June. It was the middle of 1965, and all across the rest of the city the fog rolled in to temper the effects of the sun and chart a path for the night to follow. Downtown men in office buildings snapped shut their briefcases and loosened their ties, reached for their suitjackets. Jackhammers quieted, and the song of saws crying their way through pitchy lumber; men came down off their scaffolds, hung up their toolbelts, lowered the hoods of the cars they toiled on; they wiped the grease and numbers and latest marketing plan from their hands; they handed on the shift key at the great Cargill plant out at the piers; they quit the soft ruffle of paper money counted into the drawer; they stood with their faces averted from the wind to snap their Zippos and taste that first welcome Lucky of the evening. And after a bus ride, a loose lope up the hill, pit stop at the corner bar, after a quick wink at the bay and a wistful recollection of the sailboat they had hoped to have by now and a shrug to say so what, maybe later, they went in to their women.

Lisa Fay saw the welcome green of the Rolph Playground just ahead and knew she'd need to rest. It was still sunny in the Mission, but the children had all gone home and the courts weren't livened yet by the slap of the ball and the flash of bright-clad bodies colliding midair. She had the square of grass to herself, and she settled down onto the gentle slope and waited.

When the contractions came they ran through her fast and hard and she felt whipped like a rag doll, shaken and limp. But in between? All of the city came to comfort Lisa Fay, a crazy quilt that covered her, an old dog that lay down beside her. She closed her eyes and there stood Arlyn and the other longshoremen, their muscles bulging, offloading the freighters that docked and dropped their cargo from the Orient, from Russia, enormous holds of coconut coming in from the Philippines. She saw ducks hanging in the windows of the Chinese butcher shops, whole pigs and beef sides slid from the back of trucks to the shoulders of workmen who carried them through rear doors and out of sight. She turned and moaned and caught the wail of an ambulance rushing through the streets and the crash of waves at the Lands End strand and the train whistle sliding into the station and the clang of the cable car atop the California hill and there, softly, high heels muted by stained carpet. Lisa Fay struggled to listen but the contractions took over and what she heard was her own whimper and cry and ragged breath—and the chatter, somewhere close by, of a squirrel—and then rousing, in there, not timid at all, those first awkward efforts at bellow.

Amazed, she lifted her head to look.

And then dark closed in.

The sun had climbed as high as it could and had begun to roll toward the Pacific. Lisa Fay had missed the afternoon bus to Garberville. She was huddled in the corner of a bench facing a vast expanse of green. She had brought herself back to the park, as though there were no other place in this city her legs could think to deliver her. She had no place to go but the address of a shelter folded into her wallet. Nothing to do but start over.

Lisa Fay took a long, slow look around.

Or not.

She had not opened her mouth to speak, but the words echoed as loudly in her head as if she had.

Drugs smuggled in. A homemade shank. There were women in Chino who had chosen that road. They threw themselves under the wheels of whatever train would bury them fastest. The sad girl had cried herself close to death and finished the job with a bed sheet tied over the rail. And Lisa Fay had wanted desperately to follow her, to escape on her heels and flee that place. Alone in her cell, ten years into her term, she had made up her mind. She had secured the means. And it was almost more than she could do, to pry open her own fingers and drop those small red pills into the swirl of the sink.

One by one.

Until they were all gone.

Dear Son, she thought. For you I stayed.

Throughout the city there were weathered people worse off than she was—missing teeth, missing that part of the brain that defends against fracture and theft. In spite of everything she had dragged herself along. She had protected her right to exist.

I wanted to go to sleep. I wanted it strongly. I'd been kept awake for so long my brain wouldn't think.

For you, she thought. Then, because of you.

That wasn't quite right.

Thanks to you.

If she'd eaten those pills they would surely have killed her.

Son.

Thank you.

A raven with a velvet ruff speechified from its perch on a nearby trashcan. Across the street, a cat streaked along the top of a garden wall and disappeared into an alley. She was free. She had imagined this day for a long time. In her fantasy she had sent a letter and they had said: Come. You must come. We welcome you. Your son is eager to know you. She would take the bus as far as it would go, find someone to drive her. She would arrive on their doorstep.

The raven cawed and turned his shiny eyes on her.

They could as easily say: You have no place here.

They could say: Do not set foot near him.

They would not recognize her. They would have no reason to believe her when she told them Wrecker was her son.

He would have no reason—

Forfeited. Abandoned. Betrayed. She leveled the charges against herself.

A bitter taste on her tongue.

She hadn't mailed the letter to Meg. Why would she?

Lisa Fay sat for a long time while the sun sank lower and the shadows lengthened. Her stomach was a tight fist of pain. She needed to feed herself, but the thought of eating anything made the pain worse. The thought of rising, of walking to a store or a café to purchase food—that seemed impossible. There was still the muffin stub wrapped in her bag. She reached for it and pulled it out.

A skinny dog peered warily at her from behind a shrub. She hadn't noticed him before, and she was startled at first to see him so close. But there was nothing aggressive in his manner. He had a sharp snout and black liquid eyes and medium-length hair that switched abruptly from brown to a dirty white in a line down the middle of his face, and his ribs heaved—all of them visible—as he watched her nibble at the muffin.

Lisa Fay ate what she could and then carefully wrapped the paper around the remainder to save for later.

He was the first dog she'd been close to in fifteen years.

He blinked and looked away and she studied his profile. His chin was slightly lifted and the skin beneath it made a smooth line until it ruffled with longer hair at his neck. His chest was narrow but proportionate and he sat on his haunches nobly, like a statue. Then he yawned and rolled his weight backward as his hind leg lifted and he scratched furiously at the base of his right ear.

Lisa Fay's mouth lifted in a tentative grin.

The dog caught that. He must have. Because he trained his liquid gaze on her and opened his mouth and gave a short, soft pant that resembled a smile before he looked away again.

Lisa Fay felt it like a knife to her heart. And in return, she opened the muffin shroud and carefully left the food on the bench for him as she stood to walk away.

"Nice of you," a voice said. "But he probably won't eat it. Doesn't eat much."

Lisa Fay's gaze jerked back to the dog. She was startled to see a human shape behind him, a young man lying flat on the ground. He propped himself up on one elbow to face her and flung the other arm about the dog's shoulders.

"I've tried to fatten him up, but he likes what he likes. He's healthy, I guess."

Go, Lisa Fay's inner voices told her. *Go now.* Don't talk to strangers. Don't ask for trouble.

"What does he like?" Her voice had a faint quaver.

The young man sat up. He was as slender as the dog and he was dressed in a white cotton tunic and white pants. His dark hair was loose and bushy and he wore a scraggly dark beard that covered haphazard patches of his face. He wasn't old enough to grow a man's beard. He was a boy approaching manhood, and his eyes, dark and liquid like his dog's, looked trustworthy to her.

"Weird stuff. Bell peppers. Boiled potatoes." He scratched the dog's neck and gazed at him. "My parents feed him dog food, but he doesn't like it. So I try to sneak away sometimes and take him out for a run." He reached into his pocket and offered the dog a carrot chunk. He took it daintily and then lay down and held it between his paws and licked it. She heard the crunch as he broke off smaller chunks and swallowed.

The dog was Jasper. The boy was Garth. The dog still lived

with the parents, where the boy had lived until he'd left home the year before. He'd meant to see the world but had only gotten as far as Oakland. There was an ashram there, and he found he liked meditating. He could see the world later.

"They don't take dogs?"

"He meditates," Garth said, and smiled, "but not in a conventional way."

"I just got out of prison, Garth."

It is never quiet in the city. So the car horns went on honking and the buses whooshed by on the street and over on the trashcan the raven gave a short, bored caw.

The boy's eyes never stopped being trustworthy. He said, "That might account for the clothes."

Lisa Fay glanced down.

"Not that they aren't becoming," he said, blushing slightly, "but you don't look all that comfortable in them."

She looked at him, surprised.

He put his hands to the sides of his head. "I can't believe I said that." He stood up. He was very tall. "I have to take Jasper back."

"You take care, Garth."

The dog and the boy looked at her intently. Garth hesitated. "After that, I'm going back to the ashram. You could come." He watched her face. "It's open to everybody. There's a women's dorm. You could spend the night there, if you want." When she said nothing, he reached down and patted the dog. "I'll take him home. Maybe you'll be here when I come back. Maybe not." He shrugged, and grinned. "The nature of impermanence, and all."

She didn't expect him to return. When he did, he carried a plate covered in aluminum foil. It was a full dinner, and still hot. She ate it slowly and carefully. It was the first home-cooked meal she'd had in a very long time. He waited for her to finish, and then they stood and walked down Sixteenth Street and took the subway to cross the bay to Oakland.

Dear Son, she thought. Just one night.

The next night arrived.

Just one more.

And then another. And another. And another after that.

Just until she got onto her feet.

CHAPTER TWELVE

Wrecker planted his feet in the center of the small clearing and surveyed his domain.

He was pushing eighteen. Six feet tall, solid and unstoppable, he had a tender heart, muscles on him like a Russian bodybuilder, a crown of thick blond hair, and a diploma from the home-school company so fresh the ink had barely dried. Deedee'd been jonesing for that. Payback for him was this prime little patch of land upslope and out of sight. Dig a foundation, lay up some log walls—he was building himself a house, working so far off a flat spot and a vision, trying to make up for his late start.

Wrecker glanced around and took stock of what he had. There was so much new growth it was hard to tell he'd scraped this little stretch of level ground down to dirt the autumn before. Gorse and cheat grass, yellow broom and blooming lupine, everything gone rampant, growing too fast for even the deer and the rabbits to get a handle on. Just east of him the steep side of a hill had peeled off and slid to its base in the worst of the rains. This whole place was in a hurry, same as him. He breathed in deep, caught hints of sea salt and pine sap and something sweet. All he had to do was hike a little higher up the hill, ease himself out on the cantilevered trunk of the old maple, and peer through its branches to catch a glimpse of the ocean. There'd been some wild surf out there this winter; it beat the crap out of that kid who came up from the city to try to ride it at Big Flat. Fucking crazy. Crazy like *insane*. Though he'd thought about it, himself. Was tempted by it. Those monster waves. He hated the thought of passing up a chance that might not come around again for a while.

Wrecker crossed to the northwest corner of the plot. He had a picture window sitting in Len's lumber shed that would go here. It wouldn't be hard to score some smaller windows for the rest of the views. He had laid things out so he could keep an eye on the farmhouse and the barn down below, and there was Ruthie trudging up the hill right now, the last of Sitka's pups following stiffly behind. Ruth was clutching something to her that Wrecker guessed was food. His mouth watered. There was never a time that he was not hungry. But the hill was steep and Ruth and the pup were old and they'd be wheezing already. Wrecker waved his arm in a wide arc. "I'll come down," he shouted, and he closed the distance between them like a bull elk on his way to water.

"Made you something," Ruth said. She had to sit down. Asthma, she told them. Emphysema, more likely, Melody muttered. All those damn cigarettes. Should have cut her off, and Willow had lifted an eyebrow and said, How, exactly? and Wrecker had hid a grin. They were a stubborn bunch. Not that he was any more tractable. Willow had taught him that word. "Tuna fish sandwiches."

Wrecker flopped beside her and took what she handed him. She idly scratched the pup behind the ear. "You're a beautiful boy," she crooned.

"Ain't I, though."

"You?" Ruth snorted. "You're downright ugly. Too bad you didn't take after my side of the family. Slim—"

"—svelte," he repeated with her, his mouth full of sandwich, "and so good looking it ought to be outlawed."

"Close your mouth when you chew. And get down the hill. Your mother said it's time to go."

He pushed up to standing and offered a hand. "Race you."

She'd love that, she said. She'd just hate to beat him and ruin his self-esteem.

He gave her a quick squeeze. "See you in a week, Ruth."

She held him at arm's length and looked him over critically. "Don't let them give you no guff, boy. You're better'n the whole bunch of 'em put together."

Wrecker couldn't believe that Deedee had said yes. Jack must have caught her at the perfect moment. He could tell she was feeling great, now that he'd graduated; she told people she'd managed to get her kid through high school without having to tie him to his chair to do it, but the truth was, without Melody's constant leaning on him, Wrecker would have bailed early on. And the money thing, her other constant worry, seemed to have improved steadily since she'd squeaked through the meltdown at the Merc. She'd explained it to him, how there was a balloon payment on the farm that had to get paid off at the end of this month, and how after that they'd be clear of the mortgage. She'd hit at last on something vaguely profitable—selling tie-dyed shirts she made in the barn—and with him chipping in from his timber work they splurged and paid the phone company to come string a line to the farmhouse. When Jack called and begged her to come down to L.A. for his wedding, he caught her feeling fine. "I'll buy you guys tickets," Jack cajoled. It was dinnertime, and Melody told him to shout into the phone so everybody in the farmhouse kitchen could hear. "I want you there." He paused to clear his throat. With Jack, he might as well beat a drum roll. "They're old, Melody. They haven't seen you in nearly twenty years. And Dad's been sick."

Wrecker watched Melody pause and frown at the phone handset, stretched out in her hand in front of her. "Sick how?" she shouted.

"Prostate. He got the surgery last year." Wrecker glanced quickly at Ruth and winced. "It turned out okay, though. As in, he doesn't have the cancer anymore. The rest," Jack said, his voice adopting a phony tone of reserve, "I don't ask."

"Thank God for small favors," Ruth muttered.

Wrecker grinned. Jack tended to tell all, right down to the sordid details. He finished chewing a piece of gristle. "Getting married, though." He let out a long whistle. "What's with that, Jack?"

"There's a time for everything, buddy. Listen. You guys come down, just stay a few days. So you can meet them. Ruth, baby? You come too. It'll be fun. I promise."

"More fun than I can handle." Ruth raised her eyebrows at Melody. "You two go. Bring back presents."

Wrecker had to hand it to Jack. He'd had the sense to stop there, and now he and Deedee were booked on a flight out of the municipal airport in Eureka. The plan was to stay with Deedee's parents for a bit and leave for home once Jack got hitched. He pushed his way in through the farmhouse door and Melody flinched at the noise. "What?" he said defensively.

"What what?"

He shook his head. "I'm driving," he said. "Your anxiety could get us killed."

They got there early for the flight. It was an hour in the little puddle jumper to San Francisco, another forty minutes by jet to Los Angeles. Wrecker had never been in a plane before. He stretched his legs and faked nonchalance as they bounced along in the clouds. Melody caught his eye and rested her head against his upper arm. "They're going to love you. It's me we have to worry about."

Wrecker glanced at her sideways. "What'd you do to them?"

"What *didn't* I." She straightened her neck and gave her hands a couple of good shakes.

"Worse than me?"

"No comparison."

He lifted an eyebrow. He wasn't finished yet, he reminded her.

"Yeah? Well, bring it on, baby." She poked him in the ribs. "I'm ready."

Jack met them at the airport. He hugged Melody and then caught Wrecker in a headlock. Wrecker gently squeezed his way out from under Jack's arm and examined the new car. "Dude. You got a backseat."

"I got a family, and a whopping monthly payment." Jack tossed their bags into the trunk of the BMW. "Check out the leather, bro." He slid behind the wheel and glanced at Melody as she settled herself in front. "Listen," he said, lowering his voice to a stage whisper. "Mom and Dad? They're kind of off the wall."

Wrecker caught Melody's eye in the rearview mirror. She gave him an exaggerated wink. "About me?" She yawned. "So what's new?"

"Yeah. I wish." Jack glanced over his shoulder and pulled into traffic. He looked trim and groomed—his hair cut in a lawyerly brush and an expensive watch on his wrist—but there were dark circles under his eyes and a sallow look to his skin. "They think Jocelyn's gone over to the dark side. They asked me again if I was sure I wanted to marry her."

"Not a bad question, given your track record." Deedee had her head turned to study the roadside. "Look. Remember that?" Over and over she would point to something and exclaim, and Jack would laugh and nod, or scoff.

"Third time's a charm," Jack quipped. He glanced over the

seat back. "Sport? They're dying to meet you. But let me give you a word of advice. That caveman thing you got going on under your chin? Take a razor to it. Get you more chicks that way."

"Stop it, Jack. He's proud of his beard."

Wrecker couldn't help rubbing his hand across the fuzz. "No problem with the chicks, Uncle Jack. I could give you some tips if you want."

No, no, Jack said. He had all the action he could handle right now.

Melody snorted. "Why don't you pull over right here. I'm happy to walk the rest of the way," and then Jack was pulling the car into the driveway of the house he and Deedee had grown up in, and in spite of being with two of the people he loved most in the world, Wrecker had to clamp his teeth together hard to bar the mix of dread and longing that rose in his throat.

It wasn't the disaster it could have been. They were nice, they were polite, Deedee's mother was a basket case, the old man a drunk who pretended to be joking when he said mean things—all that was normal, from what Wrecker could pick up. Jocelyn was funny and sentimental and looked terrible in that white dress, and Jack broke down and cried every time he had to speak. Jocelyn had a kid who was a couple of years younger than Wrecker and so furious she could barely say a word. Wrecker tried to befriend her but she hissed at him like he was part of some monolithic family front. Melody was so subdued in their company she was nearly catatonic. A few days there and she looked a dozen years older than the day they'd left the farm. The two of them escaped a few times—Deedee watched while he caught some breakers with Jack's borrowed board out at Redondo Beach, and they snuck out twice for ice cream at midnight on Hollywood Boulevard—but even away from her family Melody's face showed signs of serious strain. No wonder Jack seemed so worn down. Being around Deedee's family gave Wrecker a little more appreciation for his own. At least nobody was hammering at him to change the way he was.

The morning of the sixth day, Wrecker and Melody caught a cab to LAX. Deedee sighed loudly as they boarded the plane. "Well." She fumbled with her seat belt. "I'd rate that a success. Wouldn't you?"

"Pretty crazy." Wrecker had chosen a seat by the window and was keeping an eye on the ground crew. "They hardly knew I was there."

Melody nodded absently and consulted the emergency card. She hated flying, she told Wrecker. Some days she hated living, but she was old enough to realize that there was a reasonable chance the feeling would pass. "What?" she said, turning toward him. "They loved you."

"That was love?"

Melody looked up and gave a short, sharp laugh. "You bet. Close as they get to it. Mother told you you'd look better in some other color than the one you were wearing and Daddy slipped you a martini. Right?"

"A martini! *That's* what you call those things."

Melody shifted in her seat and studied him intently. "Did he say something to you?" She narrowed her eyes at him. "Don't bullshit me."

"Forget it." Wrecker ducked his head and grinned. "It's just, you know." He stroked the meager beard that dirtied his chin and cut her a quick glance. "I wonder."

"He can be an asshole."

Wrecker looked at her. "I wasn't talking about him."

Melody opened her mouth to speak but nothing came out.

"You look like your mother, Deedee," Wrecker said abruptly, and when she laughed, he said, "No. You do. You have the same—all this stuff." He reached over and waved his hand over the bridge of her nose. "Eyebrows and eyes and nose, kind of. It's nice."

Her eyes widened and she blinked at him. "And you wonder," Melody said slowly, her voice a little shaky, "who you look like."

"Yeah. Well, whatever." He turned away. It felt risky, bringing it up. His heart thumped in his chest. Maybe he should just keep his mouth shut.

"Wrecker," Melody said. She took a deep breath and let it out. Her gaze flicked toward him and then away. "There are some things I should maybe tell you." She took one more deep breath and Wrecker saw something rise in her eyes that he was suddenly certain he wanted to avoid. "Not maybe. Should." Her voice strained and he scrambled for a means to head her off. That wasn't what he was asking. If there were things he needed to know— "Should have, maybe." No, Wrecker thought, should *not*— "Should. Fuck it," she said, "you're almost eighteen," and launched in.

Wrecker felt his stomach lurch as Melody talked, and cried, and talked more. It was as though she'd held everything inside by force of will and once she let go it all had to come out. Her words rolled uncontrollably, and it took every ounce of his resolve not to reach over and clamp a rough hand across her mouth. His head spun with the information. Hello, son, meet your grandparents—and, by the way, you've got relatives you never even guessed at. Meg, his aunt? Even better: a mother who's alive and well and probably on her way to find you. As soon as she gets out of jail. Deedee stumbled over her words, said things badly, tried to correct, stumbled worse, and once the tears started she couldn't get them to stop. For chrissakes, Wrecker thought. Out of *jail*? He couldn't wrap his mind around it. Around any of it. Did he have to know this? Because of why? And what was he supposed to do now?

He sat staring at the seat back in shock, his circuits blown and his face still as a stone.

Melody slowed down, gulped another deep breath. She'd made a giant mistake, she said. She had meant to protect him but she could tell from his face she had hurt him instead. If she had told him the truth from the start—goddamn Willow for being right, again—he wouldn't be looking at her in that way right now. That way that said, *you? You? Even you?*

Wrecker dropped his chin to stare at his hands. If he kept all his attention focused there, he could try to resist the arc of electricity that cycled painfully through his body.

Melody paused. She had never before understood so deeply, she said softly, that her omission could be as gravely harmful as an outright lie.

Wrecker scowled, and jerked his arm up with an awkward effort. "Stop." He didn't want her apology. "Just say it outright. Tell me again," he said, his voice as hollow as a rotten tree.

And so she did, because she had to. What she had always said before—*I became your mother because I wanted you and your birth mom couldn't take care of you*—all of it true, in its way—became something different, told now. Everything she knew, she told him unabridged. That his birth mother was Meg's younger sister. That she—that woman, Lisa Fay—had raised him until he was three, and that she'd lost custody of him when she was sentenced to prison for serious crimes. That he had lived with foster families until Len took him in. That he was scared and angry and out of control and too much for Len to handle and so he brought Wrecker to Bow Farm.

She had let him get away once, she said, her voice quavering, and she never would again. Not until he was grown. Until he was a man, and he walked out on his own.

Wrecker's voice was tight. "What else?"

That was all she knew. Melody hesitated. There was more, she said, and stole a glance at him. But if he wanted to know it, he would have to ask Willow.

"Willow?" he said, incredulous.

Willow had been to see Lisa Fay in jail, and they had talked for a long time. "I wouldn't let her tell me," Melody said. Her voice cracked. "I wouldn't let her tell you, either." Willow had wanted Wrecker to know, but Melody had sworn her to secrecy. "You were eight," she said, and her voice trailed off to a whisper. "I had to make a choice."

"When were you going to tell me?" he asked, a fury behind his words.

"I'm telling you now." Melody turned her face away and spoke with such a small voice that he had to bend toward her and strain to hear. "I was afraid." She lifted a hand to shield her face. "I was afraid that I'd wake up one morning and you'd be gone."

The jet dropped suddenly and Wrecker reached for the paper bag in the seat back ahead and threw up into it.

When he was finished, he glanced at Melody. She looked green.

"You've got one there for yourself," he mumbled.

For the rest of the trip they said nothing. They reached Eureka, and Wrecker banged his way into the driver's seat of the car and drove without asking. He kept his eyes ahead. The sun plunged into the ocean and left a pink glow on everything, and then that, too, faded to darkness.

There was a light on in the kitchen of the farmhouse when they arrived. They shuffled in, weary, to find Ruth sitting at the table. Her hands were folded together, the backs of them a patchwork of age spots. Ruth had turned seventy this year. It took Wrecker's breath away, to see her grown old.

"Meg is in the hospital," Ruth said.

"What?" The two of them spoke together.

Ruth shook her head. "Everything's gone to hell."

A bad case of pneumonia in his wife, and Len was a shambles. He wore dark moons like badges of devotion beneath his bloodshot eyes and three days' stubble on his chin while Meg slept like a baby under her oxygen tent. She looked serene. Untroubled, Wrecker thought, gazing at her, while Len carried the trouble for both of them and bent under the strain of it. Wrecker tried to spell him, let Len spend a night at home, but Len wouldn't do it. Even a cup of coffee in the cafeteria left him jangled, anxious to return to her side.

Wrecker sat with him. It was the only place he could think to be.

"Go home," Len said again. "I mean it. You're no use to me here."

Wrecker got up and walked to the door and looked down the hall and then came back and sat down again. "The doctors said she'll be fine."

"Yes. That's what the doctors said."

"Don't you believe them?"

"Of course I believe them," Len said sharply. "I'm just making sure of it."

Len wouldn't meet his eye. The infection all those years back had weakened Meg's health, made her more susceptible to illness. Every serious bug left less of her. "Fine" was relative. Meg would likely get over the pneumonia, the doctors said, but the next thing that came along could be her undoing.

Wrecker parked himself there and passed another night in the chair. He woke the next morning with a backache. He had the sense of having dreamed something important, but he couldn't return to it. They had taken away the oxygen apparatus. Meg was sleeping peacefully. Her cheeks were pink, and Len must have combed her hair before he stepped out of the room.

Wrecker got up, stretched, and stood by the bed. He looked intently at Meg's face. He gazed at the spider veins that mottled her cheeks, the faint down on her upper lip, the translucence of her eyelids under which her eyes roamed athletically. She had a quality of softness that no other person he had ever met shared. Meg had never lied to him. She had claimed him, out of affection, and he returned it. Affectionately. Not because—

Len backed his way into the room, pushing open the door with his shoulder and carrying two cups of coffee. He nodded to the boy and passed him a cup.

Wrecker cradled it in his hands. "Meg is my aunt," he said.

Len paused mid-sip. He put the cup on the bedside table. "I see."

"You saw before."

"Yes," Len said. "I did." And then he picked up the coffee cup and slowly drank it all. When he finished he threw the cup in the wastebasket and resumed his vigil at Meg's side. He appeared deep in thought. He opened his mouth and turned his head to the side once as though preparing to say something, but nothing emerged, and he surrendered again to the silence.

"What."

Len blinked twice. When he turned to Wrecker his face was lit with a kind of defiant resolve. "Don't be so angry."

"Angry?" Wrecker got up quickly and the chair tumbled over. He bent to right it, took a deep breath, and sat down again. "I thought I knew who I was, Len. And now it turns out I had no idea. But you did. And Melody. All of you. It's just that nobody bothered to tell me."

Len held his gaze, and then he turned away. He reached a tender hand to stroke Meg's cheek. Wrecker thought he'd been dismissed. He stood to leave.

"Sit down."

Wrecker sat.

There was a long silence. Then Len said, his face still in shadow, "I've made a lot of mistakes in my life, son. But it wasn't a mistake to marry Meg."

Wrecker looked away. He had a lump in his throat that he didn't know what to do with and he wanted to break something in Len and put him back together in the same instant.

"Your aunt Meg?" Len's voice was soft and low. "She was the loveliest woman I ever laid eyes on. She worked a parts counter down there in Watsonville and she sold me a replacement taillight when I busted mine taking a curve too fast. Laughed at me for it. I was only passing through, but I knew I wasn't leaving unless I had Meg sitting on that bench seat next to me. And I managed it, too." Len rubbed his hands together like they hurt. Then he reached into the breast pocket of his jacket and drew out a scrap of paper and the sharpened stub of a pencil. From his wallet he retrieved a small, folded card. Len bent his head and painstakingly copied some numbers from the printed card onto the scrap of paper, and then he handed it to Wrecker.

"It's your inheritance," he said.

"My what?"

"I've been holding on to it for you since Meg's parents died. Willow tried to give it to your mother but she wouldn't take it. We figured to save it for you." Len shrugged. "Wasn't much then, but it grew a little." He dipped his head toward the scrap. "The account has your name and mine both. I'll call the bank and let them know to let you close it out."

"I don't want it," Wrecker said, and thrust the scrap toward Len.

243

Len turned slightly so his elbow shielded him from Wrecker's outstretched arm. He focused his attention on Meg.

Wrecker looked down at the unfamiliar numbers. "What am I supposed to do with this?" he asked, his voice cracking. He struggled to collect himself. He didn't know if he should tear it to pieces and fling it in the trash or tuck it in his pocket and leave for good. Forever. Or climb in next to Meg. Or—

"You're good with the timber, boy."

Wrecker's head jerked up. It was the last thing he expected to hear, and he looked at Len like he was crazy.

"My father taught me," Len said. "He had to." His lips pursed slightly and he shook his head, remembering. "It took all of us. My father, my brother, and me. When the blight finally got to Tennessee it took out all our trees in a short couple of years. Every single chestnut, dead. And we had to cut them all or watch them go to waste." Wrecker watched as Len laid his hand gently over Meg's open palm. "I'm just saying." Len looked up, held Wrecker's gaze. "It wasn't a mistake to marry Meg. And it wasn't a mistake to go and get you and bring you home to Melody. Two best things I ever did." He shrugged. "If it matters to you, go find out more. You'll be eighteen in a few days. You're your own man."

Wrecker felt it like a wave of grief passing over him. He stood. He bent down to kiss Meg on the forehead. He was almost out the door when he heard Len call him sharply.

"You sure as hell *do* know who you are," Len said, his voice flinty.

Wrecker looked at him and Len never dropped his gaze.

The boy drew himself tall. "Eat more, old man. You're getting skinny." He gestured with his chin to Meg. "And take care of her." He slapped the doorjamb. "I'll see you."

"Course you will," Len said, turning already to gaze at Meg's tender face.

Before he left, Wrecker called Melody and delivered a terse message. He was headed for San Francisco for a few days. If it turned out to be longer than a week he'd call again. He couldn't bring himself to say he was fine. He wasn't fine. And then he caught ride after ride, and let the miles rush before his eyes.

CHAPTER THIRTEEN

The evening air was damp with a warm fog when Willow picked her way along the path that led from her yurt to the farmhouse. She'd stayed to herself, mostly, the past few days. The night Meg got sick Willow had caught a ride to the hospital, and she'd spent forty-eight anxious hours there, trying to comfort that inconsolable man. Meg's system had been so thoroughly compromised by her illness, the doctors said, that even if she recovered from this bout of pneumonia she might not have enough strength to fight off the next bad bug that came her way. Len closed his ears to them. He focused his attention in a narrow beam at Meg, willing her back to health, and made Willow feel like an obstacle to his aim. She escaped as soon as she could.

Whatever Len did, though, seemed to have worked. They were home, now. The doctors released Meg a scant week after she'd entered through emergency, her breathing shallow and a fever raging through her system; she'd still need special care, they said, but they were amazed to see her recover so quickly. Willow shared in the relief, but she kept her distance. She turned her back to the meadow and to the strip of woods that separated her home from theirs, and counted on Ruth for updates. It wasn't pride that made her stay away. It was grief. Len was the sole reason she'd stayed so long at Bow Farm, and she was leaving, now. Leaving Bow Farm, and leaving him.

A car door slammed shut on the knoll above the farmhouse, and Willow looked up to see Melody, her arms loaded with groceries, stumble down the path in her direction. Lugging the bags was Wrecker's job. Willow shook her head. Everything had fallen apart at once. When Wrecker arrived at Meg's bedside midway through the week, reeling from the news about his mother, Len had been as brusque and dismissive with him as he'd been with the rest of them. The boy had stormed off in anger, Ruth reported, and hitchhiked his way down to San Francisco. Good for him, Willow thought. She felt a pang of guilt as Melody drew closer. Ruth said Melody grew daily more frantic with worry. But what did she think, waiting so long to tell him? Willow figured there was a good chance Lisa Fay would soon be set free. Was that what Wrecker was doing, down there in the city? Looking for his mother?

The thought made her heart skip a beat.

The setting sun put an odd pink shine on the glossy leaves of Ruth's kitchen garden. There was no place in the world like the Mattole Valley at the peak of summer, and Willow knew how sharply she'd miss it. Without speaking, she eased a bag from Melody's arms. Together they entered the dooryard. Melody bumped open the front door with her hip, crossed to the counter, and set down the sacks. She handed Ruth a packet of the ginger candies she liked. "Heard anything from him?" she asked softly.

Ruth shook her head. She was simmering something on the stove and her shoulders hunched protectively over the pot. She caught Willow's eye and then glanced back toward Melody. A look passed between them. "What," Melody said, squinting suspiciously. Ruth gazed again at Willow, and looked away.

Melody turned to stare closely. Willow watched as her eyes widened. "Jesus, Willow," she sputtered. "What's the matter with you?"

Willow stiffened slightly and angled her body away from

Melody. She had combed her hair, put herself together, but she knew her eyes were lined with red and the creases in her face cut deeper than they ever had. It had been a while since she'd slept through the night. She took off her jacket, hung it on the seat back, and rubbed her bony wrists. So she'd lost some weight. These weeks had been hard on them all. Willow set her jaw and tried to sound resolute. "We need to talk."

Melody gave her hands a quick shake, and then smoothed them through her hair. "When people need to talk, they just talk. You mean there's bad news." She leaned forward, her face tense. "Tell me. What happened to him?"

"Wrecker's fine," Ruth said brusquely, tapping the spoon on the rim of the pot for emphasis.

Melody spun to face her. "Did he call here?"

"He's traveling," Ruth said, exasperated. "When he's ready to come home, you'll know it. He doesn't need to report his every little move." She lifted the spoon and wagged it toward Willow. "Stop thinking of yourself, for once. Willow has something to tell you."

Melody's eyes widened at Ruth's tone. She sat reluctantly at the table.

Willow was annoyed to find that she couldn't stop trembling. She crossed her arms in front of herself and tucked her hands against her sides. She could get her lips to move, but couldn't count on her voice to power the words.

Ruth left her stove to scrape a chair out from the table and settle herself noisily in it. "Look," she said bluntly. "Let's not make this more than it is." She turned to Melody. "Meg's sick, and Len won't see Willow. She thinks it's over between them. I think Len will come around once Meg gets better, but she won't be persuaded." She cast Willow an impatient glance.

A fleet look of surprise and hurt skated across Melody's face. Willow swallowed and gazed away. It wasn't anybody's business but hers. Ruth was just nosy that way; she took wild guesses and then ferreted out some version of the truth. But Ruth was wrong about this. Willow knew it wasn't over with Len. "That's not—," she started, but shook her head and tucked her chin.

"So Willow's moving. Giving up on Bow Farm." Ruth frowned. She lifted both pudgy hands and cracked the knuckles, and then she stretched forward to lay her swollen digits over Willow's long, thin fingers. "I wish you wouldn't, girl."

Ruth had it all wrong. Willow's eyes glistened with tears. She was leaving because it *wasn't* over. Not for her, it wasn't. The past week had shown Willow that she wasn't willing to share Len with anyone. Not even with Meg, to whom he rightfully belonged, and who needed him, now. Needed him whole, not divided. Needed him—

Jesus. What kind of person had she become?

It had nothing to do with sex. Len's desire belonged to her alone. Willow was sure of that. But his attentiveness, the direction of his thoughts and his care and his profound hope—*Meg* was his beloved, and her illness had not changed that. She was delicate, now, her body and her mind made weak, but Len was connected to her in a way that had nothing to do with choice or intention. He could no more leave Meg than escape the compulsion that sent him to the woods each day. He was a woodcutter and a husband. Meg's husband.

To Willow he was—

It was not less. Willow felt a clot of emotion surge in her throat, and she shifted her gaze to stare out the window and force herself to calm. Len loved her. He *knew* her in a way that she had never felt known before. And when their bodies finally collided, it was explosive for her in a way she couldn't have anticipated. The potential had always been there, the tension that stretched like high-voltage wires between them—but she hadn't expected to fall in love. Willow looked from Ruth to Melody. There was no way to explain. "Please," she said. "If you could help—"

"Wait." Melody looked bewildered. Her hair had come loose from its bun and swirled around her face in disarray. "The farm payment?" She glanced anxiously at Ruth and then back. "I'm sorry. I'm really sorry. But you aren't saying—"

Willow forced herself to meet Melody's frightened gaze. "I'll need some money to get started," she said, and hated to hear her voice crack with the strain. "You'll have to go to the bank, Melody. You'll have to refinance. But I'll turn over my share in the farm to you."

"No, Willow. Please. I can't lose the farm. Not now."

"You won't lose it, Melody. Go to the bank. They'll write a new loan."

"They'll laugh me out the door!"

"You can manage without me, this time." Willow paused. She braced herself, and made her voice clear and harsh. "You have to."

Ruth huffed with dismay. "Len will come around." Her voice was a rheumy murmur. "Give him a little time, Willow. Len loves—"

"Yes." Willow stood abruptly. "That's the problem. Len loves me." She gathered her jacket from the chair back and thrust her arms into it. "He loves me, and he loves Meg, too. But he needs to take care of Meg, now. It will kill him to divide himself, and if I'm here, he'll try to do it." Willow struggled with the zipper and gave up, pulled the leaves of her jacket snug around her. "Ruth, please. I need your help." Ruth raised her head, and the wattles shook under her chin. "I need you to keep an eye on him, see him through this. But tonight, go over and take care of Meg. Tell Len I need to see him."

"Willow. Are you sure—"

"Please, Ruth. I'm begging you. Stay with Meg until Len gets back."

Ruth crossed the floor and gripped Willow hard. "Don't beg me," she said, pulling her close. "I won't know it's you."

Willow let herself huddle against Ruth's warm bulk for a little while. She could hear her friend's heart beat slow and steady, wrapped deep in that soft flesh. Then she pried herself away and escaped through the kitchen door, letting it slam behind her. Willow turned once to see Ruth's troubled face shining in the window. She knew Melody was too furious to turn toward her. And terrified. Melody might never forgive her.

That stubborn woman. If she saw what she had—

Willow tucked her chin and sloped forward across the yard.

Her yurt was a mess. As disheveled as the inside of her mind, Willow thought, as she paced the single room, dropping books and papers into half-filled boxes and turning out cabinets and drawers. She was a neat person, a meticulous person, but she had crossed a line somewhere and now her thoughts and her things alike lay scattered about her like the aftermath of a disaster. She lowered herself to the side of her bed. It was no disaster. She'd been forced to see what had been there for a long time: she was in love with a man who was married to someone else, and her children were light-years from her, living a life from which she had excised herself. Neatly. Irrevocably, maybe. Willow pushed herself up and moved stiffly, forcing herself to clear her shelves of books, stacking them in random boxes and hastily sealing them up. She needed to have as much done as she could before Len arrived. That way there would be no question. He would understand she was leaving, and he would have to agree. It was the right thing. It was the only thing.

Willow paused with her hand around a clutch of books. It was possible that Len wouldn't come. If Meg needed him—if he thought that she needed him—he'd stay and tend to her. He would send a message through Ruth that said, I'll come later. Another day. When Meg is better.

Or send no message at all.

She shook her head. She couldn't concern herself with that. She would fill boxes and protect furniture and pad the framed artwork that hung from her walls. She would disassemble the loom, stuff away the skeins of spun yarn, gather her weavings heedlessly into bags. She would ignore the vivid colors and novel patterns, her efforts to tame the wild into something that made sense. To tame herself, her own unruly heart.

Maybe he wouldn't come. Her knees softened and she sank gently to the floor.

These things, what did they matter? The tools and materials of her trade, the spun yarn and pigments of her passion, the books, the memories and small keepsakes collected from her travels, least of all the lovely, utilitarian items of her daily life—

He would come.

The cedar box lay tucked in back of a locked drawer in her writing desk. Willow got up and searched for the key. She unlocked the drawer and felt behind the boxes of envelopes and stationery for its smooth polished shape. It took some effort to tug it out, and she placed in at the center of the desk and stood for some time with her hands on its lid.

He would come. He would come, and still she would go.

Willow heard a sound outside. It was dark, and the yurt would be glowing like a lantern at the edge of the meadow. It would guide whoever had come—Len or Ruth—along the worn trail from his cabin.

The door opened, and there he stood.

"Oh," Len said.

She couldn't take her eyes from him. She had planned to be crisp, expeditious, dispassionate. That would make it easier for them both, she thought. But the fact of him interfered with her intentions.

"Oh," he said again, this time with neither surprise nor confusion.

"It's the only way, Len."

When she saw his face change, she wanted to call back the stupid words. She would recant. She would unpack the boxes and return the books to the shelves and replace the artwork on the walls and try to believe again in the patterns of the weavings.

But then his face changed once more. It darkened into an expression she'd never seen him wear before, and he stepped toward her.

Willow stepped back.

"No," he said, his voice a guttural snarl that rose from his belly.

Len caught himself, though. It took some time. Twice he turned to leave, but he didn't follow through. He waited long enough for his face to change entirely and for them both to weary of standing there, such a distance between them. And then the only solution appeared to be to reduce that distance. Cautiously, deliberately, Len took one measured step forward. And against one part of her will but in accord with the rest of it she stepped forward to meet him there, in the middle, and together they sidestepped—it wasn't a waltz, but it might have looked that way, to a stranger—to Willow's bed.

At first they were overcome with a rank urgency, their clothes still on and their bodies exacting the penalty of their anger from each other.

And then they rested, not touching, not talking, not looking at each other.

The second time Willow let Len draw her clothes from her slowly, sliding her silk shirt through the thin gap between their bodies. She let him lay his face in the crease of her neck and against the swell of her belly, felt his desire rise with the scent of her skin. When he reached for her she climbed onto him and held his wrists against the sheets and dragged the sway of her breasts across his lips; and when he couldn't—would not—wait any longer she let go of him so he could grasp her hips and slide himself inside her. He watched her move above him, watched his own work-hardened hands run up her sides to lay dark on her pale breasts, and then he turned and carried her beneath him, drawing out the sweetness for as long as he could last.

The third time, she took him in that other way and he came again so suddenly and violently she thought that he would shake apart.

The fourth time was no time at all. They had slept for hours. Len woke first when the faintest light glimmered through the east windows, and he gazed at Willow for a long time. She opened her eyes to find him like that. Willow reached a hand to stroke the stubbled line of his jaw. She felt him stir against her thigh. But her face changed, softer still, and she moved away from him and slowly eased herself from the bed.

Wearily, Len rose.

She threaded his arms through his shirt. She snapped the buttons together with tenderness and care. He pulled on his jeans and Willow fastened the buckle of his belt. Then she sat him in the armchair and she gently eased on each sock, fit each boot to each foot, and wept.

"Go," she said, pointing to the door.

And Len did.

Willow slept then, for some time. She was pretty sure a day had elapsed—a whole day of sun and heat and brilliance and the night that followed it, lost to her—and that when she woke it was not the same dawn but a new one. It helped her to believe that. It seemed to lend a kind of hope to the prospect that she might make it through.

She finished packing, and then there was one final thing to do.

She sat at her desk and opened the box. Slowly, thoughtfully, Willow gazed at each of the photographs. She spread them across her desk so that no one obscured another. Her son Teddy at nine, the lead in the school play. David at thirteen, stiff in a suit and tie, going off to a debate tournament. Emily before she could walk. All three of them holding a large carved pumpkin the year she left, grinning their goofiest grins, the black patch covering Teddy's eye. Dozens of photographs, her children caught posed or candid by the camera lens, alone, with each other, with Ross, with herself, all together as a family, without the slightest thought that harm would come, that something—a small thing, really, what did it matter?—would rise up to split them from one another, send them to live separate lives.

And the one that didn't match. The little blond boy in the baseball jersey and cap, eating an ice cream cone on a set of cement stairs, his mother beside him.

Willow shuffled the others gently back into the box and closed the lid. The last one she left before her on the desk. She drew a sheet of paper from the desk drawer and lifted a pen from the cup. *Dear Wrecker*, she began.

It seemed important to me to leave you this photograph. I think you can guess who the people are, in it.

She didn't know how, exactly, to speak to him of this. But she was leaving, now. She had to do this. For him. For Lisa Fay. For Melody, she hoped; and not against her. Willow dipped her head and continued, trusting to what would come.

By now you may have already met your mother. If so, she will tell you the story herself. If not? I hope that one day you will meet her, and that you'll give her the chance to explain to you what happened, and why, and what it meant to her. It's not for me to do that. I can only tell you my story.

Willow leaned back in the chair. She wasn't sure why she needed to tell him this. It didn't concern him, really. He didn't know these people. It was possible that he would never meet them. But if she showed him this—that she had made a mistake, and that she knew it, and that it had nothing and everything to do with love—maybe he would understand that there were things that happened that could not be helped, and that all they could do was go on.

And so she went on.

When I was not very much older than you are now, I met a man. We got married, and after a little while our son David was born. After David came Teddy, two years later. And then, four years after Teddy, Emily was born. Ross was a good father. I was a good mother. Our kids were good kids. Ross and

I had our disagreements but we never let them get in the way of being parents.

And then one day (a Sunday, I remember, because I was driving the children home from church), something happened. The car hit a patch of ice and spun out of my control and went over an embankment. And the kids were fine. Miraculously, the kids were fine. Except Teddy, who was 12, and it was just that a piece of shattered glass from a Coke bottle he'd held in his hands found its way to his face. It lodged itself in the fold beneath his eye. And even though I got them all out of the car and up the embankment to the road and flagged down help and got Teddy to the hospital, my son lost his vision in that eye.

Willow lifted the pen from the paper. Her hand was shaking slightly and she placed the pen carefully on the desk. She hadn't told this story to anyone for so long. Not since all those times of repeating it in the courtroom, to the evaluator, to her lawyer.

The accident had changed her. It had changed the way she could mother them. She became fearful, smothering the children more than they could tolerate. The boys were growing older and needed the room to branch out on their own, needed to take chances. And she and Ross—things fell apart between them. Ross drank more. One night, when he'd had so much to drink that his speech slurred and his skin flamed an ugly rose color, Ross turned to her. His voice was thin and incisive, a hot wire laid upon her brain. It was your fault, he said.

Of course it was her fault. Whose fault could it have been? She was driving the car. She had lost control. She knew it was her fault. She hadn't done anything wrong, but she'd been in charge. Her children had been in her care. And one of them had been harmed in a way that could not be set right.

She did everything she could to set it right, and all it did was make things worse.

I'm leaving, Ross said.

Willow secured a lawyer. She couldn't make Ross stay, but no judge would take custody from a mother. A good mother, who had done nothing wrong.

She's unfit, Ross said.

Willow almost laughed. She was fitter than anyone, at anything. She was fitter than Ross.

As far as the judge could see, she was fit.

Our son was blinded as a result of her actions, Ross said.

Accidents happen, the judge said, and besides, he's got one eye left to see through.

The children are afraid to be with her, Ross said.

Ross was lying. Wasn't he? The judge ordered an evaluation. The children were questioned. They were old enough, the judge deemed, to choose which parent they would rather live with, and they chose their father.

Well, all right, then, the judge said, and let his gavel fall. Weekends and holidays with their mother.

We'll fight it, Willow's lawyer muttered. Don't lose hope.

It wasn't hope she lost. It was heart. No, Willow said.

What? Her lawyer was shocked.

I'm leaving, Willow said. Her limbs felt like lead but she forced them to move. They'll be safe with him. Let them grow up normally.

No mother is not normal, he reminded her. You have weekends. You have holidays.

But she turned her back on him and left, and it had been eighteen years since she'd seen them.

She had not driven once in all that time.

Willow picked up the pen and bent over the page.

Later on, when my husband ~~lost faith in~~ and I were separated, our children were forced to choose between their two parents. At the time, I didn't see the error of that. I was overwhelmed with shame and anger that they did not choose to be with me.

That was my mistake, not to see. And then I made a bigger mistake. I walked away from them. I told myself they'd be better off without me.

Wrecker. Listen to me. Don't choose. Melody is your mother. Lisa Fay is your mother, too. It's not fair, what happened to you as a little boy. But what happened to you after that

She stopped there. *May have saved your life*, she meant to write. But it hadn't only saved him. It may have saved them all.

What happened after that was a good thing.

I'm leaving now to see if I can find my children. They'll all be grown, now, which seems impossible. But if I can find them, and if they'll see me, I won't let the time we lost stop us from spending the time ahead in whatever kind of together they allow.

I hope I'll see you again some day.

Love,
Willow

Willow set the pen aside. She ran the tip of her finger lightly along the deckled edge of the photograph, and straightened it beside the letter. Then she stood and slowly walked the perimeter of the yurt, pausing at each window to gaze at length at the view.

259

She had been looking out these windows for eighteen years. It was time for a change.

Wrecker stood in the motorcycle showroom in downtown San Francisco and let his gaze run over the shiny chrome of the new Triumph.

The salesman approached. "Hell, yeah," the man said, tipping his head toward the bike. "If I were a young buck like you? I'd be riding something like this."

Wrecker glanced at him. The man was balding, gone to pot, with bland hazel eyes and a manufactured smile. Wrecker pegged him for a Honda 750, with a fairing and a sound system and maybe a little trailer he towed behind for long road trips. "I've been looking at that Ducati," Wrecker said.

The salesman stepped over toward the Italian bike and laid a proprietary hand on its gas tank. "This one? Hell of a lot of motorcycle. You'd want to be sure you could handle it."

Wrecker had a bank check big enough to buy the Triumph outright. His inheritance, compounded quarterly for ten years. He thumbed the check in the front pocket of his jeans. As if life weren't absurd enough already. An inheritance, from grandparents he never even knew he had. "How much did you say you want for it?"

The man chuckled deep in his throat. His eyes had an unexpected gleam in them. "This one's a honey, brother. Open her up on the highway and you'd better be hanging on. One forty, one forty-five, and the motor's just purring like a cat." He patted the leather seat and fixed Wrecker in his gaze. "Listen to me. You buy this baby, she'll take you anywhere you want to go."

Wrecker looked at the bike. Then he looked out the window.

He had been where he thought he should go. When he arrived in the city he had gone to an arcade and played foosball all afternoon, let the chimes and bells of the machines and the shouts of the men and boys who stood shoulder to shoulder with him in the hall cover his thoughts with white noise. He had careened like a tourist from one district to the next, wearing down his rubber soles, flashing his transfer at bus drivers and Muni men. He snuck a bike past the monitors at the rental stands and rode it fast through mud bogs in the park. He went to the top floor of an old apartment building and threw glass bottles down the trash chute just to listen to them smash. He found a place in Chinatown where he could buy M-80s; he wired them to a makeshift raft and tried to blow it up offshore. And then he turned eighteen, and found himself standing in the rain outside the big stone building that housed the records downtown.

He could go inside. Tell them his name. And they would hand him his file.

He would learn about the prison, Len had said. He could go there, ask to see her.

But Wrecker had turned away. He had walked faster, turned corners with abandon. He didn't know if he was running away from or running toward. Or which would work out better.

Wrecker blinked, and looked again at the motorcycle salesman. All of a sudden the only place he wanted to go was home.

"Maybe," he said, backing toward the door. It had been over a week, longer than he'd ever been away.

He would give it some thought, he told the salesman. And then he stepped out to the street, settled his cap on his head, and pointed himself toward the Mattole.

Melody had driven the hatchback to Eureka, parked it in the lot of the Piggly-Wiggly, and used the pay phone on the corner to call her brother. "Jack?" she said anxiously.

If the answer were yes the news would have leapt out the minute he recognized her voice. "Hey, Mel," he said.

Her hopes crashed. There was no place to sit down. She leaned
her weight on the small metal counter and tried hard not to cry.

"I made your case," Jack said. "I told him it was the right thing
to do. I vouched for you, but he wouldn't budge."

Melody nodded.

"You all right?"

She had to focus on breathing. She'd been to see the man who
held the note on the farm, and the best he could manage was a
two-month extension. If she didn't come up with the balance by
then, he warned, he'd have to file for foreclosure.

"I tried, Mel. He said—"

"Don't. Jack?" Melody put a hand to her forehead and looked
out the glass at the clear sky. "Probably better not to tell me."

He was silent for a moment. Then he said, "Listen. I could cash
in some paper. Get you a grand or two."

Melody shook her head. "That won't do it. But, thanks. I ap-
preciate it."

There was a longer pause, and then Jack said, "Dad respects
you. That you've made it on your own. He says he's confident
you can make it through this too, and that it'll—"

"Tell him fuck you." Her voice was sharp. "Okay, Jack? Can
you remember that? Fuck you very much."

"You're back in the will, Melody."

"A lot of good that'll do me if I lose the farm."

There was a charged moment of silence. "Okay, then," Jack
said. She could tell from the sound of his voice that someone had
entered the room. "Okay. Good luck. I'll talk to you soon." And
he hung up.

Melody pushed her way out of the phone booth, stuffed both
hands in her jacket pockets, and forced back the tears she felt rise

against her eyelids. How was she supposed to go about any of this? Willow was the one who held things together, who kept it all under control. She had finessed the financing all those years ago, had insisted Melody save for this day. Melody, who couldn't keep two dimes lodged in one pocket for fear they'd talk each other into leaping out. But she had scrimped and saved and denied herself and put Wrecker's less pressing needs on hold and squirreled away just enough to meet her end of the payment. She had worked shitty jobs when the Merc folded and got involved in complicated fruitless moneymaking schemes and had nearly killed herself and Wrecker those months they'd ventured into the soap-making business, the fumes unexpectedly overcoming them; and then she'd slowly paid those doctors' bills, eked out enough to invest in the tie-dye equipment, found a way to turn a small profit at the end of an exhausting season of work. She had met her end of the bargain.

A solid vein of grief ran like an unmined ore straight through the center of Melody's heart. Bow Farm was the only place she had ever lived that felt like home. It had made a mother of her. She'd turned the corner from a wild, unhappy youth to a middle age that felt like something she could settle into, something that would let her, even, even, okay, *blossom*, was there a better way to put it?—late bloomer that she was, let her grow into someone she wouldn't mind spending the rest of her life with. As.

Alone, maybe. Her son gone AWOL, furious with her—and her best friend falling to pieces.

Melody stopped in the middle of the sidewalk and pictured what they stood to lose. Her ramshackle barn. Ruth's kitchen, clean as a whistle. The little clearing upslope of them all where Wrecker had started to build himself a house. A home. *His* home, a home he could count on for the rest of his life. Every little patch of ground was soaked with who they were. And if they lost that?

Melody shoved her hands deeper in her pockets and kept walking.

Wrecker hitched a ride with a cement truck that got him as far as their turnoff from the Mattole Road. He hoofed it the rest of the way.

The hatchback was gone from its parking spot. He felt a little stab at its absence. He trudged down the hill and pushed his way through the farmhouse door. Ruth looked up from the lump of dough she was kneading at the kitchen table and Wrecker tried to read her expression. Something was wrong. "Meg?" he asked, his heart in his throat.

"She's fine. She's home with Len."

He flashed her a tentative smile.

Ruth wiped her hands on the sides of her jeans and came around the table. "I'm glad you're back." She hugged him. "I missed you." She held on to the sleeves of his shirt and stood back to look at him. "You don't look any older. But happy birthday, anyway."

Wrecker shrugged. "Not so happy, really. Nobody made me a cake." The corner of his mouth tilted up in a grin. "You still could, Ruthie."

"Maybe I will. Chocolate, with chocolate frosting. That's what I'll do." She squeezed his shoulder. "I'll never lose weight living near you, boy." Ruth crossed back to her dough and resumed kneading. "Did you find her?" she asked casually.

Wrecker's face clouded. "Did Melody say something?"

"She did."

"She shouldn't have."

"Maybe not. But you don't really think she could keep a secret around me, do you?" Her eyes crinkled, and then softened into seriousness. "Listen. Why don't you go see Willow?"

"I'll talk to her when I'm ready."

"I think you should go now," Ruth said gently.

Wrecker turned sharply and poured himself a glass of water from the tap. He opened the refrigerator door and studied its contents. Ruth kept a tender eye on him.

"Leave it alone, Ruthie," he muttered, and walked outside.

The yurt had suffered in the last few seasons. Flickers had taken a new interest in it and had hammered sizable holes in much of the cedar trim, and the waterproof top had proved no match for the rain that drenched the Mattole Valley. The deck was softening with pockets of rot. Wrecker stood outside in the meadow. There was a stillness that said no one was home. He called Willow's name, and when no one answered Wrecker climbed the steps and ducked through the door.

Inside, a corner of the floor was stacked with moving boxes. The shelves were empty. All of the books had been packed away. Willow had broken the loom down into its composite pieces, gathered them in bundles with twine. The place smelled of lemon oil. Wrecker made a circuit of the room. It seemed smaller, so much plainer, without her. He had never noticed how shabby it had become. He had not been there in some time. He and Willow—it had never gone easy for them, but he hated the thought of her leaving. And then Wrecker paused at the old trestle table she used as a work desk. There was no way he could miss the sheet of paper addressed to him. Or the photograph beside.

Wrecker felt his anger rise. He hadn't asked for this. If he'd wanted to know, he'd have gone to find out on his own. He looked around in a mounting fury. The yurt was a flimsy structure, never meant to last this long. He could rip it from its anchors, send it asail in a stiff wind. He could burn the place down. He could destroy the letter before he glanced at it again and never know its contents.

Wrecker waited for his anger to ebb. Then he picked up the letter and read it through to the end.

When he finished, Wrecker sat in the only chair and let his head rest in his hands. He heard soft footsteps cross the deck before Willow appeared in the doorway, and he lifted his head to meet her gaze. She was thinner than he ever remembered seeing her. Her face was pale. She had dressed for town. "You came back," Willow said.

Wrecker gestured to the letter. "You're leaving." It jumped out of his mouth like an accusation.

She crossed her arms loosely on her chest and leaned in the doorframe. "It's time to go." She gestured to the boxes. "I've hired someone to come get my things tomorrow."

Wrecker looked away. Why now? he thought to ask, but he didn't think he wanted to know the answer to that. "Where to?"

She gave a little twitch of her cheek. "Eureka, temporarily. I rented an apartment there. I have some things to take care of." Wrecker glanced down and fingered the page, and she nodded. "I was out in the meadow," she said, and smiled softly. "I saw you come inside."

"Were you waiting for me to read this?"

Willow gave the slightest shrug. "Some things can't be said." She waited for him to lift his head and slowly added, "And some things have to be. I want you to know this, Wrecker. I thought Melody was making a mistake when she took you. I thought she would grow to regret it." She hesitated. "I was wrong about her. I was wrong about you, too."

Wrecker struggled to keep his face impassive.

"I'm hoping to be wrong about myself, as well." She slowly

rose and crossed the room. She turned at the door. "That photo-graph? I know you don't want that. I've kept it for you for a long time. If you'd rather, I'll hold it until you're ready." She watched his face. And then she nodded and she turned and left.

Wrecker gave her time to cross the meadow and make her way toward the road, and then he stood and stepped outside and gently pulled the door shut behind him. He looked out at the evening fog beginning to wisp its way in off the ocean, and it gave him the courage he needed to look down at the object in his hand. It was a small, square black-and-white photograph. The stamp on the back read "June 30, 1968," and there were two people in it.

One of them was him.

Wrecker walked back to his cabin. It was lonely there. It was a boy's room, and he didn't feel like a boy any longer. He lifted the quilt with its sails and waves from his bed, felt its familiar heft, and folded it. He set it on top of his dresser. He looked at it there and then he picked it up and shoved it onto a high shelf, out of sight.

Ruth was in the farmhouse. She watched him warily as he dragged himself up the steps and into the kitchen. "So you heard?"

"Willow's leaving."

Ruth nodded her head. "I guess we all are." Wrecker looked at her sharply. "Didn't she tell you?"

"She told me a lot of things."

"She didn't say anything about the farm?"

"Like what, Ruth?"

"Oh, honey." Ruth sighed and it sounded like the end of the world. "Without Willow's half, Melody can't afford to make the payment. She's trying to find a way to keep the farm out of foreclosure." She bit her lip. "She thought she might have to sell the place."

Wrecker paled. He would need to borrow the truck, he said.

Melody was outside, sitting on the stone steps of the savings and loan. When she saw the truck she slowly stood up. He had come back. She waited quietly while he parked and crossed the street to approach her. He was taller than he had been the week before. He was more beautiful than she remembered. He was his own man. She had not ruined him. That she had managed that— "Well, look what the cat drug home," she said wryly, and let her happiness spread across her face.

Wrecker reached into his back pocket for the check. He unfolded it and handed it to Melody.

She shook her head. "Six thousand dollars. Where did you get this?"

"Len kept it for me."

She looked again at the check and slowly realized what he meant. "Your mother's money," she said softly. She folded it in half and passed it back to him. "That's yours, son."

"Deedee." His face looked pained. "If the farm is in trouble, let me help. It's my home." He paused, and his voice lowered, took on a grudging tone. "And you're my mother."

Melody searched his face. "I know that," she said quietly. "You think I don't know that?"

"I know, but—"

"You think I don't know that?" She reached up and patted his cheek. She grabbed him around the middle and fake-pummeled his ribs. "You think I don't know that, bub?"

Wrecker's face wrinkled like he'd suddenly been exposed to too bright a light. He gave a small, asymmetrical pant. "The farm?"

"The farm is ours." Melody shrugged, and gestured to the building behind them. "God knows why, but they gave me the loan." She took his arm. "Come on," she said, dragging him into the street. "You drive. Let's get home."

CHAPTER FOURTEEN

Dying felt to Ruth like a physical thing, a tickle in her throat or a ringing in her ears that she couldn't locate precisely but that wouldn't go away, either. It wasn't painful. She was used to pain. Her whole body was going to hell, and it was taking the slow road, making time for scenic detours. Her joints ached, her ankles swelled, and once in a while her bottom leaked without prior notice. Her lungs made room for only half a portion of air with each breath. On some days, the worst days, even her sense of humor seemed under attack. Things weren't as funny when you saw them through the lens of decrepitude. And once that was gone? What was the point? Better to lie down in the road and let the next speeding truck wonder what made the bump when it took the corner fast. She had given Bow Farm twenty years of her life, and that ought to be enough. Of course, they were bonus years. Twenty years she hadn't expected to have. And Bow Farm had given her—

Well. It had given her Wrecker.

But the day was fast coming when he would leave, too. The boy was twenty years old—a man, almost—and the world beckoned. He was talking Alaska. He was tossing around the idea of a winter down near Jack, surfing the breaks at Redondo Beach. He had gotten a roof on his new house and was holding off on finishing the inside until he was ready to spring for materials. Wrecker had matured into a man's body, solid as a stump, with a good mind and a growing command of his emotions. His judgment was ripening, he was capable beyond compare, he had a little money banked from working with Len and a motorcycle he loved with a passion. He rode the Ducati, Ruth could only hope, with more caution than he had the little Enduro that lay wrecked and rusting under a tarp behind the barn. Caution wasn't his strong suit, Ruth knew, but he made up for it with quick reflexes and a modicum of luck, and she kept the prayers rolling. Once she crossed over, she'd be able to keep a closer eye on him. If it didn't work that way, she'd be seriously pissed. She'd want to have a word with whoever had set things up.

It was a bittersweet thing, watching Wrecker launch; and it was painful, too, for Ruth, watching Melody seesaw between wanting it for him and dreading it at the same time. Melody was slowly getting the hang of letting go. She had more or less given him free rein to make his own choices, to live as he pleased. She'd never been much good at discipline, anyway. But the idea of him going? Being physically away? Melody couldn't stand to think of it. She said stupid things and flapped her hands more when the topic came up, and then berated herself afterward for reacting that way. Wrecker took it all with a grain of salt. He was certain he'd be leaving, Ruth suspected, and he seemed to know Deedee would come around. Ruth had to marvel. There was a degree of trust there that looked more like grace than the result of any effort. Not that they hadn't both had to try hard.

Melody was more sentimental than any of them, Ruth had come to realize. The summer before last, when Willow left, it cut a hole in Melody's heart that still needed some mending. By the end of the first week there was no trace of Willow but the ruts the moving truck left in the soft dirt of the meadow and the piers and wood floor of the yurt. It was all of them at Bow Farm, and then a week later it was one less. Ruth was surprised to see how Melody pined for her. It had been some years since the two of them had exchanged much more than a civil word, but let Willow leave and all of a sudden the loss registered for Melody, a gaping hole that made her mope around and second guess every decision she made. A whole year passed, a year of no communication. And then Ruth made sure the phone rang while Melody was standing in the farmhouse, and it was Willow, just calling to say hello. As easy as that, they picked up where they had left off. The two of them spent the better part of an afternoon on the telephone, said things they'd never thought to before. Willow was living up near Seattle, Ruth already knew. She'd made contact with her sons and had begun spending regular time with them and their families. Her daughter worked for a high-powered law practice in New York and had let Willow visit once, but it hadn't gone well. Willow wouldn't give up trying, she told them. Her kids were everything to her. Ruth didn't say much to that. Privately, she thought, ha. *Everything*. And Len?

But Willow was gone from Bow Farm for good, it seemed; and before long Wrecker would slide away into adulthood; and sometime in the not-too-distant future, Ruth knew, she'd be leaving, too. Checking out of this earthly hotel. The process had already started. She was being gently stalked, her attention drawn from the people and places she walked among toward the ones she'd been parted from, so many years before. She felt for Melody. It was a lot of good-byes for a girl who loved family. For all her oddity, Ruth thought, Melody was cut out for motherhood. She loved the bustle, loved living daily in the rough embrace of the people she adored and fought with. It would be hard for her to adjust to living alone.

For herself? Ruth thought: Any day. That buzz, that whisper—it had already begun. And that would be all right. Cremate her, strew her ashes at the beach, and she'd finish the work she'd started all those years ago.

But it wasn't Ruth who went first. It was Meg.

It wasn't as though they'd lacked warning. The doctors had expressed their concern. But Len had nursed Meg, and spoiled her, and bullied her into regaining her health. Already she'd outlasted their predictions by twelve good months, so what did the doctors know? Len let himself believe she'd beat the odds. Until the strokes began. Brief ischemic episodes, the doctors called them; unwelcome little visits from an invisible thief who robbed Meg of her meager speech and then stripped from her every shred of capacity and personality. It would be a blessing, Melody thought, if Meg were to pass quietly in her sleep. It seemed that way to Ruth, too, whose prayers asked for a merciful end, and to Wrecker, who didn't think Len could stand much more.

And yet it came as a shock to them all, the morning Len ran through the woods and across the meadow to find Wrecker. He still had no phone, and the poor man had had to leave his wife's body cooling in the bed and go for help. To Wrecker, to Ruth and Melody, it was a surprise, and mixed in their sadness was a measure of relief. But to Len, it was a travesty. It was a brutal error and a mark of failure. *He* had failed—but at what, he couldn't tell them.

Len crossed again to the home he'd shared for all these years with Meg, and Wrecker gathered them together, Ruth and Melody, and shared the news and split the tasks. Melody took charge of the telephone, notifying neighbors and planning the ceremony. That done, she joined the others and together they moved Meg's body to the lumber shed, covered her with a flowered sheet, and supported Len back to the cabin. He collapsed on his bed, comatose with grief. Ruth would stay with him, it was decided. Melody would attend to Meg's body. Wrecker, who could neither console the living nor prepare the dead, offered to dig the hole for Meg to lie in.

"Out back by the edge of the woods," Len whispered, and Wrecker nodded.

Ruth left Len for a moment and stepped outside with the others. She mopped her face with a handkerchief and blotted the sweat at the base of her neck. It was warm enough to fry an egg on the tin roof of Len's lumber shed. She took Wrecker's sleeve. Charlie Burrell had a backhoe he could use, she suggested.

"No," Wrecker said. He stood tall and wouldn't be swayed. "I'll dig it myself."

"Then dig fast," Ruth said, and made sure he understood. It was August and Meg was in a hurry to rot. They would have to get her to ground before she liquefied like an old tomato. Wrecker nodded soberly and turned from them. At the edge of the porch he lifted a shovel and they watched him walk away, his shoulders broad and his tread heavy.

"I'll send Jack to help when he gets here," Melody called after him. "For all the use he'll be," she added, her voice low and ironic.

"Maybe he can make the time pass quicker," Ruth murmured.

Wrecker turned once and flashed them a smile, and then passed out of sight.

Ruth patted Melody's hand. "I'd better get inside. Do you know what you're doing?"

"Figured I'd start with a washcloth and a bowl of warm water, and pray for inspiration."

Ruthie smiled. "That should do it." She turned toward the door. "Melody? Light some incense. Meg's going to get ripe."

"You did everything you could, Len," Ruth said. She did not move far from his side for the long day and night and half a day

277

again it took to prepare for Meg's burial. It was the living who needed the vigil. The dead was lying on cleated planks in the lumber shed, washed by now, and oiled, and wrapped. A neighbor woman had arrived with skill and experience to share with Melody, and together they made sure that Meg would go out in style.

"I know," Len answered, as he did each time. There wasn't much more for either of them to say, but Ruth thought it was good to keep Len's larynx from closing up from lack of use. She prodded him with this every hour or so when they were both awake. He didn't cry. She suspected he didn't know how to. Sometimes men lost the knack for it when they moved past boyhood and into the narrowed expectations of their later years. Or maybe Len was just cried out. The Meg he'd lived with for the past eighteen years was a sweet girl, and Ruth would miss her. But the Meg he'd married? She'd been long gone. That was the shame of it, Ruth thought. He'd spent all these years unable to mourn the loss of the woman he loved, and now that he was finally laying her to rest he had nothing but regret to grieve her with.

The goose? She knew how to cry. They let her grief speak for them all. She was an elderly bird and her voice wasn't nearly as strong as it had been in her youth, but she'd been heartbroken by the loss and was determined to let the world know. She waddled around their frequent haunts, her plaintive honk echoing in the yard and threading through the saplings that had sprung up in Meg's vegetable garden. Len didn't think he could live with that, he said. It was the longest sentence he'd strung together since he'd woken to find Meg still beside him.

Len was vertical, now. He'd tired of lying in the bedroom, and now, the second day, they had moved together into the kitchen. Ruth was cutting banana slices into an enormous bowl of Jell-O while she boiled macaroni for a salad. She gazed at him with pity and irritation. "Wait and see if you change your mind," she said. "We'll take her if you still want." She glanced out the window, and sighed. "All right, then. People coming," she reported. She crossed to him and ran her fingertips along his temples to smooth his errant hair. "You'll have to speak to them. Are you ready?"

All of Mattole, it seemed, assembled in Len's yard to honor Meg. The neighbors came with their arms burdened with the food they'd cooked and the flowers they'd picked from their gardens, and they milled through the small cabin and mumbled whatever words they had to offer their sympathy. The women hugged Len and the men clapped him on the shoulder in shared sorrow. Len wasn't an easy man to comfort, but he showed them his gratitude. He straightened his back and he received them with a somber grace. Late in the afternoon, after Meg had been laid to rest and the food had been eaten and the small talk had been made, they went home and said *That poor man*, and weren't sure why.

Ruth kept looking around, but she never came.

Melody had thought that she would. She'd called Willow as soon as she heard the news and the two of them had spoken briefly, just long enough to relay the information and discuss arrangements before she got off the line to make the rest of the calls and go attend to Meg's body. Willow had said she'd come down to say good-bye to Meg. She said she thought she would. She said she'd think about it and either she'd come or she'd call to say she wouldn't make it. Ruth frowned. She pinned Melody with a stern gaze and made her promise not to say anything to Len. If she comes, she comes, Ruth said. It wasn't right to get his hopes up.

So many people *did* come, finally, that they almost forgot about Willow. Even DF Al showed up, looking older and more hand-some after a three-year stint building water systems in Nepal.

There'd been a few men in the ten years since Al went on his footloose way, Ruth knew, but she could tell Melody couldn't escape the feeling it gave her to see him again. He left often but he couldn't seem to get completely free of the Mattole. Once in a while, Melody had confessed to Ruth, she wondered what it would be like if he changed his mind and gave in to its pull in a permanent way. She might get tired of him, then, she thought. Better they spread things out.

When the time came to bury Meg, the men gathered in the lumber shed and gravely and graciously negotiated their positions. Wrecker and Jack and DF Al and Charlie Burrell's son Charlie Jr., who'd turned out all right after all, each took hold of a handle. They carried the cleated plank with Meg's body slowly through the yard, leading a procession of mourners, and wound their way to the edge of the woods. Len walked alongside, his body held as straight as he could muster, which wasn't very straight at all. When they reached the graveside, the men lowered their burden to the ground.

Len stooped to lay his spread hand gently on the part of the wrapped corpse that had been Meg's clavicle. He closed his eyes and left his hand there for a good long time, and the others had to struggle with the dampness that sprung to their eyes. And then Jack and DF Al and Charlie Burrell Jr. and Wrecker each took a corner of the blanket Meg rested on, lifted her weight from the plank, walked as carefully as they could to the hole, and eased her softly in.

Ruth worried about Len. He came to dinner at the farmhouse every night because they insisted on it, but he rarely spoke and never smiled. It had been two weeks, already, and he showed no interest in resuming his normal life. He wouldn't step into the woods, not even with Wrecker; he wouldn't go to town or read the messages the boy picked up for him at the new general store adjacent to the post office. He cleaned house with a fury. It seemed to Ruth that he was trying to scrub every last evidence of human habitation from the cabin and the outbuildings. She didn't take it as a good sign. She knew how grief could shove you off your moorings. She was afraid that he would drift so far afield he would lose his way back.

Late August, the light was the rich hue of clover honey, and the green leaves seemed worn out by the long summer's effort to make sugar. It had not rained in a month. The river was sluggish. Dusk came earlier and there was in the air a suggestion of change, a kind of impatience with the way things were. Ruth could sense it in Wrecker. He was ready to push off. He wouldn't leave Len in this state, but his body was eager to move.

It was Sunday. Ruth had a chicken dinner simmering on the stove inside, and the four of them sat out on the front porch while she ran the clippers expertly about the bowl of Wrecker's head. His summer mane fell in golden hanks to the floorboards. Short hair made his face look younger. His blue eyes shone brighter and his ears emerged as the hair fell away. Ruth silenced the clippers and ran her hand over the soft nap. "Ha," she said, laying her fingers to points on his scalp. "How many scars have you got, now? Nine? Ten?"

"A hundred." Melody got up from the glider to examine them herself. "Here's that nasty one from tumbling down the barn ladder," she said, tapping a point near the crown of his head. "Remember how long it took that gash to heal?" She blew on the nape of his neck to chase away the shorn strands and covered his ears with her palms, gave his head a mock shake. "Hey. How about you stop knocking yourself on the head from now on?"

"Yeah. I'll just quit cold turkey."

"I raised a reasonable man."

"Off the stool," Ruth demanded. "It's Len's turn."

But Len had his head cocked to listen to a car engine approaching on the drive. "You expecting anybody?"

Melody shrugged. "Jehovah's Witnesses, maybe." She reached for the porch broom and started sweeping the golden strands off the floorboards.

"Came by last week," Ruth said. "They wouldn't be back this soon. Plus it's Sunday." Ruth enjoyed the local missionaries. She served them tea and cinnamon toast and then systematically and tactlessly but with plenty of mitigating humor disabused them of their beliefs.

The car glimmered through the spaces between the trees and then came to a stop atop the hill. It was a late-model sedan, dark colored, not flashy, but with good lines and an understated elegance. "Is that who I think it is?" Melody said, when the driver's door opened and a woman emerged.

Ruth peered, blinked twice, and then looked at Len.

Len stood stiffly and clutched his hat. He kept his eyes on the visitor. His face grew pale.

Wrecker stood up from the stool. "Since when does Willow drive?" He raised an arm. "Willow!" he shouted. "Damn!"

"Leave the swearing to me, boy," Ruth growled, and walked to the edge of the porch.

Willow did not rush to close the distance between them. She was dressed as smartly as ever, her hair a silver cap that sat stylishly upon her head, and she moved with the same liquid grace that had always distinguished her stride. She had gained a little weight. It softened the angles of her face and made her look more permanent. She had always been elegant but she seemed to have relaxed into a kind of stately ease. Willow climbed the porch steps and stood before them. "Hello, Len," she said softly.

What happened next, they each remembered differently.

Wrecker said that Len resembled a tree trunk newly severed from its base that teetered and then fell. Melody thought it was a different kind of gravity; that Willow's presence exerted some kind of pressure on Len that drew him toward her like iron filings to a magnet. Len himself understood that he had no control over what was happening and that any effort he made would only result in his hurting himself or her. And Willow just opened her arms and prepared herself to accept the weight of him as he collapsed toward her.

Miraculously, she kept him from crashing to the floor. Even when Wrecker stepped quickly forward to try to relieve her of Len's weight, Willow motioned him back. Len still had his feet to hold him up, and she wasn't willing to be parted from him again.

They stayed bound together like that for a long time, and Wrecker and Melody and Ruth stood quietly by, unwilling to break the spell. They looked at the floorboards and then off in the distance. Melody realized she still held the broom in her hands, and she made an idle effort to sweep the few remaining strands of hair off into the bushes. They could feel how their presence made a kind of protective shield for Willow and Len, and they weren't going to jinx it by looking at each other or at them. They let the evening air course in and out, through them and among them. And then a squeak sounded atop the hill and the passenger door opened and another figure stepped from the car.

Willow eased slowly out of Len's embrace. She kept her eyes fastened on his face as he found his balance apart from her. And then she turned from him to face forward, to face the yard and the hill and the car atop it, and leaned her weight back against his body and draped his arms over her shoulders and did not let go of him for one minute. She raised her chin to acknowledge the woman who approached them.

Melody stilled the broom and squinted toward the woman as

she made her way carefully aside the ruts and rocks down the incline. There was something vaguely familiar about her. She had short, curly, colorless hair, and a wide, deeply lined face, and a calm expression that suggested a serious nature. She wore a simple cotton blouse that fit loosely on her sturdy frame, and rumpled cotton slacks, and on her feet a pair of what looked like Chinese slippers. No one in the Mattole Valley dressed like that. Her gaze swept over them all as she came to stand at the edge of the porch.

Willow spoke softly. "This is Lisa Fay," she said. "I'm sorry we're so late. It took me some time to find her."

Ruth's hand flew to her mouth in surprise. Then she extended it and, roughly but congenially, she used her grip to pull the woman up onto the porch.

The woman had her clear gaze fixed on Wrecker. "I'm looking for my son," she said.

Ruth cleared her throat. "Well," she said. "You found him."

Ruth, being Ruth, eventually got the whole story. Or as much of it as each of them was willing to tell. There was the electric moment of meeting when Ruth wasn't sure if Melody was going to go berserk and shove Lisa Fay off the porch or if Wrecker would become a pillar of salt, standing there as still as he did, or if Willow would ever let go of Len (and she did not, not really, ever again), or if she herself would have some kind of attack and drop dead right there just from all the excitement of the afternoon. Any of those things could have happened, and Ruth had to believe the reason they didn't was because Lisa Fay stood there so calmly and anchored them all. Her heart must have been beating a stampede, Ruth thought. How she kept it contained was a mystery. Those two years in the ashram helped with that, she found out later. The fifteen years in jail, she told Ruth much later, had not helped with anything. And then she said no more about that.

Lisa Fay didn't say much at all, actually. Ruth realized she had food on the stove and she herded them all inside, made them sit at the table like civilized human beings and share the chicken and rice. Melody, too, was nearly silent. The color had risen in her cheeks and a combination of fear and desperation flashed first in her eyes, and Ruth watched her carefully, poised to intercede if something like that was necessary. Ruth knew fear. She knew desperation. She watched it subside. Something softer arose. A look of surrender. And then a look of entreaty, followed by a look of relief, a look of investigation and assessment and consideration, a trace of terror and then again a kind of cautious semi-trusting regard, and all the while Lisa Fay waited politely, accepted the food that was offered to her, snuck looks at Wrecker, and did not ever let Melody out of her field of vision.

Len was entirely speechless. He looked like a man from whom an enormous weight had been lifted, and whose body ran the risk of floating off were it not held to ground by the constant contact with the woman at his side. Ruth was pretty sure he would cry, soon. Not at the table, probably. He could probably wait until he was in something closer to privacy. But it was coming.

Willow murmured softly, and Ruth realized that this was the first time in all the years she'd known her that she'd ever seen Willow truly happy.

No one said anything. Even Ruth could not seem to find words to fit the day. They sat at the table and dished the food and gazed at one another in a kind of temporary paralysis.

And then Wrecker started to talk. He just opened his mouth and began. Sweat sprang out on his forehead. He talked so steadily, so long without interruption, and so eloquently—if a twenty-year-old boy-man could be said to be eloquent—that they riveted their attention on him out of amazement and a little alarm. His customary reticence gave way to a flood of words so unstoppable that even his food remained untouched. He talked to them all, about everything. He told stories about Meg and reminisced about the walks they'd taken and the structures they'd built, forts woven from twigs and mud and fortified with tin cans and with mushrooms pilfered from the forest floor that he had to make sure Meg didn't eat. He talked about the things he loved best about his motorcycle, the intricacies of its shifting mechanism and the speeds it could attain if the road were straight and no one blocked the way. He described reading he'd done on the great forests of Alaska and the presence of muskeg and permafrost; he discussed the species of trees he might expect to encounter and the different practices they used to bring them down, and how cold it got and what people wore and ate to ward it off. Wrecker talked about Jack and why Jack thought this marriage might work even when the others had failed; he chuckled at his own jokes and backed up to correct his information and mused on the implications of the facts he'd gathered and as an aside mentioned that he thought Ruth should get a dog and if she found one like Sitka that was the one to choose. They all stared at him, watching his mouth move and his eyes brighten, his ears and his forehead all naked and exposed by the haircut, his sunburned face a stark contrast, and could not help but realize that his being there—his being, in fact—might serve not to make enemies of them but to bring them together.

Lisa Fay leaned toward Melody. "Does he always talk this much?" she asked softly.

"Almost never," Melody responded, in a whisper.

Len and Willow shared a quick glance and looked away, blushing. And of course Ruth caught it, because Ruth missed nothing.

There were details to work out. In time, they would work them out. They had each other, and they had him. And though they missed Johnny Appleseed and mourned Meg, and though

Wrecker would leave them all soon and only come back to visit, as even the best children do, and though the goose would die not quite as peaceful a death as Meg had (but quickly, and they all hoped painlessly) and the dog Ruth chose would not be quite as profoundly good as Sitka, and though Len would develop arthritis in his hands and have to trade the chain saw for the softer work of starting seedlings to regrow the forest he had cut down, and though DF Al would never stay long, and Yolanda would not be seen again, and Lisa Fay would not regain the years she'd lost to prison, they would know that together, and in spite of themselves, they had done this.

But all that would come later. In the kitchen, sitting at the table with his family, Wrecker's flow of language gradually slowed. He glanced around at each of them and then down at his plate. Methodically, he cut the meat and lifted the fork to his mouth and chewed. He finished his piece and then he looked up. "I guess I'll have some more chicken, Ruthie," he said.

She stood and took the plate he extended. "Anything you want, boy," she said.

ACKNOWLEDGMENTS

This book has been a long time in the making. The story was sparked years back by an unexpected encounter, and the process of writing it became a path toward making peace with that experience. The end result is fiction. Lucky for me, the people who have helped along the way are incontestably, blessedly real.

I offer my deepest thanks to:

- The Barbara Deming Memorial Fund, for a grant (and a vote of confidence) early in the book's creation.
- A Room of Her Own Foundation, for faith and support, in the form of the Gift of Freedom Award, to see it through. When I didn't know how I would ever finish, you all stepped in and opened a way. Darlene Chandler Bassett, you are a visionary committed to the understanding that no vision is ever realized without a leap of faith and a lot of hard work.
- The friends and colleagues who have read chapters and drafts and revisions and more revisions and still more revisions. Anne Costanza, Veronica Golos, Kim Ponders, most especially Kathy Namba, and others unnamed but no less appreciated—your comments have reached to the heart of the matter and made this a truer, better book.

- Pam Houston and the PAMFAs—year in, year out, you listened, offered insights and encouragement, and fed me the world's best mashed potatoes.
- Everyone at Bloomsbury, who took a bunch of words and turned them into a thing of beauty. Most of all to the best editor an author could ask for, the tough-minded and tender-hearted Kathy Belden.
- Dan Conaway, my brilliant, generous, savvy, insightful, tenacious agent. Not just for representing the book, but for seeking it out, loving the characters, and challenging me to love them more, too.
- Richard Torres, extraordinary storyteller and one heck of a great father-in-law.
- Silvia Rennie, for friendship, support, and encouragement.
- Michèle Shockey, who first led me to the Lost Coast and who, decades later, listened to what grew from those crazy adventures.
- My mother, Ellen Wood, my father, Norbert Wood, my sisters, Winton, Harper, Elaine, and Uma, and my brother, Peter—for teaching me the meaning of family, and for sticking with me through thick and thin.
- The four small boys who shared our home for a while and our hearts for always; and to their parents. Wherever you are, bless you.
- Tetsuro, Kan, Yohta—this is yours. You put up with it for a long time. I'm so proud of you all.

Thanks most of all to Kathy. Without you, none of this. With you, everything.

A NOTE ON THE AUTHOR

Summer Wood is the author of *Arroyo*. In 2007 she received the
Gift of Freedom Award from A Room of Her Own Foundation
for her work on *Wrecker*. She teaches writing at the University of
New Mexico's Taos Summer Writers' Conference, and in 2009
she directed the first NEA/Taos Big Read. She has lived with her
family in Taos for the past twenty years.

www.summerwoodwrites.com